Look for More Titles by Cassandra Chandler

Lingering Touch

The Summer Park Psychics
Book Three

Cassandra Chandler

Copyright Page

Lingering Touch
The Summer Park Psychics, Book Three
Copyright © 2016 by Cassandra Chandler
Print ISBN: 978-1-945702-54-9
Digital ISBN: 978-1-945702-55-6

First eBook edition: August 2016
Second eBook edition: May 2017
First print edition: August 2016
Second print edition: May 2017
10 9 8 7 6 5

cassandra-chandler.com
P.O. Box 91
Mission, Kansas 66201

Cover by Cassandra Chandler

Dedication

For those who dare to try again.

*Don't miss out on any of
the eerie romance in Summer Park.
Subscribe to Cassandra Chandler's newsletter at
cassandra-chandler.com now!*

Prologue

Summer Park—May 2015

Time travel was impossible. There was no such thing.

Finn had worked plenty of weird cases as a private investigator. This one might break into his top ten.

He picked the lock on the theatre's back door, then slipped into the building. The most recent production had wrapped almost three weeks ago. That meant only construction crews would be around. They'd be focused on the stage. Finn was interested in the theatre's seating.

All he needed was a few minutes in the box reserved for Elsa Sinclair—famous novelist and professional recluse. His best friend, Garrett, had hired Finn to figure out if Elsa was being conned by the guy she was living with—Dante Lucerne.

It seemed likely. For starters, Dante Lucerne had been dead over a hundred years. Finn turned up that little gem of information within an hour of working the case. The original Dante had been killed in a fire in London in 1881. Finn couldn't find any other men matching the name and description Garrett had provided. And it was a very

1

unusual description.

Six foot tall, short dark hair, thin build, blue-green eyes, and scarring over a quarter of his face centered on his right temple. Oh, and he dressed like a guy from the 1800s… who chose to wear a *Phantom of the Opera* mask.

Yeah, this case had definitely cracked his top ten.

Garrett had turned around and told Finn to drop the case right away, but it was too late. Finn's curiosity had been piqued. The more Finn learned, the more curious he became. He had even already brought out his secret weapon—psychometry. He'd used his psychic ability to read what had happened in the limo Elsa rented the night Dante appeared in her life.

Finn snorted and shook his head as he remembered Elsa telling Dante that she had basically teleported him from 1800s London to modern-day Florida.

Time travel. Yeah, right.

Finn could buy into a lot of things—psychometry and telepathy, for instance. His very personal experience proved those were real. But going back in time and bringing someone to the future? No way.

Dante had been really convincing, though. Not only had he been wearing the old-timey clothes Garrett had mentioned, but Dante had been covered in soot and sweat. He had the accent down, speech cadences sounding like something from a period piece.

Only one explanation seemed plausible—Elsa was

researching a new book. She was going all out and had hired an actor to help her get into the spirit of things. For all Finn knew, this was how she researched all of her stories. It would explain why everyone talked about how real they felt. Hell, even Finn's dad was a fan.

Finn might have to read her next book. The horror novels he usually read right before sleep were finally getting to him. It had been decades since he'd woken up screaming from a nightmare. He was a grown man, for crying out loud. He couldn't quite remember what had happened in his dreams the night before, but he felt in his gut that it was somehow related to this case.

He'd never had an investigation get under his skin like this. He'd been on edge all day, jumping at the smallest things and feeling…honestly, kind of terrified. He didn't understand where it was coming from. He did understand that it needed to stop.

If sifting through the memories of the dozen or more people who had been in the limo since Elsa and Dante would help him figure out the mystery, it was worth it. Even the ones that were a graphic and unwelcome reminder of his last encounter with Jazz. They had broken up after a disastrous date in a limo.

That was Fate's punchline. Elsa wasn't just tight with Garrett—who was as close to a brother as Finn was going to get this lifetime—she was best friends with Finn's ex, Zhou Jazz.

Who was he kidding? Jazz wasn't just an ex-girlfriend —she was *the* ex-girlfriend. The only woman Finn had ever wanted to spend the rest of his life with. Their relationship had escalated so quickly, even though they'd only been together for a couple of months. He'd been certain she was the one he was meant for. Part of him still thought so.

Normally, he used his work to avoid thinking about her, letting himself get lost in the puzzles his investigations presented. With this case, everything reminded him of her.

He had even seen her a few times, talked to contacts that he introduced her to. For some reason, she was putting together a fake ID for Dante. If Dante was conning Elsa, he was conning Jazz too. Finn took a deep breath and willed his body to relax, his hands to uncurl.

If Dante was conning Jazz, if he tried to hurt her in any way... It would not end well for him.

Finn made his way to the box that Elsa had reserved for every single showing of the play. It was unlocked. Two chairs sat facing away from him. The curtains were already closed. Apparently, she insisted they were kept that way—yet another of her eccentricities. No one had bothered to open them yet.

It worked in his favor. He could check things out without being seen. Her memories should be all over the place.

Finn closed the door behind him and set to work. He

held out his hands and shifted his awareness, letting the feel of the place soak in. A few deep breaths would open him to…

Holy shit.

The tiny room was bursting with energy. Finn felt like he was on a roller coaster, his stomach lurching and doing flip-flops. He staggered forward and grabbed one of the seats in front of him to stay upright. A jolt of energy lit him up like the Fourth of July. His eyes were electrified, his body tingling from head to toe. He blinked a few times, waiting for his perspective to shift as his powers kicked in.

Normally, he felt like he was floating above the place he was viewing—his awareness on the shoulder of whoever had touched what he was touching. This time, he was booted out of his body like someone rammed him in the gut. The vision was different too—the colors more vivid. Too vivid to be real.

He looked down from the ceiling to see Elsa standing in the same spot that Finn's body must be occupying. She was staring at…nothing. Between the no-blinking and standing completely still, she looked like a mannequin.

It would have been creepy if not for the ribbons of golden light whipping around, centered on her. They cast off little fireworks of energy that filled the space. Finn felt like he was inside a glitter-filled snow-globe that was being swirled around.

The light started to gather in front of her, taking on the

shape of a man. Elsa's arms shifted so that she was embracing him, clinging to him. The light was painfully bright. In a final flash that made Finn wish he had eyelids to shut, Dante appeared in her arms.

What the fuck! What the flaming flying fuck!

Dante collapsed. It looked like he was convulsing.

"Dante? Dante, are you all right?" She grabbed a dark cloak from the back of the other chair. "I'm so sorry. I didn't think it would be this bad."

She draped the cloak over him, then dropped to the ground. She snuggled up against his back, spooning him and rubbing his arms and chest. He was shivering and breathing heavy.

"Stay with me. Please stay with me," she said.

Finn watched, dumbfounded. After a few moments, Dante's tremors subsided. He gripped Elsa's wrist and said, "I assure you, I have no plans to go elsewhere."

They sat up slowly. She knelt next to him, hovering like a hummingbird, her face pinched with worry. The pair finally faced each other, and damn, Finn could sense the chemistry even without his body. A much dimmer version of the golden lights was hovering around their bodies, linking them together like she was still holding on to him.

"How do you feel?" Elsa asked.

"I scarcely know where to begin."

"Are you hurt?"

"I do not believe so. For the most part, I am confused."

That made two of them.

"That's understandable. I'll explain everything as soon as I can. But right now, we have to go."

Elsa rose to her feet and offered her hand to help Dante up. Of course, he took it. The two stood close, staring into each other's eyes like...

Like Finn wished he and Jazz would have. He groaned at himself, then forced thoughts of Jazz out of his mind.

"Where is it we are going?" Dante asked.

Elsa smiled. Finn realized he had never seen her look happy before. Not that they'd spent much—or any—time together. Jazz wasn't keen on incorporating Finn into her life.

"Home," Elsa said.

She stepped toward the door. The vision faded as she and Dante moved away. Finn blinked a few times as his awareness returned to his body. He was sitting on the floor where Elsa and Dante had been talking. When had Finn fallen?

The conversation Finn had viewed in Elsa's limo took on a whole new depth of meaning. She really *had* brought Dante forward over a century, had saved him from the fire that supposedly killed him.

Finn stood, careful not to touch anything. Once was enough for being pulled into the current of such a powerful memory. He staggered out into the hall, closing the door behind him. His thoughts whirled as he leaned against the dark wood, still clutching the doorknob.

Finn's hearing cut out suddenly, his perspective shifting so he was looking down at the door. Another vision? What the *fuck* was up with his powers today?

A blond guy was standing in front of Elsa's theatre box, stroking the door. Yeah, that wasn't suspicious at all.

Finn recognized him as one of the people he had sifted through when finding Elsa's memories in the limo she rented. He remembered the guy because he had just sat there, completely still, for a long time the day after Elsa and Dante rented it. That was too much of a coincidence.

Finn made a note of the guy's height and weight, his build, his clothes, anything that might help ID him later. The vision ended gradually, letting Finn sink back into the awareness of his own body again.

He had a call to make. Garrett needed to know that Dante wasn't the one Elsa should be concerned about. And after that, Finn would start looking for the blond guy.

Chapter One

Summer Park—July 2015

Garrett's car was in his driveway. Jazz parked her SUV behind it, clutching her wheel with a white-knuckled grip. The day was already oppressively hot. His car was going to be an oven. Why wasn't it in the garage?

The garage. Right.

She had never really thought about garages before. Now she hated them. She couldn't imagine how they made Rachel feel after what had happened to her.

No, Jazz could. She just didn't want to.

"Get off your ass," she said. Rachel was waiting for her.

Jazz grabbed the green bag sitting in the passenger's seat. Apparently, Rachel was in the mood for some metaphysical arts-and-crafts. If it helped her feel better, Jazz was all for it. She opened the door and slid to the ground.

Heat reflected up from the white concrete of Garrett's driveway. Her leather pants held on to the cool from the AC, deflecting some of it. The big black sweater she had decided to wear—not so much. She stood for a moment as the humidity penetrated the fabric, baking her.

Today's wardrobe choice brought to you by yet another lapse in judgment.

"Fuck. This."

She slammed the door shut. It was even more satisfying than swearing—a habit she had picked up from Finn.

Don't think about Finn.

She repeated the mantra a few times as she marched up to the house and rang the doorbell.

"Coming!"

Rachel's voice. She sounded...happy. How could that be possible after everything she'd been through?

Rachel opened the door. She had a broad smile on her face. It was almost like nothing had happened. No, not quite. The lines of tension around her eyes had deepened.

She always had a haunted quality about her that made Jazz want to kick her parents' asses. It had never been this bad before. She ran through a quick, assessing check.

Rachel's hair was brushed but otherwise left alone. Simple blue shirt, jeans, sneakers. No jewelry, no makeup... Yeah, Rachel was still healing. The dark circles under her eyes weren't the only sign. She kept one hand behind her back, as if she was hiding something.

"Hi!"

Jazz knew Rachel's enthusiasm must be at least partially forced. Probably to benefit Jazz. Her eyes were burning. She was grateful that Rachel was okay. Would be, anyway. They would all make sure of it. Especially now that Rachel was at Garrett's.

"Hi."

Rachel's brow knitted and her smile vanished. "What's wrong? Did something happen?"

Did something...

"Are you kidding me? Yes, something happened. I haven't seen you since you left the hospital, and you've barely texted or called!"

Jazz walked into the house and shut the door, then grabbed Rachel and hugged her. Rachel stiffened as the awkwardness of the moment sank in. Dammit, Jazz needed to start hugging people more often. The idea that she could have missed the chance to make up for it...

It was too much. Her eyes were still burning. No way in hell would she cry. If she did, Rachel would try to comfort Jazz, and that was not okay. Rachel was the one who needed comforting.

"Are you okay?" Jazz asked. "You look better."

"I am better. Getting there, anyway."

Jazz sniffed to keep her nose from running. The air was thick with incense. Not freshen-the-air incense, either. It was the same scent that Chloe used at her metaphysical bookstore, Bookwyrm.

"Why does it smell like a temple in here?" Jazz asked.

Rachel laughed and stepped back. "That would be from this."

She held up a small brass incense holder with holes punched in patterns along the sides and lid. Three tiny chains attached to it led to a small hook at the top that Rachel had looped over one finger. The thing—a censer, Jazz remembered—was used in rituals and religious observations. Smoke trailed out of it, slowly wending its way up Rachel's arm.

"If you don't mind, I need to smudge you," Rachel said.

How did Rachel know what smudging was? Jazz was the only member of her group who was into metaphysics. Well, aside from Elsa. But Elsa wasn't so much interested in the topic as forced into it from first-hand experience. Maybe Rachel didn't know what she was talking about.

"You want to cleanse my aura?" Jazz asked.

"That's the idea."

Okay, she does *know.*

Jazz stepped back toward the door and lifted her arms to give Rachel space to work. Like a pro, Rachel wafted the smoke around Jazz's body, clearing and cleansing her energy field.

Auras were kind of mainstream. Lots of people knew what they were and Jazz wouldn't have been too surprised for that topic to come up in conversation. But smudging was a level deeper.

The question of "how Rachel knew" wasn't as disturbing as "why was she doing this?" Jazz actually cleansed and combed her aura on a regular basis. She smudged herself and her apartment every month during the dark moon, banishing thoughts and attachments she wanted to clear out.

Finn's smiling face popped into Jazz's mind—his cocky grin surrounded by dark brown stubble and those pale blue eyes that she could dive into. She had never been able to bring herself to try to clear Finn's energy from her life, even though she constantly told herself to stop thinking about him.

He and Rachel had the same exact eye color. It had unsettled Jazz at first. Now she found it weirdly comforting. Nostalgic even.

Bullshit.

It just gave Jazz an excuse to think about him—let her blame it on an external stimulus instead of the soul-deep longing that kept her up at night and made her that much more dedicated to her work.

Dammit, stop thinking about Finn.

Her mantra wasn't working. Then again, it seldom did with him.

One month, three weeks, six days, and twenty-two hours. That was how long they had been together before he left. Even after all this time, she still thought of him every day.

She needed to be thinking about Rachel.

"If you need me to open the bag to cleanse the stuff inside, let me know," Jazz said.

Rachel paused briefly with the censer under the bag. She let the smoke float up around the green plastic.

"That should be good enough." She laughed abruptly. "I know we've never discussed paranormal stuff before, but I have to say I'm very grateful you're into it and already know so much."

"I didn't know you were into it at all."

"It's kind of been a necessity for me. Let's sit down and talk." Rachel took the bag and led Jazz into the living room.

Necessity. Like Elsa.

Jazz wondered if Rachel might be psychic too. It was pretty common in Summer Park. Something about the place seemed to call to people with gifts, drawing in whole families sometimes.

Like Finn and his dad, Tommy.

Her stomach tightened as she remembered sitting around their kitchen table and laughing till her sides hurt. Finn hadn't just given her his heart—he'd given her a family. She had messed up and lost them both.

She modified her standard mantra, trying to get a better handle on her emotions.

Do not think about Tommy.

"Can I get you a drink or anything?" Rachel asked.

"I'm good."

Garrett's coffee table was covered in an impressive library of metaphysical texts. Jazz recognized several of the same books she had in her collection. Chloe was doing good business.

Jazz sat on the couch and said, "I'm guessing this isn't a passing interest."

"No."

Where was Garrett? Jazz broadened her attention and heard water running at the other side of the house. He must be in the shower. While she was scanning the room, she noticed a poppet hanging above the sliding glass doors that led to the patio.

A poppet?

It was made of plain white cloth and shaped like a person, but didn't have any other defining characteristics. Jazz checked the kitchen window with her limited view from the couch. Sure enough, a poppet was hanging there as well. Rachel was warding away spirits. Not just a specific spirit—otherwise, there would have been more detail to the things. She was keeping away all of them.

That explained the smudging.

"I see you're already redecorating," Jazz said.

Rachel's smile faltered and the tension around her eyes increased. She'd said she wanted to talk metaphysics, but maybe she was like Elsa and new to the whole thing.

"It's a poppet," Rachel said. "They keep away spirits."

Maybe not-so-new.

Rachel made herself a workspace on the coffee table, then sat on the floor and opened the bag. She placed what

Jazz had picked up at Bookwyrm on the table. Silver jewelry wire, a wire cutter, a silver chain, and three stones.

"Snowflake obsidian, fluorite, and opal, as requested," Jazz said. "I picked out three that looked like you could make them work in a necklace."

"These are perfect, thanks."

They were in a small sealed plastic bag. Rachel opened it, then let the stones tumble gently onto her hand. She set them on the table reverently.

The snowflake obsidian was black with little gray speckles that looked like snow. Obsidian was used in metaphysical work with the subconscious. Snowflake obsidian specifically could be used in meditation and rituals designed to help a person manifest their most authentic self.

Fluorite, on the other hand, was about boundaries and concentration. Jazz used it when she really needed to focus on a project and didn't want to be distracted by outside influences.

The one she'd picked out had lots of blue and purple flowing through the translucent body of the stone, which would bring out the iridescent qualities of the otherwise milky-white opal. Opal was used for journeying and balance.

Journeying... Was the necklace meant for Elsa?

Rachel was linking the stones together, wrapping the jewelry wire around each one to hold it in place. While she worked, she said, "I spoke with Elsa on the phone today. She told me what she can do."

Yup. It was for Elsa.

The choice of stones suddenly made sense. No, not just sense—they were genius. Opal to aid journeying, fluorite to aid focus. Using those stones together, Elsa's psychic ability of astral projection would be heightened. They would give her more control. Jazz wasn't sure how the snowflake obsidian factored in, though.

She also wasn't completely certain that she and Rachel were on the same page. Until she was, Jazz wouldn't spill Elsa's secret, even though Elsa said she was planning to tell Rachel eventually.

"Elsa can do a lot of things," Jazz said.

"So can I."

Rachel let her hands drop to her lap and stared at Jazz intently. She had never seen Rachel look so serious.

"I can hear spirits," Rachel said. "Sometimes I see them in reflections. Especially mirrors."

Damn. Was Jazz a psychic magnet or something? She knew she didn't have any abilities herself. She would have discovered it over her years of practicing, researching, trying to reach the other side.

Plus, Chloe had tested her.

One of the reasons Jazz settled in Summer Park was to be closer to Chloe and work with her. She had been the most promising lead in Jazz's ultimately futile quest.

Aside from "having a heightened sense of people's character", Jazz was within the normal levels of sensory perception. And even that ability hadn't helped to avoid—

Do not think about Michael.

Her mantra didn't keep her stomach from knotting. She hated that Michael could affect her so viscerally. She took a slow, deep breath through her nose and let it out through slightly pursed lips, hoping that Rachel wouldn't notice.

"Aren't you going to say something?" Rachel asked.

"I'm being inscrutable," Jazz said. "It's an Asian thing."

As she hoped, Rachel laughed. Jazz felt her own face pull into a stiff smile.

"Okay. I need more information."

Rachel nodded. "You know how I sometimes get distracted? That's usually when I'm hearing spirits having a conversation. Florida is filled with ghosts. That's why I'm making this for Elsa."

How did ghosts intersect with astral projection?

"I don't see the connection."

"Elsa travels astrally. She leaves her body behind, ready to be occupied."

The knots in Jazz's stomach tightened.

"Occupied?"

"It's easy for a spirit to enter an empty body."

"You're talking about possession."

Rachel nodded. "Some ghosts can even take over bodies that have souls in them. If they have a strong enough personality, they can overcome the existing consciousness. All they need is an opening or conduit. It would be easy for a spirit to take over Elsa's body while she's traveling."

Shit. Jazz should have thought of that as soon as Elsa had told Jazz what she could do. Jazz had been too dazzled and happy and proud of Elsa's ability.

Elsa didn't just use her power to let her soul travel through space—she traveled back in time *on a regular basis*. No wonder her novels were so rich in historical detail.

As if that wasn't enough, she had discovered Dante, basically fallen in love with him while observing him, and saved his life by pulling him forward through time *physically*. Jazz had never heard of anything happening on that level. She was still kind of in awe of the whole thing. Even so, she should have realized the danger inherent in Elsa leaving her body empty.

Jazz knew that mediums could channel spirits through their bodies during séances and that sometimes the spirits didn't want to leave. She had studied the phenomenon of walk-ins, even a bit about possession. Finding out more about how spirits and the living could interact had been a near-obsession of hers for years after her father's unexpected death.

Never think about Father.

Her mind shied away from the topic instantly, like the

thought was made of shards of broken glass. She pulled her focus back to Rachel again.

The snowflake obsidian finally made sense. The necklace wasn't meant to boost Elsa's powers. It was meant to keep her safe.

Jazz pointed at it. "Are you sure this will protect her?"

"It should," Rachel said. "She's been lucky."

"What about a salt circle? Would that help?"

"If she can control when she travels, yes, that would keep spirits away. I'm not sure how the circle would affect her, though. It might trap her inside or keep her from being able to get back. We can run some experiments and see."

Chloe needed to be there when that happened. Her experience would be invaluable. But Jazz was getting ahead of herself.

"She's not going to want to try anything until Dante is better. Since she can control her ability by not being around any art, it shouldn't be a problem."

"Art?"

"That's what triggers her ability. I guess it's like you only seeing spirits in reflections."

Rachel nodded. "That will buy us some time."

The knots in Jazz's stomach lessened a tiny bit. Elsa was safe for the moment. Dante was doing well. Garrett was apparently at-ease enough to take a shower, which was a relief, since he'd been so busy taking care of everybody else he'd been neglecting himself for the last two months. That left Rachel.

"What about you?" Jazz said. "Are these poppets enough to keep spirits from bothering you?"

"That plus spraying salt water on all the doors and windows. Florida is so humid and there's already salt everywhere from the ocean being close. It doesn't take much extra to ward entryways."

Jazz had never bothered warding anything. She'd fix that as soon as she went home.

"I'll keep that in mind. What do you do when you leave the house?"

Rachel paused for a moment before saying, "I don't."

What?

"You can't stay here forever."

"I'll figure something out. If Dante and Elsa are staying in the city for a while, maybe I can stay at their place."

"That isn't what I meant. You can't let ghosts keep you imprisoned for the rest of your life. They can't hurt you, can they?"

"It's difficult for them to hurt people physically through direct contact. They're more likely to try to startle me so I jump out in front of a car or maybe impel an animal to bite me or something."

"That's not reassuring."

"It's hard for spirits to control animals. They'd have to be extremely willful and focused. Death tends to distract people and scatter their thoughts. It takes them a while to regroup and be able to think rationally."

The most recent ghost that Jazz could think of was also the worst. Michael.

You will *think about Michael if it helps Rachel be safe.*

Michael Angelo, the brilliant artist whose works inspired such a visceral response in viewers because his paintings were made from the blood of women he *killed.* Jazz felt her stomach heave, but clenched her muscles, willing herself not to be sick. His works had been set to exhibit in Jazz's gallery—*her own fucking gallery.*

He had targeted Rachel and Elsa, kidnapping Rachel first. Elsa's ability had been triggered when she went into Michael's exhibit room. She'd traveled to where Rachel was being held in Michael's garage.

On one level, Jazz was grateful. If Elsa hadn't seen the paintings, she and Dante wouldn't have been able to run to the rescue, having Jazz call in reinforcements in the form of EMTs and the police. But if Jazz hadn't brought Michael's pieces into the gallery, her friends might not have been hurt at all.

Heightened ability to read people's character. Right.

Michael had shot at Dante and injured him, had strangled Elsa, and had…tortured…Rachel. And then Rachel had shot him. A lot. If Michael's spirit wanted revenge, she would be his first target. The first of many.

"What about—"

"Michael is dead and gone. His body was cremated.

Without any remains, his spirit can't linger." Rachel recited the information as rote. She and Garrett must have already covered this ground.

Jazz let out a huge breath and nodded. "Okay. What about these other yahoos? How do we get them to stop bugging you?"

"I'm still working on my long-term plan."

"There's more you're not telling me. I want to help."

"The best thing you can do is get this to Elsa."

Rachel held up the finished necklace. It was gorgeous. The stones were secure, but still showcased. She had even added little flourishes with the silver wire, making spiral patterns on the stones.

"You are a miracle worker," Jazz said. "I keep telling you I could sell your work in the gallery easily."

"I have a trust fund, remember?"

A trust fund from parents that didn't give a damn about Rachel. Her dad was absent except for photo shoots, and her mom was a grasping, conniving, undercutting woman. Jazz wasn't into hating people. It took too much energy. Rachel's mom had earned it, though, after too many gallery openings where she attended seemingly just to humiliate Rachel.

Even with a trust fund, Rachel had wanted a job. Wanted to contribute. How the hell had such a beautiful person come from that pair?

"Is that why you fought me so hard on getting a

paycheck?"

Jazz almost managed a smile at the memory. Rachel worked hard at the gallery. Jazz had to shove a check in Rachel's purse and threaten to fire her if she didn't cash it.

"The knowledge you've shared with me is worth more than any paycheck. You've given me a chance to do something meaningful that I love."

Something that had almost gotten her killed.

"How's that working out for you?"

"Are you kidding? I've learned more from you than anyone."

"If knowledge is all you wanted, you could have gone back to school," Jazz said.

"There are no schools that could give me the experience I've gained working with you."

Experiences like being chained to a wall and exsanguinated for a painting. Jazz bit back the acerbic comment. When Rachel was ready to talk about what happened to her, Jazz would be there. But she wasn't going to bring it up herself.

Dammit, she was tearing up again. Rachel didn't need to see that. Jazz coughed to clear her throat, but it was still tight when she spoke.

"Is there anything special I need to do when I give the necklace to Elsa?"

"No, but I need to charge it with an intention first. If you give me a moment, I can do that now."

Jazz nodded, then leaned back. Rachel held the necklace in her closed hands, presumably to block out any of the ambient energy floating around the room. She shut her eyes and murmured something so quiet Jazz couldn't make it out.

After a few moments, Rachel opened her eyes and set the necklace on the coffee table. She flicked her hands to shed any residual energy. Yeah, she knew what she was doing in the energy-manipulation department. That still seemed like a very small-scale ritual.

"Seriously?" Jazz asked. "That's it?"

"The simplest solutions are usually the most powerful."

That sounded like something Chloe would say.

"I might have taught you about running a gallery, but I'm guessing you had other mentors."

"I had two teachers," Rachel said. "One on each side."

"Each side of what?"

"One was a spirit. The other was a medium."

"I suppose that makes sense. Actually, a lot of things I wondered about you are making sense now. Like why you try to get people to think you're scatterbrained when you're actually brilliant."

Rachel's eyebrows hiked up her forehead and her mouth dropped open. She let out a fake laugh, trying to throw Jazz off her scent. It was way too late for that.

"I don't know about that," Rachel said. "But I appreciate the compliment."

"It wasn't a compliment. It was a statement of fact. And you're doing it right now." Jazz sighed. "I wish you would stop."

"I don't know what to say."

"Forget it. I'm just glad you're away from your mother. I've been trying to get you out of that pit since we met. Garrett's going to get a deep discount on his next piece for accomplishing that."

"A pit? I've been living in a mansion."

"That's putting lipstick on a pig. Your mom could suck the joy out of a sold-out opening show. I've seen her do it. Belittle your accomplishments and demean you in front of a room full of people."

Rachel's laugh was tinny and hollow. Jazz could only imagine the things echoing in Rachel's mind. Ghosts were probably easier to deal with than memories of her mother's passive-aggressive abuse.

"You're the one who makes the sales," Rachel said.

"Stop. Now you're doing it to yourself."

"You sound like Garrett."

"Good. If we all remind you to disregard the crap she's told you over the years, it might help you to stop telling yourself the same lies she taught you."

Rachel's eyes filled with tears and she muttered, "Thanks."

This topic was too sensitive. Jazz needed to distract Rachel. Immediately.

Jazz nodded and asked, "Will it disrupt the energy if I touch the necklace?"

"It's best if others handle it as little as possible."

The silver chain had come in a velvet bag. Rachel slid the finished necklace into the little pouch and handed it to Jazz.

"I'll see that she gets it tonight," Jazz said. "But what about you? How do we get all these ghosts to leave you alone?"

"I can take care of myself."

Jazz grabbed Rachel's hand and held on tight. "We take care of each other. Now more than ever."

Rachel was trying to say something, but only little coughing sounds came out. If her throat was as tight as Jazz's, it was no wonder.

No more talking. No more thinking. Just this offer of comfort.

She knelt next to Rachel and pulled her into a hug. Rachel buried her face in Jazz's hair and hugged her back, hard.

Jazz pulled away and sniffed. "You need me—you need anything—you call. Understand?"

Rachel nodded.

"Okay." Jazz put her hands on Rachel's cheeks and kissed her forehead as she stood. They both needed time and space to collect themselves, to give the emotions and memories they had stirred up a chance to settle. "Give

Garrett my regards. And be sure to lock the door after me."

Rachel nodded. She didn't walk Jazz to the door. It was probably for the best.

Chapter Two

Finn splashed cold water on his face, hoping it would chase off the aftereffects of his latest nightmare. It didn't.

He dried off, then chucked the towel on a pile of dirty clothes. He needed to do laundry, but hadn't been able to motivate himself to do much of anything lately. Dad was stuck doing all the dishes and Daphne was cooking for them both. Finn needed to get this under control.

Letting out a snort, he shook his head. Nothing was under control.

He ran his fingers through the tangled mess of his hair and it stayed standing on end. He needed a shower. Dammit, he was *going* to shower. And get dressed. And leave the apartment. Today.

"Finn! Get in here."

After he found out what Dad needed.

"Coming."

In his thirties, and his dad still shouted for him like he was a kid. Finn shook his head as he headed for the kitchen.

Dad was sitting at the table, a grim expression deepening the lines on his face where time had left its mark. His hair was almost entirely gray, though it had once been dark brown. He was chewing on his lower lip. The upper was hidden beneath a full mustache.

"What's up?"

Finn was already in the room when he noticed Daphne leaning against the counter. Her dark curls hung loose around her shoulders and she stared at him with warm brown eyes. She was already dressed for working the bar downstairs—jeans and a plaid flannel shirt with the sleeves rolled up.

Finn was in his boxer-briefs.

"Dad, warn me next time."

"It's nothing she hasn't seen before. Sit down."

Finn paused, already halfway back out of the room. He looked at their faces again. Very unhappy. Nervous.

"What is this, an intervention?" Finn laughed.

Neither of them smiled.

"Something like that," Dad said. "Sit down. Please."

If he hadn't added that "please" at the end, Finn might have balked. But the strain on their faces was too much for him to walk away from. He sat across from his dad.

"What's going on?"

"That's what we'd like to know," Dad said.

"What do you mean?"

Dad tapped his finger on the table. "You aren't taking cases. You're not looking after yourself."

Finn shook his head and started to rise. He did not have

it in him to deal with this right now. Dad reached for his hand, but Finn jerked it away. It was too dangerous for them to touch at the moment. The last thing Dad needed was to see the messed-up thoughts in Finn's head. Since they shared the same psychic abilities, Dad would be able to read Finn in a heartbeat.

"Son, I know you're still having nightmares."

"Yeah, so you know it's not a good idea to touch me right now."

"Tommy." Daphne's quiet voice cut into the conversation, reminding them that they had an audience and shouldn't just let each other have it.

Dad leaned back and took a deep breath. "I'm not trying to read you. Yet. But I'm getting close."

He didn't need to see the nightmares that were plaguing Finn or feel the hopelessness that grew every day. He wasn't sure his dad's heart could take it. If they touched, Finn wouldn't be able to hide the darkness he was struggling with. He wouldn't burden his dad with that knowledge. Not when they'd almost lost him a few months ago.

Anyway, whatever this was, it would pass. It had to.

He thought about the nightmares—of the woman chained to the wall and being tortured. The woman whose awareness Finn shared during his dreams. He felt every shuddering breath, every stab of the needle. He could feel death surrounding him. Every night, he saw her killer's face.

It was too late for Finn to go after the guy. The serial killer known as Michael Angelo had not only been caught but killed. That case was solved, but not closed. Not for Finn. He had no idea why this one victim's memories were so firmly implanted in his mind. He didn't even know who she was.

On good days, when he felt like he might be able to accomplish something, he tried to find out more. He was amazed at how little media coverage there had been after Michael's murders were discovered. Usually, serial killers were all over the papers, reporters swarming the story and splashing it on every TV screen they could reach. Not even the local media had run with the story. It had been buried.

Finn had learned more from Garrett, who had been at the scene when the cops arrived. Elsa and Rachel, two of Garrett's other friends, had both been targeted by the killer. Bad move on his part. The pair had teamed up and taken him down—permanently.

Good for them.

They both had considerable resources. Elsa could probably buy and sell Dad's bar a dozen times over. Rachel was both rich and the daughter of a powerful lawyer. The papers weren't shy about her dad's upcoming political campaign. In a town as small as Summer Park, the local papers couldn't afford to piss him off by plastering pictures of his daughter next to a serial killer.

Garrett was torn up over the whole thing and sketchy on the details. Finn knew that Dante, the guy Garrett had originally thought was a threat to Elsa, had been hurt pretty bad. Finn had cleared Dante as a suspect when Garrett first became aware that someone was after Elsa.

Finn's investigation had revealed that he and his dad weren't the only people in Summer Park with special gifts. Summer Park was a happening place for psychics.

Garrett was supporting Elsa as best he could, and now that Dante was in his good graces, Garrett would do everything in his power to help. From the sound of things, his friend Rachel needed him too. So Finn would get by on his own.

He wouldn't call, even to check in. Garrett knew Finn too well and would be able to tell that something was wrong. It would have been great to have Garrett to talk to, though. Finn missed him.

Garrett had a tight circle of friends who all supported each other. Finn was more like a satellite on the periphery. He would have loved the chance to join their club, but since he and Jazz split, that wasn't an option anymore. It never really had been.

He couldn't believe how much it still hurt that she didn't want to include him in her life anywhere outside the bedroom or Dad's bar. Finn had been in the same room as Elsa, but never been introduced. He'd never laid eyes on Rachel. Garrett didn't know Finn and Jazz had been a couple. She had insisted on secrecy.

Finn had offered her everything he had, everything he was. She hadn't wanted to be seen in public with him. Not as a couple, anyway.

In private, though… He could feel the warmth she kept locked away. Her smiles would make him forget whatever had been bothering him. Her touch had ruined him for other women, and not just because she was the only person he'd ever met that he couldn't read.

"Finn?"

Dad's voice snapped him out of his thoughts. Dammit, it was so hard to focus.

"I didn't say anything when you buried yourself in your work or when you dropped most of your friends except Garrett. But you're not even hanging out with him now. You don't talk to Daphne. Or to me."

"Dad—"

"You're isolating yourself. It's not healthy. You wake up screaming every night and drag around here all day. You haven't been right for years. You've been living like a monk ever since—"

"Not everything is about Jazz, okay!"

Finn picked up the salt shaker on the table and chucked it at the wall across the room. It embedded itself in the cheap plaster. Daphne gasped and stepped away from the counter, as if she was concerned Finn wasn't done with his tantrum.

Shit.

Finn took a deep breath and let it out slowly. He covered his eyes with one hand as he tried to get control of himself.

Nothing was in control.

Dropping his hand, he said, "I'm sorry. Look, I'll fix it later. Today." He was going to get a handle on this, dammit.

"I'll take care of it," Daphne said.

"You don't have to."

"I know," she said. "But I will."

"If you don't want to talk to us, fine," Dad said. "But you need to talk to someone. Call Garrett."

Finn was glad *that* was the name Dad had chosen. Usually when Finn was in a funk, Dad bugged him to call Jazz and see if he could patch things up. Beg her to come back to him. If only Dad knew—Finn was the one who had broken things off. Still, he doubted she'd be coming back any time soon. Or ever.

For some reason, Dad never urged Finn to move on. It was like he knew that wasn't an option.

Three years. Three years and Finn thought about her every damned day. When he wasn't thinking about the woman from his nightmares.

Finn had seen a news story about Michael Angelo the day after he'd been killed. The details were sketchy, but Michael's picture was in a little box on the screen as the reporter spoke.

"A serial killer who went by the name of Michael Angelo was caught and killed yesterday evening. Police are investigating several missing persons cases that may be related..."

Finn was shocked to recognize the killer from his nightmares. It didn't take long for him to realize he was the creepy blond guy that had been stalking Elsa. Maybe it was the readings he did trying to track Michael down, but something about the guy had made it under Finn's skin.

Even Finn's powers had gone crazy. When Finn tried to read objects, he saw the memories attached to them as if he was the person involved—not as a detached observer. It was visceral, like he was there in that moment.

Touching someone to read their thoughts was even worse. The only way he'd made it out of their heads was when they jerked away, looking at him like he was nuts.

He had to get his powers back under control. Otherwise, he really would have to become a monk. Being around people was too dangerous.

Finn stood and started toward his room. Daphne stepped in front of him.

"Where are you going?" she asked.

"Out."

He had a sudden urge to do something, to get out of the house, to leave. It was overwhelming.

The nightmares were tied to one of Michael Angelo's

victims. Finn was sure of it. He had to figure out why she was haunting his dreams. To do that, he needed to find out more about who she was and what had happened. He looked back at Dad.

"I do have a case," Finn said.

And it started with Michael Angelo. That was Finn's only lead.

Chapter Three

The gallery had been her life for almost a decade. Now, Jazz could barely stand the thought of stepping inside. It had been rough after breaking up with Finn, with so many memories of the two of them together when no one else was around. That was nothing compared to this.

To hell with it. This was *her* gallery.

She unlocked the door and stalked inside, heading for the alcove that hid the alarm panel. She keyed in the code to shut it off—Finn's birthday. She should really change it, but that would mean letting go of one more part of him. At least she could keep this little piece in her life.

Ugh. Maudlin thoughts.

"Enough!" She actually waved her arm in the air to cut herself off.

Great. Now she was talking to herself.

She flipped on the lights for the foyer, then pulled her sweater over her head and walked to the front door to lock it. The white T-shirt she wore reflected from the glass.

She was trying to put on a show of having her shit together. Same black leather pants as always, matching boots up to her knees, the V-neck shirt, minimal make-up, and the same attitude. She wanted her friends to know they could count on her.

They didn't really seem to need much help anymore. That left her alone with her thoughts, which would not shut the hell up.

Peering out at the dark street gave her the creeps, especially after her conversation with Rachel. Jazz already believed ghosts walked among the living. Hearing Rachel's firsthand account of encountering them— knowing they were *everywhere*—that was a bit much.

Not the ghost I was looking for, though.

But that was a good thing. Her father had crossed over. Chloe told Jazz during their first séance. It had taken a while for Jazz to accept it, but after all these years, she was glad. She believed he was in a happier place.

Her eyes filled with tears again. She was sick of it. People were counting on her, people she had already let down. She had to find a way to make it up to them.

Rachel was staying with Garrett. That was a huge blessing. Elsa had the necklace that would protect her during her travels. Dante was in good spirits, considering…

Jazz clenched her eyes shut and turned back toward the gallery. She didn't want to remember seeing him with his face covered in bandages. She really didn't want to remember what he had looked like when the EMTs had taken him away.

She had been so proud of Dante. So happy for him and Elsa and the life they were about to start together. A life Jazz had helped them create.

A wave of anxiety rippled through her. She had wanted Elsa happy. Wanted her to find love. That was part of what had blinded Jazz to Michael in the first place. Setting him up on a date with Elsa had been the first mistake—the one that let him into their inner circle.

How much had she talked Elsa up to Michael? What had Jazz said to Dante? She couldn't remember. But if she had been too ebullient in her praise, too obviously affectionate in her own feelings toward her best friend...

This could all be her fucking curse again.

Every fortune-teller Jazz had ever been to had given her the same reading. No matter what divination method they used, the message was always, "You are an implement of Fate." They said Jazz would play a vital role in facilitating the fates of the people in her life, helping them on the paths to their destinies.

She wished they had warned her about how dark those destinies could be.

Jazz had thought the readings were weird and amusing the first few times she visited psychics, until Fate struck her down over and over again—any time she bragged too much about someone she loved. And the stronger her emotion was, the worse the consequences would be.

It would have been easier to handle if Jazz was the one

who bore the brunt of it, but the curse targeted the object of her affection. Whenever she was too happy and let anyone know, whoever she loved most paid the price.

At least this time no one had died. Well, no one who didn't deserve it.

Her friends didn't deserve what had happened to them, though. They were good people. They shouldn't be suffering.

Even doped up on medicines, Dante seemed to sense Jazz's distress and tried to ease her conscience, making jokes and pleasant conversation. It only made her feel worse.

She was used to his mask. The Phantom one was her favorite. The first time she saw his scars, she hadn't reacted well. He'd caught her off-guard, and she had already been worried about Elsa at the time.

What would he look like when the bandages came off?

"Goddammit, Jazz," she said. "Get it together."

He would still be gorgeous. He would still be Dante.

Watching Elsa dote on him earlier that afternoon should have been hilarious—like Winston's running commentary while he made everyone dinner. How could they laugh so soon? Jazz was still raw, especially after visiting them. She practically vibrated with the need to *do* something.

God, she missed Finn. If they had still been a couple, going back to his place would have been the first order of business. Or heading to the office in the gallery. She needed an outlet for her frustrations. Finn had always been so great about that, sensing when she'd had enough with talking and thinking and needed to just feel—even if he obviously had more he wanted to say.

And you wonder why he bailed.

She would be grateful to have him as a friend at this point. He was the only person she ever felt she could talk to. She gave Rachel orders, teased Elsa, chatted with Garrett, but only really talked to Finn. He knew her plans for the gallery, everything she hoped to accomplish with it.

She wanted to build up her business so that she could become an integral part of the community, could change Summer Park for the better. Hell, she had even shared her dreams for retirement—filling her twilight years with travel and new experiences.

If they were still hanging out, she could ask him for another self-defense lesson just to have someone to wail on. He'd encouraged her to let herself go as much as she wanted. He told her he could take whatever she dished out.

Apparently not. It didn't take long for him to decide he didn't want her in his life at all.

She was supposed to be over him by now. Dammit, she *was* over him. She had moved on.

She threw her sweater down on the bench seat near the door, then headed for Dante's exhibit room. Looking at his paintings would help clear her head and calm her. It might help her feel less alone.

She turned on the lights for his room and took a deep breath as the soothing artwork entered her peripheral vision.

A portrait of Elsa at her writing desk hung on the wall opposite the entrance to the exhibit. In the painting, Elsa's blonde hair glowed with gold tones that warmed her brown eyes. She was dressed in a pale pink tank top and pajamas that picked up splashes of color in the sky visible through the windows of her solarium.

Jazz loved the piece. If she thought Dante would sell it, she would buy it in a second. He had beautifully captured Elsa's balance of vulnerability and strength. The cautious hope on her features left Jazz breathless. The brushstrokes were bold and gentle at the same time. How did he do it?

She stood in the center of the room, turning to look at Dante's landscapes. She felt herself smile, her cheeks stiff and bewildered. It had been a while. His paintings lifted her spirits. If she had Elsa's ability, that lifting would be literal—Jazz would be able to go back in time to when Dante had made the pieces.

She still wouldn't be able to warn them.

This wasn't helping. Not her, not anyone. She needed a plan, a focus. Some sort of direction.

One of Dante's landscapes caught her eye. It was Elsa's backyard, which seemed as big as a freaking football field. Jazz didn't want to know how much her friend paid to make the grass green and thick in such a large space.

Normally, Jazz thought of it as wasteful. But it had helped Dante create this masterpiece.

There was a wistfulness in it. He had captured the gentle swaying of the palms and pines along her property line. The painting almost seemed to move. Garrett's house was right on the other side of those trees, a much smaller dwelling on a bit less land.

For a moment, Jazz actually felt homesick.

Maybe she should throw in the towel and move back to Kansas. Join her mom on a swing on the front porch and watch her little sister raise those three adorable nieces. The idea was good on paper, but the reality would be anything but peaceful. Her sister would light into her immediately, like she always did.

"When are you going to have kids? You should really settle down with someone. You're not getting any younger you know. My kids need more playmates."

Their mom would just sit and stare at them, letting them work it out between themselves and not taking sides. Jazz knew what that side would be, though. Her mom had married and had kids, after all. Jazz just wasn't interested.

Her sister wouldn't take no for an answer. Even when Jazz had confided that she'd already gone through with a tubal ligation and had no interest in government-sanctioned ceremonies to legally bind her to another person, Mei had just said, *"You can adopt. Hire a nanny with all that art-money."*

Mei could really be a pain in the ass.

"Dammit!"

This is not helping.

Jazz needed to get out of her head. Or at least switch what she was focusing on.

There was a mountain of paperwork waiting for her in the office. Bills, schedules, emails—all the gallery work that she'd been putting off while focusing on getting her friends back on an even keel. Everyone else seemed to be doing better, but Jazz felt like she was drifting around in a fog. She was sick of it.

She headed for her office, stopping long enough in the alcove to turn off the main lights before scaling the stairs two at a time.

Chapter Four

Finn couldn't believe he was doing this. Breaking into Jazz's gallery in the middle of the night.

All his leads had come up empty. He was sure the Montgomerys were the ones burying the story. Everyone Finn talked to had been nervous. Enough so that he was considering looking into that family when he was done with this case. Bribery only went so far. The people he spoke with acted more like they were being threatened.

He didn't dare try to read their minds with his powers out of control. He had to solve this case first and get back to normal. The gallery was the only option he had left. He hoped he wasn't getting in over his head.

Luckily, he'd helped Jazz design and install her security system. He knew where the cameras pointed, where the blind spots were, and the interior layout. He even had a key to the back door, though he was sure she'd changed the lock.

He walked up to the edge of the back camera's field of view, which was a few feet away from the door. Black gloves protected him from picking up random memories and leaving prints anywhere. If anyone reviewed the footage, the long raincoat and his dad's fedora would disguise his features once he was visible. Of course, if he could get in and out like he hoped, no one would think they needed to look…

His thoughts trailed off as he looked at the doorknob. Same shade of gray, same model, same scratch on the handle where Jazz had lost her grip on an unwieldy metal sculpture and dropped it—a secret he was sworn to take to his grave, even though it hadn't been damaged.

She'd felt so bad about it, she'd purchased it from the artist and then donated it to the local hospital. And sworn to him that she'd hire people to help her move heavier pieces in the future. It was a big concession for her. She was a hands-on kind of person. In many, many ways.

He shook off the slew of memories that floated right at the back of his mind. The gallery was full of them, like when she'd given him the key on their one-month anniversary. At the time, he'd thought it was a great sign— that they were on the same page and headed toward a lifelong partnership. Turns out, she trusted him with her business. Not her heart.

It still didn't make sense that she hadn't changed out the lock. She'd had years to do it. Maybe she'd only replaced the tumbler and kept the rest of the hardware. Maybe she'd expected him to come crawling back after he left. If so, he doubted these were the circumstances she had in mind.

He pulled out his key ring. The gallery key was still on it. Ducking his head, he quickly walked to the door, then slid the key in the lock and turned it.

Click.

There was no time to reflect on what that meant— which was probably nothing. He slipped into the dark gallery and shut the door behind him, then turned to look at the motion sensors.

Green light. Bad news.

That meant someone was already in the gallery. Unless the alarm had been left off. He doubted that was the case. Jazz loved her gallery. She wouldn't leave it unprotected. At this time of night, she was probably the one hanging around. He hoped so…and he hoped not. Seeing her would be too much to deal with right now.

He needed to be quick.

The streetlamps outside the big front windows gave him just enough light to see vague shapes and doorways. Finding Michael Angelo's exhibit room was easy. It was the one roped off with police tape. He couldn't believe Jazz hadn't dealt with that yet. The doorway leading to Michael's room wasn't visible from the front foyer at least.

It wasn't like her to let anything interfere with her business. Two months was a long time to keep the gallery closed.

He pushed aside his unwelcome concern as he ducked under the yellow ribbon of plastic crisscrossing the doorway and turned on his flashlight. The small beam cut a weak line of light through the darkness.

The room was cold. Colder than the rest of the gallery. Colder than it should be. The hairs on his arms were standing on end, even under his coat. He half expected his breath to come out as fog.

What the hell?

It was probably his imagination. He was already dreading what he had to do. Terrified, actually. He was going to try to read the walls.

The chance of him getting anything was slim. He wasn't reading an object—he was reading a wall that had touched an object. And the paintings had been removed months before. The more time passed, the more the energy dissipated.

But this was a special case. The paintings that had hung on these walls were covered in blood. Blood put in place while Michael's victims were dying. They watched it flow from their bodies and be spread on the canvas.

Sick fucking bastard.

Finn was glad Rachel had killed Michael. After reliving the memories of one of Michael's victims every night for two months, Finn wanted to kill the guy himself.

What he didn't want was to read these walls. He almost hoped he would come up empty. Except then, he'd be stuck like this indefinitely. At least reading the walls would be safer than reading the paintings. Finn was counting on that.

The paintings had to be filled with terrible energy. Too much energy—memories that were so dark, Finn was afraid of becoming trapped in them, of taking on more and losing himself entirely in the memories of Michael's victims. The residue left from the paintings would be easier for him to pull back from.

Please, let me be able to pull back from this.

Best to get it over with quickly. He put away his flashlight, then pulled the glove off his left hand and stuck it in the pocket of his jeans.

He did not want to do this. He so did not want to do this. But he touched the wall anyway, his fingers splayed over the smooth surface.

Voices began to echo in Finn's mind, their words distorted as he strained to listen. Yelling. Jazz's voice mixed in. Elsa's name. A man's voice as well. Accented. Crisp. *Dante.*

Finn pushed back farther. Sweat broke out on his forehead. He was keeping as tight a hold of his powers as he could, holding on to the tenuous threads of the past while trying to not lose control in the present.

A man and a woman speaking quietly. Her voice—her energy—was so familiar, but he couldn't place her. Dante again. They were talking about Michael's paintings.

Finn pushed more.

Jazz barking orders. Just her—in her element.

His breath hitched and he felt himself leaning forward, wanting to be closer to her, even now. He stopped himself, the strain increasing as he tried to control his body and his powers at the same time.

This used to be so easy.

He paused at that moment, listening to her voice. The measured cadence of her speech was comforting. It was the last comfort he was going to have for a while. He pushed again, rewinding the memories imprinted on the wall.

The room became colder. His skin prickled and he felt a pull, like gravity was shifting and the wall wanted to suck him in. His stomach lurched and his knees weakened. He had felt similar things working some of his early cases— before he had learned how to spot trouble and brace himself for it. Domestic investigations that had gone south. Way, way south.

He sensed death. Violence. Fear.

His stomach kept churning. He didn't want to hear anyone die. And if he became lost in the memory... He sure as hell didn't want to experience it with them.

At least in his nightmares, he always woke up before the victim died.

He couldn't feel his body anymore.

The wall was sending out ripples of energy, like it wanted to cleanse itself of the paintings it had touched. Then the ripples became a spiral, pulling him in, thick as tar.

He heard someone yell. He thought it was a memory beginning, but it was male. All of Michael's victims had been women, hadn't they?

The whirlpool that ensnared him vanished. Finn was on all fours on the floor, his right knee sending sharp spikes of pain to his brain. Before he could register what was going on, a strong, slender hand clasped his right wrist and pulled that arm out from under him, then twisted it around behind his back. His assailant jammed their knee into his back, further throwing him off balance so that he fell forward onto his face.

"Struggle and I will dislocate your shoulder."

Jazz.

Christ, her voice was sexy even when she was pulling his arm out of its socket. Trying to, anyway. She twisted his arm a bit further, just like he had taught her, making pain arc through him intense enough to beat out the throbbing in his knee for a moment.

"Ow."

The pressure lessened a miniscule amount. "Finn?"

Dammit. Why was he flattered that she knew it was him from one word? His idiotic heart was doing flips in his chest, as if it didn't remember her stepping on it. Repeatedly.

"Hi, sweetie," he said. "Thought I'd drop by and check out the gallery for old time's sake."

"In the middle of the night."

"I was trying to avoid an awkward encounter."

"How's that working for you?"

Man, he'd missed the snarky sarcasm. Truly, he had. He chuckled, face against the hard wood, waiting for her to be ready to let him up. Her weight disappeared from his back. She kept her grip on his wrist, though, and used it to help him turn over.

She was standing above him, long legs silhouetted against light that filtered in from the doorway. If she dropped to her knees, they could pick up right where they left off. More meaningless sex. More dashed hopes.

Not this time.

"Do you mind?" There was a bite to his tone that seemed just about right for how he was feeling.

Instead of stepping away, she bent down, sending his heart and other body parts into overdrive. Maybe meaningless sex wasn't such a bad thing. But then she gripped both his hands to help him up, and his lust instantly flipped to panic.

They were touching skin-to-skin. Their *hands* were touching skin-to-skin. At least, one of them. It might be enough for him to be pulled into her thoughts, to lose himself there.

Jazz was the only person in his life he had never been able to read. But that was before his powers went off the rails. He didn't want to read her thoughts now. He didn't want to see that she really didn't give a damn.

"Let go!"

She jerked back her hands as if he was made of lava. "Fine. Keep your ass on the floor."

"Come on, Jazz. Could you just give me a minute to try to get my bearings?"

"Once you do, find the door and get the hell out of my gallery." She walked to the wall near the door and flipped on the lights, blinding him.

He held up his arm to shield his eyes. "Right. Go for the weak spots to disable your opponent."

"That's what you taught me to do." She let out a sigh. "What are you doing here, Finn?"

Something in her voice was off. She sounded tired in a way that went beyond the physical. He'd never known her to be anything but charged with enough energy to power the state. Lifting himself on his elbows, he finally laid eyes on her again.

Damn...

Her skin was flawless, shining over her smooth cheekbones and highlighting the graceful curve of her jaw. Her black hair fell over her shoulders in thick locks. It was longer than he remembered. She looked thinner too. She didn't have the weight to spare, and his worry grew.

Her eyes were the same, though. Two spheres of onyx sparkling with intelligence and passion. Her lips were full and lush. He couldn't stop staring at them.

Memories flooded his mind, but at least this time, they were his own. He remembered those lips pressed against his body, how her long legs felt wrapped around his waist, how she would smile at him and make him feel as if he was the only man on Earth.

Finn's breath caught in his chest. Gorgeous wasn't a strong enough word to describe Jazz. Her presence filled the room, commanded him to focus on her and her alone.

"Stop looking at me like that."

Finn didn't have to ask what she meant. He scowled and lay back flat on the floor, covering his face with his hands. Jazz was forged from iron. Unyielding. No wonder he could never read her.

"Are you okay?"

"No, I'm not," he said.

That tentative edge was in her voice again. She almost sounded vulnerable. Shit, what the hell had happened? Where was her unshakeable confidence? Finn rolled onto his side, then rose on all fours.

"Let me help you."

He probably still couldn't read her. If she only touched him through his coat, he'd be fine either way.

"Thanks."

She held on to his arm as he tested putting weight on the leg she had kicked out from under him. Even when he was steady, she didn't let go.

He wanted to bury his hands in her hair and kiss her

and never stop. Hell, maybe melting into her wouldn't be such a bad thing. Except the unshakeable woman of iron he had dated was holding him with a trembling hand, and for the first time since he'd known her, there was uncertainty in her eyes.

Which only made him want to kiss her more. To hold her close and tell her he would make it right. Whatever was wrong, he would fix it.

One case at a time…

There was someone else he needed to help first. As much as he could at this point. The woman from his nightmares. He had to know what happened to her, why she was haunting his dreams. Hopefully then his powers would come back under control and the nightmares would stop.

"I'm working a case that involves one of Michael Angelo's victims."

"One of…" Jazz's gaze became unfocused for a moment. She shook her head brusquely. Her lips tightened and her eyebrows pinched together. Her eyes started to blaze.

Uh-oh.

"What do you need?" she said.

"I was just going to read the walls and see what I picked up."

Jazz was one of four people who knew about Finn's ability. The others were Garrett, Daphne, and Dad—who shared the gift. Apparently, it was hereditary and passed through sons. His line would end with Finn, which was okay by him. He had family up north to carry it on.

"You think you can get something from the wall even though the paintings are gone?" she asked.

"I'm hoping so. Especially since you've kept the place roped off." He gestured toward the yellow ribbon. "You thinking of making this a permanent display?"

"I'm thinking of burning it to the ground."

Shit. That was…extreme.

She crossed her arms and nodded. "Hurry up and get it over with. I don't like being here."

Finn felt his hatred of Michael ratchet up another notch. The bastard had driven Jazz out of her own gallery. There was no way she would have let this room stay as it was if she'd been around. It shook him to realize how deeply Michael had affected her. Finn didn't want to keep her there any more than necessary.

"I don't suppose I could get a little privacy?"

"I'm staying. Deal with it."

His jaw clenched at his most hated catchphrase. The only thing about their breakup he had been whole-heartedly grateful for was that he would never hear those words from her again.

And now she was about to see him use his wonked-out powers. This night was getting better and better.

He would have to stay in control. He *could* stay in

control. Repeating that thought, he turned back to the wall and pressed his hand to its cool surface.

Chapter Five

Jazz had returned to the gallery to try to set at least one corner of her world right. Instead, everything had been turned upside-down by finding Finn in the Cursed Display Room. That was what Jazz was going to call it forevermore. At least in her head.

Finn Connelly, the great love of her life. Who had kicked her to the curb before they had a chance to experience how great they could be together.

He looked like hell. Well, in an *I'm-too-sexy-to-do-laundry-or-shave* kind of way. The white tank top he wore under that ridiculous raincoat was rumpled and she wouldn't be surprised if he'd been wearing those same jeans for a week. His level of stubble was dangerously close to becoming a beard, and... She wanted to kiss him. Her skin burned from it, her heart pounded, and even her stomach seemed to be trying to reach out and touch him.

Just touch him...

Every part of her body was in agreement. But not her mind.

This was the guy who had broken her heart. He was the one who walked away. And she would *not* go crawling back to him. She wouldn't beg him to take her back, no matter how much she wanted to.

Even obviously exhausted, Finn was the most gorgeous man Jazz had laid eyes on. And hands... And mouth... And...

Something was wrong. His breath was coming out in little grunts. He raised his right hand slowly, as if someone or some*thing* was trying to hold it down and he was fighting against them.

He punched the wall. Hard. Hard enough to hurt. She was surprised the drywall held. The impact propelled him backward, away from the wall. He ended in a crouching, fighting stance, eyes wild, glancing around the room as if he expected to be attacked.

Jazz knew better than to approach anyone standing like that, even before Finn's lessons. She waited for his breathing to calm, his body to straighten and relax.

"Are you okay?" she asked.

He didn't reply. He seemed to be looking right through her.

"Finn?"

"Yeah?" He spoke as if he hadn't heard her.

"I asked if you're okay."

She watched his throat work as he swallowed. He put both hands on his face and shook his head, then dropped his arms to his sides and let out a huge breath.

"I'm fine," he said.

"Seriously? That is the biggest load of bull."

He glared at her, but she didn't care. He had scared her. She was sick of being scared for people she cared about, and dammit she still cared about him.

"What the hell was that?" she asked.

"That was me using my powers."

"I've seen you use your powers before. It never looked like that."

"This is a special case."

No kidding. What had he seen that affected him so profoundly? She couldn't believe that even an echo from the paintings would do that to him. Then again, she'd seen with her own eyes what Michael had done to Rachel. The mangled flesh on her wrists, the waxy cast to her skin from so much blood loss—blood *theft*.

Jazz didn't let herself think about what had happened in that garage before she and the police showed up. She couldn't bear it. She wasn't sure she could stand watching Finn try to read the wall again, either.

You can and you will, if it helps him.

"Did you find what you're looking for?" she asked.

"No."

Her stomach sank. "Finn…"

"You don't have to stay."

But she did. She absolutely did. Dante still had multiple surgeries ahead of him. The bruises on Elsa's neck had only faded a few weeks before, and Rachel was trapped in

Garrett's house until they could figure out a way to keep ghosts from haunting her. Michael might not be among the ghosts bothering her, but even the residue of what he had done was still hurting people.

There was no *fucking* way she would let Michael hurt Finn from beyond the grave. Not if she had anything to say about it.

"I'm staying. Tell me how to help."

His mouth opened, then snapped shut. There was something she could do, but he didn't want to tell her.

Typical. They had never really been partners.

She might not want a marriage contract, but she still wanted a companion. Part of that was having someone to lean on and part was wanting to be the one giving help. It had never been easy for either of them to ask.

"I'll get it out of you," she said. "You know I will."

"Yeah." He sighed. "If I seem to get…stuck, snap me out of it. Just go for the left knee this time. The right one's already taken a beating."

He gave her his best cocky grin. She saw right through it. Still, that flash of teeth, all the memories that gorgeous fake smile brought out of her made her stomach flood with butterflies. Her heart was pounding again and heat started to build deep within her.

And she'd thought she was over him. What a joke.

Finn must have grown tired of her meaningful stare. He headed to another spot where a painting had been. The track lighting was still set up for the exhibit, making it obvious where the pictures were supposed to hang.

Jazz had considered Michael's work dark, brilliant, and compelling. Her stomach cramped at the thought.

Each space represented a lost life. Each one had left a family grieving that would never find closure. Michael had carried the names of his victims to the grave. She hadn't thought of that, either. She'd been too busy taking care of her friends. Still in shock over what had happened.

All those people… If Finn could help even one family find closure, Jazz wanted to help him. Finally, she could *do* something. Something to try to make things better. To set the scales right. It was a start, at least.

Finn shook his left hand, like he was trying to remove any residue from the first spot he'd checked, then he placed it on the wall. He was wearing a glove on his right hand. She'd never seen him wear gloves before. That and the coat were weird wardrobe choices for Florida.

Says she of the leather pants.

Working on such a disturbing case, it made sense that he'd want to protect himself from seeing things when he wasn't ready. Maybe the gloves were supposed to help with that.

When he'd told her about his powers, he said they worked primarily through his hands. He could read memories off objects and actually read peoples' minds if he maintained contact. Luckily, he couldn't read her for some reason. The idea of having sex with someone who could read her thoughts during skin contact was not a turn-on.

Jazz wasn't sure how he was getting anything from a wall that touched a painting. The energy imbedded in the paintings must have been intense. She thought of Elsa and her ability to travel through art by using the emotional energy infused into creating or even observing it.

Finn's powers didn't seem to be based on any kind of heightened emotion, though. He could read anything that happened around an object. He said the further back he went, the blurrier the memories became. The paintings had been gone for almost two months. He had to be pushing his limits.

He started to lean toward the wall he was reading. That didn't seem good. He pressed his forehead against the surface, bringing his right hand up to help support himself. He shifted his weight to his left leg. She had kicked his right knee pretty hard when she'd thought he was a burglar.

"Finn? You okay?"

He didn't respond at first. When he did, his voice sounded strange. Lighter, more breathy.

"You are so beautiful."

He turned his right hand and ran the backs of his knuckles over the wall's surface. That was weird.

"Look at me," he said. "Look at me!"

Jazz jumped at his sudden shout. The change in his demeanor was so fast and unexpected.

"What the hell, Finn."

But he didn't turn. He didn't even register that she was there. Did that mean he was stuck or was he just immersed in a memory? She didn't like that he was acting things out. Besides being creepy as hell, he was reading the memories of *a murderer*.

Finn pinched his index finger and thumb together, like he was offering the wall a treat. She had seen that gesture before. Michael used to tip Rachel's face toward him by putting his hand under her chin that way.

"There, now. Isn't that better," Finn said. "You shouldn't have spilled the blood, Nicole. I can't finish your portrait without more."

"Shit!" Jazz's stomach seemed to drop through the floor.

"Don't worry. I'll get you something to eat and drink. We'll spend a bit more time together than I planned. That's all right, though. I forgive you. This is my first masterwork. Delays are to be expected."

Was this what Finn meant by getting stuck? She thought he meant he could get stuck viewing a memory, not that he'd actually become part of it. She never would have let him read the wall if she'd known.

She grabbed his shoulders and pulled, but he didn't budge. She yanked on just his right arm, but that didn't work either. He was half a foot taller and at least a hundred pounds heavier than she was. She'd always loved how his body was all muscle, admired how he sculpted himself. Now she just wished he was smaller.

He shifted closer to the wall, as if he was going to lie against it. She had no idea what that would do to him. There was still a narrow space, and she slipped into it, putting herself between Finn and the wall.

His body pressed against hers, bringing back her own memories. They hadn't been able to get enough of each other. Any closet, any private space was fair game. They'd had sex in her office in the gallery more times than she could count.

This time, her skin crawled at the close contact. This time, it wasn't Finn.

Finn was thick with muscle—carefully controlled muscle. He had always seemed to envelop her, melding himself to her body as if they were made for each other. It made her feel delicate and strong at the same time. Finn owned himself, his body and his movement. The body pressing against hers was tense, hesitant.

"Finn, look at me."

She put her hands on his cheeks, forcing him to face her. The pale blue-gray of his irises had hints of a brighter, darker blue bleeding in around their edges.

What the hell?

"Dammit, Finn!"

Pain had snapped him out of it before. Maybe it could again. She slapped him, hard. He didn't even blink. The blue kept seeping into his eyes as he murmured disturbing things to a woman long since dead.

"Finn, please…"

She slapped him again, even harder. This time, he blinked and shook his head. Jazz used the opportunity, bracing herself against the wall and shoving his chest as hard as she could. They stumbled away from the wall together.

He shook his head, then turned toward the ceiling. He covered his face with his hands as he took deep breaths. On the last burst of an exhalation, he lowered his head and hands, then opened his eyes.

Pale blue again. He was himself.

Chapter Six

"What the hell was that?"

Finn had never heard Jazz yell so loud. His head already hurt, and the noise was like a jackhammer on his skull.

"Could you keep it down a little bit?"

"No, I can't keep it down! You need to tell me what just happened."

Finn ran his hands over his face. His cheek stung like crazy. "Why does my face hurt?"

"Because I slapped you. Twice."

He let out a snort, then walked to the low viewing bench that ran along the middle of the room and sat down.

"I hope you didn't enjoy it too much."

Her rage kicked up higher, rolling from her in palpable waves that he didn't need his powers to detect. The volume of her voice lessened, but that just made her more intimidating.

"Fuck you."

Damn. Yeah, that was past the line.

"Sorry."

"Your eyes changed color," she said. "The things you

were saying, it was like you were *turning into Michael*. You just scared the shit out of me."

His eyes had changed? That was scary for him too. He knew he was having trouble pulling himself from other people's memories, but he didn't think it was manifesting externally. He didn't think his powers *could* manifest that way. It brought up too many terrifying possibilities.

"I'm sorry. I didn't know that would happen." He leaned forward with his elbows on his knees and put his head in his hands. "I don't know what I'm doing, Jazz. I'm trying to fix things, but I just can't put them right."

"What are you trying to fix?" The fire had left her voice.

"Me. My powers."

In his periphery, he saw her stoop to pick up Dad's hat. He hadn't even realized it had fallen along with him earlier. She set it next to him, then joined him on the bench.

"Start at the beginning."

Feeling her body so close to his, he didn't trust himself to look at her while he spoke. The need to touch her was almost overwhelming. He stared at the floor, clasping his hands in front of him. He wished he could hold her. Hell, he wished she would hold him, but it was way too late for that.

"Two months back, I woke up from this screaming nightmare. Dad came running into the room, asking what was going on. I didn't know. I tried to shake it off. Told him it was nothing."

"But it wasn't."

"Yeah." Finn nodded. "It was something. Big time."

"Did Tommy believe you?"

Her tone warmed just mentioning Dad. It was so obvious how much they loved each other. Finn never understood why she was fine with becoming part of his family, but wouldn't tell her own or even any of their friends they were dating. Old indignities tried to rise up in him, but he was too tired for them to take hold.

"At first. But the nightmares didn't stop. Every night, I'm either sleeping so hard no one can wake me, or I wake everybody up screaming. It's been wearing on them."

"Them?"

Right. Daphne had moved in after Jazz was out of Finn's life. He didn't know why the thought of telling Jazz made him uncomfortable. There had never been the tiniest spark between him and Daphne. She was much more interested in Dad. If he'd stop being blinded by the difference in their ages, he'd see it.

"The new bartender has been living in our guest room."

He glanced over at her in time to see her smile, the tension easing in her features. He caught a glimpse of the face she had shared with him and his dad and no one else —not that he'd ever seen, anyway. No cockiness, no bravado. Just Jazz. It only lasted a moment, but it was enough to send him reeling.

"Finally." She let out a brief laugh. "I told you guys you needed more help."

"Yeah, you were right, as always. Daphne's been a big help in and out of the bar."

Jazz went completely still. From what he could see, she wasn't even breathing.

Crap.

"We're not…together. Never have been."

Goddammit, why was he compelled to explain himself? He could practically hear ice crackling around her, a thick coat of cold blocking her off. That was another thing he hadn't missed—her freezing him out.

"Not my business," she said.

Yeah. That was a familiar sentiment.

She launched herself from the bench and headed for the wall. He expected her to lean against it, cross her arms, and glare at him. Her arms were already lifting when she balked, then turned away and started to pace. She didn't so much cross her arms as hug herself as she walked.

That was new. She probably didn't want to touch the walls after what she had seen and heard from Finn. He wished he could un-see it himself.

Nicole had been a thin blonde woman with blue eyes. Similar to the one in Finn's dreams, but not the same. Nicole was much smaller, for one thing.

In his dreams, Michael used a needle, tubing, and jars

to siphon blood from his victim's body. Nicole...

Her body had been covered in cuts. Michael was using a knife.

Finn ran his hands over his face again. If he thought this case was about bringing Michael down, he would be all over it. He'd be charging in and reading everything he could to bring the bastard to justice.

But Michael was already dead. Finn seriously didn't know what he was accomplishing with any of this, aside from figuring out the identities of the victims. Like Nicole.

Did she have a family somewhere? Were they still hoping, waiting for her to come home? How would they react if Finn walked in and told them she was gone? He hoped they never found out what had been done to her.

"Tell me about the nightmares." Jazz's clipped voice was commanding. Somehow, that reassured him—made him feel that he wasn't in this alone. At least for the moment.

"I'm inside someone else's body, sharing their experience. I'm chained to a wall in darkness. My wrists are burning, my arms sore where they aren't numb. There's cold cement under my knees and my lungs are full of stale air."

Jazz stopped pacing and stared at him. He knew that look. It would be a while before she spoke. She wanted more information. He could provide it.

"I've only been able to see and hear things in dreams

before. These are different. I have all my senses. I can feel everything, and I... Whoever it was, she was so scared. They always end the same way. Light floods the room, and this guy comes in."

"Michael Angelo." Jazz said the name like a dirge. Appropriate.

"I recognized him from the news. I can see his face clearly in the nightmares. I know he was the one hurting me. Hurting her."

"Do you know who she was?"

He looked over at Jazz and let out a short chuff of breath. "I wish. Maybe then I'd have a clue what the hell is going on. I mean, why am I having these dreams? I didn't touch anything or anyone related to this case. I would have known if I did. Nothing like this has ever happened before."

"What did Tommy say about it?"

"I haven't told him."

"Why not?"

Finn let out a sigh that felt like it emptied him out. "Dad had a heart attack not too long ago. We almost lost him." Finn's voice cracked a bit, but he didn't let it slow him down. "It scared the crap out of me. He's worried enough already. If he finds out my powers are..."

He paused when he looked up at her. All the blood had drained from her face and her mouth was hanging open.

"You okay?"

"I...um..." She shook her head and swayed on her feet.

Finn leapt up and grabbed her, pulling her against his chest. She gripped his arms tight, taking slow, steady breaths. She murmured something too quiet for him to hear.

"What was that?"

"You should have called me!"

She shoved him hard. Pushing him away. Always fucking pushing him away. She staggered to the bench and sat down with her head between her knees.

After a few moments, she said, "Is he going to be okay?"

Affection and jealousy were fighting it out inside of Finn. She loved his dad so much. Why the hell couldn't she love Finn that much? Like he loved her—passionately, completely.

"The doctors say he needs to be careful. Dad did their rehab and is seeing a specialist." And the bills were still rolling in. Bills Finn was doing his best to intercept so Dad didn't worry more. "He's exercising more and we're watching what we eat. And he isn't working so many late hours."

"Okay." She let out a shaky breath. "That's good."

She was worse off than he thought. It made sense, though. She had almost lost Elsa and Rachel. Hearing about Dad when Jazz was already off her game... Yeah, he understood why it was hitting her hard. He was glad to know at least she still cared about his dad.

"Has Tommy ever been haunted?" she asked.

Her voice was a little muffled since her face was pointed at the floor. Finn couldn't have heard her right.

"What?"

"Haunted." Jazz sat back up, looking more stable. "Has he ever run into any ghosts?"

Finn laughed and shook his head. Jazz didn't join him.

"Oh, you're serious."

Her stare turned into a glare and he cleared his throat.

"He's never mentioned it. And he would have told me when he taught me about our powers."

Jazz nodded. "We need to talk to Tommy. I get that you don't want to worry him. We'll figure out a way—"

"Hold up." Strolling down his own memory lane had been...awkward and uncomfortable. But he was done. Jazz was a distraction. Being around her was too damned painful. "There is no *we*. *I* will figure out a way."

"Not this time. I'm in, whether you like it or not."

"All I need is more time with this room. I already have a name now. Nicole. I can check with missing persons files and see if I can find more leads."

"I'm. In. And there is no way in hell I'm letting you read more of these walls. Not after almost losing you like that."

"Look, your concern is touching, but—"

"You try, and I'll have you arrested for trespassing."

He stared at her, stunned for a moment. "You wouldn't."

She cocked an eyebrow at him, then stood and pulled out her phone. Yeah. She would. He shook his head and smiled.

"Same old Jazz."

If he could manage half of her self-control and determination, he doubted his powers would be acting up at all. Maybe having her along would help. She could keep him from losing himself in the memories he read. He just needed to be sure he didn't lose his heart again.

Right. As if it wasn't already hers.

He rose to his feet without realizing how close she was standing. A few inches of space separated their bodies. It might as well have been an entire universe.

Chapter Seven

Jazz wished that Finn was farther away. Or closer. She wasn't sure which she would prefer. He was too close for her to ignore the effect he always had on her, but not close enough for her to really enjoy it.

Now that he wasn't trying to crush her against the wall, she was back to appreciating his size. He wasn't nearly as tall as Garrett—then again, who was?—but Finn was packed with muscle. She could see the outlines of his pecs through his tank top, traces of his chest hair peeking out.

Do not think about Finn's chest.

She needed to focus on the issue at hand. He was trying to shut her out again, and she wouldn't stand for it.

"I'm not going to let this go," she said.

"I kind of figured."

She felt herself relax an infinitesimal amount. At least their history helped him know when she wasn't about to back down.

"I'm not saying you shouldn't try to figure this out. I'm just saying you can be smarter about it. If these walls are pulling you into Michael's memories so strongly that you can't find your way out on your own, maybe you should try less visceral spots."

The paintings were physically linked to the women Michael had killed. Strongly linked. It would be as bad as reading the chains in his garage. Jazz stifled a shiver at the memory of red-crusted metal—Rachel's blood on the manacles attached to those chains.

There would be other places in Michael's house that Finn could read, though. Places that might not be as strongly connected to Michael but could still give them useful information. She doubted Finn would have come to the gallery if he knew where Michael lived. They could go there and try to find another lead. Very carefully.

"You sound like you have something in mind," Finn said.

"I do, but I'm not telling you until we've talked to Tommy."

Tommy. She couldn't believe she'd get to talk to him. She had missed him too. Her head started to swirl again as she thought about his heart attack. She could have lost him without having a chance to say goodbye. Just like she'd lost her own father.

Never *think about Father.*

Tommy. Think about Tommy.

She wanted to see him with her own eyes—to know he was okay. There was no way Finn could move on without her this time. He was stuck with her.

"I'll drive," she said.

"Aren't you afraid people will see us together?"

They were *not* going to have this argument again. Not after all these years. Not now.

"I have tinted windows."

He glared at her, but then let out a sigh and shook his head. "Fine."

She had expected more of a fight. Finn giving in so easily only made her more worried.

"Come on, then."

Her SUV was parked right in front of the gallery. In this part of town, shops closed up and people went home early. At least, on a boring Wednesday night. She could actually find parking on the street.

"That is a big-ass SUV," Finn said. "I thought you didn't want to own a car."

Jazz shrugged. The car beeped as she hit the button to unlock the doors. "I need it for transporting art."

She had removed all but the front seats right after buying it and laid out a tarp for extra padding. She wasn't even sure where the other seats were anymore. Maybe somewhere in the gallery or the storage unit for her apartment. At the moment, the back space of the vehicle was empty and roomy. Big enough for two.

Dammit. Stop thinking about Finn. Especially that way.

They climbed in and buckled up. Finn was sitting next to her. It was like a dream. If only the circumstances were different.

The bar was halfway across town. He broke the silence after a few minutes.

"Dad's been reading tons of Westerns since the doctors told him to take it easy." Finn fiddled with the brim of Tommy's hat. "When the library ran out of new ones, he started reading romances set in the west. Now he's hooked and reads anything he can get his hands on, no matter where or when it's set. He especially likes the historicals, though."

"I can absolutely picture your dad reading a romance novel."

Jazz laughed, and Finn joined her. She couldn't believe how good it felt to hear. Her heart skipped from the sound. What kind of a fool was she?

"Yeah, he's not shy about liking them. He's been chatting up the regulars, going on and on about the stories."

She imagined Tommy leaning across the bar, holding a dog-eared paperback with the cover bent backward as he pointed out a particular passage. Tommy had a way with people. He was always kind, an incredible listener, and gave good advice when asked. Everybody loved him.

It warmed her heart to think of Finn and his dad still living together and taking care of each other. Talking to Finn like this… It was bringing back memories of the first few weeks when they were dating, before things had become complicated.

"You're still above the bar?"

"We like it above the bar," he snapped.

And the moment passed. "I know you do. I didn't mean anything by it. I just thought you might have moved into your own place at some point."

"Dad needs me."

"I get that. I was thinking about before his..." She couldn't even bring herself to say it. She shook her head. "It's been years, Finn. Things happen. *Change* happens."

Finn let out a huge sigh and ran his fingers through his hair. It was down-soft. She knew.

"I'm sorry. It's been hard to keep a lid on my temper with all of this crap going on."

"It's understandable." Rather than wade into the nebulous waters of their emotions, she pulled on her pragmatic façade. "When did your powers start acting up?"

"The day Michael Angelo was killed. I ran it down with the little bit of information I could find. I never would have guessed such a big story could be squelched like this was."

"It was a good thing. The people involved have been through enough."

Jazz felt her fingers tighten on the wheel. She wished she could break it in two. It might make her feel better since there wasn't a damned thing she could do to change what had happened to her friends.

"I know Elsa was involved." He spoke gently, but Jazz felt as if she'd been slapped. She stared at him, wondering how he had found out.

Elsa had ridden in the SUV a couple of times since that night, but Finn's hands were carefully folded in his lap. His gloves were on. While she stared, he suddenly reached for the wheel, jerking it toward him.

"Watch the road!"

Adrenaline flooded her system. Jazz looked back through the windshield at the parked car she had almost side-swiped.

When her heart stopped pounding in her throat, she asked, "How did you know?"

"That we were about to crash? I looked out the window."

"You know that isn't what I meant."

She heard him sigh.

"I didn't read your car, if that's what you're worried about. I know how you feel about that." He was quiet for a few moments, then said, "Garrett told me."

She let out an exasperated burst of air. The more word spread about Elsa and Rachel's involvement, the more chances there were for people to start bothering them about what had happened. Jazz was going to have to remind Garrett of that fact the next time she saw him.

"I know you're blaming Garrett, but I would have figured it out anyway. I can see how upset you are about the whole thing and know the only person you care about that much is Elsa."

Jazz let out a snort and shook her head. "I care about a lot of people."

Including the dumbass sitting next to her. She bit her tongue before saying more. Fate was always listening.

"Yeah."

That edge of tension she hated so much was coming to his voice again. It had always preceded their fights.

Instead of a snarky retort or escalation, he asked, "Is she doing okay? I haven't heard from Garrett in a while."

"She'll be fine. Her boyfriend got the worst of it."

"How's Dante doing?"

"He'll be fine." She refused to believe otherwise.

Finn seemed to sense that he shouldn't push that line of inquiry. He let out a little scoff. "I still can't believe Elsa's shacking up with someone."

"She's an amazing woman. Why is it so hard to believe?"

"I don't know. I guess I just imagined you two becoming spinsters together."

"You think *spinster* is part of my life's plans?"

She glanced over at him. He was glaring at her. Then he looked away.

Yeah. There it was.

She had always guessed that Finn wanted the whole package. Marriage, kids, picket fence. Jazz wasn't interested. She didn't need rings or ceremonies to bind herself to Finn. He shouldn't either. And even though Jazz loved her nieces and kids in general, motherhood was not for her.

She'd tried to bring up the subject once while they were dating. He'd scared her off from the topic before she could ask if it was a deal-breaker.

"Kids? Kids are great. I have all of these cousins with bunches of them. I wish I had nieces and nephews to enjoy, but...you know. Curses of an only child."

The whole conversation had been so awkward and his reference to curses had freaked her out. They'd only been dating for a few weeks at the time. His position seemed pretty clear, though. She had hoped maybe after they'd been together longer if she brought it up again it wouldn't be an obstacle. He'd left her before she had a chance.

She'd known she was fooling herself anyway.

"Yeah, well, I guess it's just going to be me knitting on the porch in a rocking chair."

He let out a sharp laugh.

"What is it now?"

He ignored her cutting tone.

"That is the funniest mental image. No matter how I try to picture it, I always see you standing up and throwing aside the needles, and saying, 'Seriously?' before storming off the porch."

At least he understood that domesticity wasn't for her.

They didn't have a chance to say more. Jazz pulled up to the curb in front of his place. A few cars still dotted the street. The bar had probably just closed. Her heart beat in her throat as they walked toward the front door.

Tommy had named the place Connelly's and their name was painted on a tasteful and understated sign that stuck out above the street. Jazz had tried to get Tommy to let her upgrade the storefront, but he wouldn't budge. He had teased her that she'd have to wait till Finn ran the place, since she had more sway over him.

The windows were coated with opaque dark green paint to give the people inside privacy. Finn popped his dad's hat onto his head and opened the door, then held it in place with his foot. Even wearing gloves, he seemed not to want to touch anything for too long. That handle was probably layered with memories, some of them recent, most of them clouded from drink.

She slipped past him quickly so he could get away from the door.

Connelly's... She had missed this place too. The smells had changed. At closing, the scent of cleaner was front and center. But instead of the air being thick with grease, it was lighter. The sharpness of smoked meat was the main note she detected instead of the fryer.

"When did you guys start doing BBQ?" she asked.

"Daphne talked dad into setting up a smoker. She's a really good cook."

Daphne again. Jazz's replacement.

"I know how you feel about BBQ outside of KC," Finn said, "but you really should give it a try."

There was laughter in his tone, and for a moment, Jazz could almost believe things were back to the way they had been before. They used to meet at the bar most weeknights. The three of them would eat dinner together and talk, then Tommy would go to bed. Finn and Jazz would sit up and talk before finding their way to his room.

Jazz couldn't care less about Daphne's BBQ. She *could* care a hell of a lot less about Daphne cozying up to the Connellys.

The woman of the hour stepped out from the kitchen— at least, Jazz assumed it was Daphne. She held a plastic tub that reeked of bleach in one hand and a rag in the other.

Why couldn't she be ugly?

No such luck. Her black hair was lustrous and hung down to her shoulder blades in soft curls. She had a pale complexion and eyes that were a rich mahogany brown. Her bone structure was delicate, like the rest of her.

Great. The pair of them were Snow White and Prince Charming. Finn said they weren't a couple, but it was only a matter of time.

Not my business. Not anymore.

"Hi Finn." Daphne had a soft, gentle voice. "Who's your friend?"

Finn hesitated. Yeah, they weren't a couple.

"This is Jazz."

Daphne's big cartoon eyes widened and her jaw dropped.

Enough! Jazz pulled her uncharitable thoughts to task.

Daphne was helping Finn and his dad with the bar. That was more than Jazz had been able to do the last couple of years. If Finn and his dad were happy and Daphne was part of that, Jazz should be hugging the woman, not letting catty thoughts run through her mind. Jazz wouldn't heap her own issues on someone else. She would deal with it.

Daphne set her cleaning supplies on the bar. "You're Jazz?"

Daphne knew who Jazz was? Why would Finn and Tommy still be talking about her after all this time?

Daphne stammered and smiled. A genuine smile. Jazz didn't want to trust it. She felt herself warming up to Daphne anyway.

"It's nice to meet you," Daphne said. "I've heard so much—"

Daphne looked over Jazz's shoulder and shook her head as if parroting someone else's movement. Changing tack, she said, "I mean...I've heard nothing. Nothing at all about you."

Jazz couldn't stop herself from laughing. "Wow, you are a terrible liar."

Daphne gave Jazz another of those heart-melting

smiles. "I've never put much effort into it. The truth is usually good enough for me."

"That makes two of us."

"Daphne, when you're done wiping down the bar—" Tommy stepped through the door that led to the kitchen.

Jazz felt like she'd been punched in the stomach. Tommy had acted like a father to her—had *felt* like a father. He had helped fill that gaping hole in her heart. She had thought she and Finn were headed toward a lifelong commitment. She had let herself get attached. Too attached. And she'd been paying for it for years.

She should have known better—that she and Finn wouldn't work out. There were too many obstacles.

You don't name your bar "Connelly's" without expecting a long line of heirs to run the place.

Tommy smiled at her. "Well, I'll be. Jazz Zhou. Sorry, I mean Zhou Jazz. I never could quite get the hang of that."

Dammit, she was tearing up. She forced herself to smile back. Not that smiling at Tommy took much effort.

"Hey, Tommy." Her voice was high and tight.

Tommy made her feel like a teenager. Ever since the moment he'd walked in on her in Finn's bed—naked after they'd slept together for the first time. Tommy had blushed furiously while trying to make conversation until Finn walked in and introduced her.

Tommy had quickly retreated saying, "You kids have fun."

Her father had never walked in on Jazz with a boy. Jazz hadn't started dating till college and her family couldn't afford visits back then. They had planned to come out to celebrate Jazz's graduation.

They hadn't made it.

And now Tommy was staring at her with that quirky smile half hidden under his ridiculous mustache. He looked older. More frail, but still strong. Like time was slowly wearing him away.

Tommy walked over to her and stared at her for a moment. Then he said, "Come here," and pulled her into a hug.

Keep it together. Keep it together.

How was she supposed to do that when everything she ever wanted was right next to her and completely out of reach? Finn was a few steps away, she was surrounded by the place that felt more like home than anywhere she had ever lived, and she had let it all slip through her fingers. She had messed up.

"It's good to see you." She forced out the words.

Finn put his hand on her shoulder. Clenching her eyes shut, she fought the tears away. They didn't need to see how much she...needed them.

Deal with it, Jazz. You made your choices. Now live with them.

Chapter Eight

"We need to talk," Finn said.

He might have underestimated how much Jazz cared about his dad. She was clinging to him like her life depended on it. Finn shoved down the jealousy that was trying to rise up in him for the millionth time.

"In a minute, son. I'm not quite ready to let go."

Neither was Jazz, from the look of it.

Finn used to try to comfort himself by thinking that Jazz wasn't affectionate with anyone in public. He wanted to believe that was why she only ever scowled at him when other people were in the room. He had seen her give Elsa and Garrett quick hugs, though. And she was never shy about hugging his dad in front of people.

When it was just the three of them in the bar, she seemed to smile all the time. She'd pat their shoulders and give them hugs. Hell, she would even sit in Finn's lap with a beer when they were having their late-night discussions. She'd acted like they were a family.

And when it was just the two of them…they'd been so much more. He could never read her, and yet always felt more connected to her than anyone he had ever known. He didn't think he'd ever understand how she could seem so open one moment, then build a wall of ice the next.

He'd ask to take her out on the town, and she'd respond with stony silence. He would yet again beg her to tell Garrett or anyone that they were dating, and she'd shake her head and tell him no. Any time he tried to talk to her about it, she shut down. It drove him crazy.

Finn had to stop thinking about the past. She needed him right now. He would be there for her. He had never seen her so shaken. He knew she loved his dad, but still...

He kept his hand on her shoulder, hoping to lend her support and for a moment feel that connection they had all shared. Jazz finally stepped back. She actually ran a fingertip under her eye and leaned against Finn's side.

He wanted to wrap his arms around her and nuzzle her hair. If Daphne hadn't been in the room, he might have, but Jazz had conditioned him too well. No affection in front of anyone but Tommy.

Anyway, it only took her a second to realize what she was doing. She stiffened and moved away.

"It's damned good to see you, Jazz." Dad cast a glance at Finn that was all too clear. *"Don't screw this up again."*

"I can finish in the kitchen," Daphne said. "Why don't you three go upstairs?"

Dad shook his head. "No. We're all family here. Come on and pull up a chair."

"It needs to be upstairs, Dad." Finn started for the front

door, but Jazz ducked in front of him.

"I'll do it." She locked the door, keeping Finn from having to touch it again.

"Thanks."

Dad was staring. Better to get this over with and keep him from building false hopes.

"Is that my hat?"

"Yeah." Finn took it off and handed it over.

Dad ran his fingertips over the brim. He was reading it, trying to figure out what was going on.

Finn sighed. "Can we go upstairs? There's way too much…ambient energy down here."

"All right."

Dad looked worried. The last thing he needed was more stress. Finn followed the group up the stairs, letting Jazz and the others go first. Once they reached the kitchen, Daphne took up her favorite spot leaning against the counter in front of the sink. Dad hung his hat on its hook on the wall, then sat at the table with Finn. Jazz sort of hovered nearby.

How to begin? Finn rubbed the bridge of his nose briefly, feeling a headache starting to build. He needed to just come out with it.

"You guys know something's wrong. I didn't want to worry you, but I haven't been able to fix things myself."

Tommy nodded. "What's going on?"

"My powers aren't working right. I'm getting stuck in

memories. I don't always remember…myself when I'm in a vision. And when I touch people, I read their thoughts almost instantly. Same deal. It's like I'm them instead of me. I'm getting lost." He raised his hands and wiggled his fingers. "That's why I'm wearing gloves."

Dad narrowed his eyes and looked at Finn's hands intently. "Then why did you go with leather?"

Shit. Finn realized his mistake as Dad started explaining for Daphne and Jazz. This was rookie stuff Dad had taught Finn when he was a kid.

"Leather transmits. These gloves might muffle readings a little, but you want silk to block energy."

"I've read that before," Jazz said. "You're supposed to keep tarot cards and other metaphysical tools wrapped in silk to protect them from stray energy and cleanse them after use."

Finn let out an exasperated sigh. He took off the nearly useless gloves and tossed them on the table.

Yeah, he should have come to his dad sooner. Even talking to Jazz about it more would have helped. She'd never taken him to her favorite bookstore, but talked about Bookwyrm often. She had studied all kinds of paranormal phenomena.

"I forgot about that," Finn said. "Thanks. My head hasn't been right for a while now."

"We noticed." Dad laughed.

He was trying to ease the tension, help Finn feel more

comfortable. Man, Finn was a lucky bastard to have such great people in his life. Topping it off, Jazz stepped up behind him and put her hand on his shoulder, prompting a sigh that was anything but exasperated.

She gave his shoulder a squeeze and said, "Finn's powers are somehow being disrupted by a connection to the serial killer from a couple months back."

That was way too blunt. Finn was trying to figure out how to tell Dad without giving away any details. He just… hadn't worked out how to do that yet.

"Dammit, Jazz! I can tell them myself."

She jumped, as if his outburst surprised her. Funny, they never had before. Sure, they'd prompted plenty of freeze-outs, but she had barely registered them in the past. A brief look of hurt crossed her face. That was new too.

"I'm sorry."

It was too late, though. She crossed her arms and walked to the other side of the room, glaring at him.

"I'm sorry. I'm just raw."

"We get that, son, but lashing out isn't going to help anyone."

Dad was probably more concerned about Finn chasing away Jazz than anything else.

No, that wasn't fair. Dad was worried about Finn.

"I wish you'd come to us sooner. You shouldn't have let it eat you up inside like this."

"Yeah, well hindsight's twenty-twenty."

"There's nothing wrong with asking for help now and again," Dad said.

Not this again.

"And if your powers aren't working right, this is serious."

"I know. I get it." Finn could hear his voice rising. He closed his eyes and took a deep breath, then let it out.

Dad turned to Daphne. "Can you run to Finn's closet and bring back that dark blue silk shirt of his?"

"Sure."

As soon as she had left, Jazz said, "You kept it?"

"Yeah, I kept it." Finn would never let go of that shirt.

Jazz had given it to him early on. It reminded him of their best times together, when they had just switched from a professional relationship to a personal one. They had met when Jazz hired him to investigate an artist she thought might be a fraud. The case had been…complicated.

She'd learned about his powers before it was over, they'd worked together, and after the case was closed, they'd pretty much jumped each other. He still wasn't sure who had started it.

Finn stood and took off his coat, then draped it over the back of his chair. He was wearing a cotton long-sleeved shirt over his tank top. He took the shirt off too and set it on top of his coat.

The silk shirt had short sleeves, but would still do a better job protecting him from random readings. Daphne returned and handed it over.

"Thanks." He slid it on, aware of the many stares on him as he did. They were waiting for him. No more stalling. "The connection isn't to the killer. It's one of his victims. I'm having nightmares about what happened to her."

As soon as Finn sat back down, Dad started his interrogation. "Was she someone you'd met before?"

"I don't know. I guess she does seem familiar somehow, but that could be because I'm dreaming about her every night."

Dad leaned on the table. "What happens in the dreams?"

"I basically experience what she did when she was being held by Michael Angelo. I'm chained to a wall and he's... Well, the dreams are unpleasant and I can say wholeheartedly that I'm glad the sick bastard is dead."

Daphne shifted her weight and said, "Could you have touched something the victim came into contact with? Maybe in the bar?"

"I thought about that. I don't know how that could have happened. For these memories to be available, it would have to be something that she touched while she was being held captive. Only one person escaped, and I doubt she kept any mementos."

"Two escaped," Jazz said. "If you count Elsa."

"You know one of his victims?" Daphne asked.

"I don't know any *victims*," Jazz said. "I do know both of the women who took him down."

"Are they okay?"

Jazz nodded at Daphne. "They're going to be fine. I'm more worried about Finn right now."

What an admission. And after only knowing Daphne for a few minutes.

"Rachel's the one who shot him," Finn said.

"That's Garrett's friend," Dad said. "I've heard him mention her."

"Yeah, and if you would watch the news or read anything other than your books, you'd know Rachel's dad is running for office soon. The whole thing has been swept under the rug. The lid they're keeping on this is insane. They have to have something they're using as leverage on a whole lot of people."

Dad shook his head. "I can't fault a man for trying to protect his daughter."

Jazz let out a snort and everyone turned to her. She shrugged. "Rachel's parents don't give a crap about her. She's a prop they use to appear like a perfect family. They're covering their own asses, not hers."

"That's a cheery thought," Daphne said.

"It's the truth."

"Where's the connection, though?" Dad tapped his finger on the table. "Break it down for me."

Finn's dad was even more of a hidden weapon for his

investigations than Finn's powers. Finn could always count on him to give new insight into cases. Dad was the one who told him to start tracking Elsa when Finn's investigation into Dante hit a wall. And really, that was when this had all started.

"Okay. So, Garrett calls me to look into Elsa's new roommate."

"He did *what*?" Jazz broke in.

Finn sighed. "It was after the break-in, when she refused to call the cops."

Jazz looked like she was about to light into him again, but then cast a wary glance at Daphne.

"I already know about Dante being from the 1800s and Elsa's ability to time travel," Daphne said. "Finn was kind of flipping out when he figured things out, and the walls are really thin up here."

"Great." Jazz glared at Finn. That was going to cost him.

"Could we maybe stay focused?" Dad said. "You worked Garrett's case and found the creepy guy, but never told me what came of it. You just said he was out of the picture."

"Yeah," Finn said. "Permanently. That was Michael Angelo."

Jazz took a step toward him. Her hands were balled into fists at her sides.

"You knew that Michael was stalking Elsa?"

"I knew *someone* was stalking Elsa," Finn said. "You all did. And I let Garrett know what I'd found out as soon as I could. Turns out it was a little too late."

"Come on now." Dad tapped the table harder. "Let's focus here. That was the first time you felt the guy's energy. When did the dreams start?"

"The night he was killed."

Dad leaned back, crossing his arms and staring at the ceiling. "So, you've got the killer's energy signature on you. He dies."

Jazz cut in. "It can't be his ghost."

Everyone turned to stare at her.

"I'm just saying, it can't be his ghost. His body was cremated. What?"

Finn finally turned back to Dad. They hadn't really talked about ghosts before. But if psychometry and time travel were possible, why not ghosts?

"I can't be haunted, can I?" Finn asked.

Dad turned back to stare at Finn.

"Michael killed a lot of women," Jazz said. "Maybe one of them is trying to communicate with Finn. To get closure or something."

"Why Finn?" Daphne asked.

"She could be sensing his power," Jazz said. "Using it as a conduit."

"No," Dad said. "There would have to be a stronger connection than that. Something or someone that links them."

"I really *really* hate to ask this," Jazz said, "but has anyone in your family ever gone missing?"

Finn turned back to look at her. He had talked about his family a lot when they dated—not that there were many running around locally. Only Finn and his dad were in Florida. The rest were from Boston.

Of course, Jazz never bothered to share more than that she was from Kansas City. He didn't even know which side of the state line.

Focus, Finn. Focus.

"Do the police know if Michael worked anywhere else?" Finn asked. "Any other states?"

"Not that they've mentioned," she said. "The last I knew, the only clue they had is that Elsa and Rachel are both blonde. The police said maybe he had a type. They're compiling a list of missing persons—" Jazz glanced over at Dad. "Tommy, wait!"

Finn turned to his dad, only to see him lurching across the table. He grabbed Finn's hand and pulled him forward, holding it against his chest.

"Dad, let go! You don't want to see—"

Shit, he hated it when Dad read him like this. It hadn't happened since he was a kid. He felt the pull, the feedback from both of their powers colliding, then the click as they synched up.

Then Dad drew out the vision.

The rattle of chains. The weight of the manacles digging into her flesh, tearing it as she struggled to get free. The prick of needle after needle in her arms. Darkness. Fear. Knowing that death surrounded her—feeling it close. Michael Angelo's smiling face. And blood. So much blood.

Finn could feel Dad's hands trembling even through the vision. Then something strong yanked him back from it, pulling him free. He landed on the floor, sitting between Jazz's legs. She had her arms wrapped around him and was crushing him to her chest.

He might have enjoyed her warmth, her closeness, except his dad and Daphne were on the floor right in front of him—and Dad was clinging to Daphne's arms, sobbing.

"Dad. Dad!"

Finn scrambled to his dad's side and wrapped his arms around the pair. Dad was shaking so bad. Finn had never seen him cry. Ever. And this? This was a complete breakdown.

The vision was terrible, but Finn didn't understand his dad's reaction. Had he seen something Finn couldn't? Was that even possible? They had always shared the same visions when he read Finn before, the same memories or experiences, like Finn did when reading objects.

"Dad, come on. You have to calm down."

Jazz put her hand on Finn's back. He closed his eyes to let her calm sink into him. Except her hand was shaking too. He looked at her over his shoulder.

The blood had all drained from her face again. Her lips were set in a grim line. Instead of looking like she was about to pass out, she looked like she wanted to kill somebody.

She reached between them all and pressed her fingers against Dad's neck. Checking his pulse. Finn's heartbeat skyrocketed. He should have thought to check that first thing.

Jazz's face seemed to relax a bit and she nodded. Finn closed his eyes and took a deep breath, letting it out slowly. When he opened them again, he mouthed, "Thank you."

She actually gave him a tiny smile. She dropped to her knees and pulled Finn's head against her neck. They were touching skin-to-skin, and all he felt was comfort. No memories, no thoughts. He still couldn't read her. He swore he felt her press a kiss to the top of his head, though. Then she wrapped her arms around the group.

They sat in a heap on the floor for what felt like eternity while Dad cried it out. Finally, exhausted, he leaned into Finn.

"I thought it was for the best," Dad said. "I thought she'd take care of her. Give her a good life. Protect her."

"Who, Dad?"

"Your sister."

What the...

Shit, had Dad picked up some part of the memory and lost track of who he was? Finn had been able to shake off other people's thoughts and memories as soon as he stopped touching them or whatever object he was reading. At least, so far. Surely Dad could do the same.

"I don't have a sister."

"You do. You did. Oh God, how could your mom have let this happen? I thought I was doing what was right."

"Dad, you're not making any sense."

Finn's heart was in his throat. Dad had never mentioned Finn's mom before. Whenever Finn tried to bring up the topic... It didn't go well. It didn't go anywhere. He'd stopped asking when he hit his teens.

"I recognized her," Dad said. "The connection. I felt it." Dad's blue eyes were bloodshot and lined with red. Tears were still streaming down his face. "I know my own daughter. That was Siobhan. Your sister, Finn. Your twin."

The blood rushed from Finn's head fast enough to make him dizzy. Luckily, Jazz was right there, keeping him steady.

"Your mom wanted more than I could ever give her," Dad said. "I thought maybe when we had you two, she'd settle down. Be happy. But it made her miserable. We were living in Boston with my family. She took up with some lawyer and told me she was divorcing me and taking Siobhan with her. She said I could keep you as long as I didn't try to find them, but if I did... She said they'd take you too. And I knew her new husband could do it."

"Christ, Dad. Why didn't you ever tell me?"

"I didn't want you to know that she didn't want you. Didn't want *us*. When Pat and I got the chance to open the bar down here, I moved us away so we could start over."

Finn's uncle Pat had passed away a decade ago, leaving his half of the bar to his brother.

"You never looked for her?"

"How could I, when I let your mom take her? When I..." Dad swallowed hard. "When I kept you for myself rather than making her take you too. They could have given you so much. Anything you ever wanted. But I couldn't let you both go. I was afraid if you found out about the kind of life I had kept you from you wouldn't forgive me."

Finn thought of all the years barely scraping by. Hell, he thought about the stress he'd been under the past few months, trying to make sure they had what they needed and could pay for Dad's medical bills, let alone be ready if something else should happen.

He thought about all the fights they'd had, when Finn wanted to use their powers to make some money and finally be able to stop struggling. How Dad had stayed strong and never once wavered or seemed to be tempted.

Then he thought about the woman who had given birth to him. Who he finally had learned something about.

She didn't want him. Worse than that, she was willing

to use Finn—her son—to blackmail Dad into abandoning his daughter.

No matter how bad it was, Dad was always crystal clear in how much he loved Finn. How much he wanted to be part of Finn's life. Not many adults could stand to live with their parent when they were grown. Finn loved spending time with his dad. They relied on each other, took care of each other.

What had Siobhan grown up with?

Finn was reeling. Too many emotions were running through him. He was too shocked to process them all. Anger passed by his awareness and he latched on to it.

He couldn't let himself be angry with Dad. Not after almost losing him. So he directed it at the woman who had torn their family apart—a family Finn didn't even know he had.

"Are you kidding? If she didn't want us, that's her loss. I'd rather have been raised by someone who wanted me."

Dad wrapped his arms around Finn's neck and held on. Finn hugged him back hard.

He couldn't imagine what it must have been like to hold on to this for all these years. He wished his dad had told him, had come to him with the truth before it came out in such an awful way.

"We have to find out what happened to her, son. If she's haunting you, we have to help her find peace."

Chapter Nine

Tommy had been so exhausted he had passed out as soon as Finn and Jazz tucked him in bed. Jazz didn't want to leave. Even more, she wanted to have answers for Tommy when he woke up.

Finn stepped into the hallway with her and quietly closed the door to Dad's room. Daphne was downstairs finishing up closing the bar. As soon as they were settled, Jazz would...do something. Figure out a way to help, whether Finn wanted her to or not.

He paused with his hand resting on Dad's door. She couldn't imagine what he must be thinking. Seeing his dad go through that, finding out about his twin—knowing he'd lost her and that he was feeling her death over and over again. Jazz was amazed at how well he was holding it together.

She kept her voice as low as she could. "What do you need?"

He looked wrung out. She wanted to take care of him too. Food, water, sleep. Those were at the top of her mind.

He turned around and grabbed her, molding her against him and covering her lips with his.

Right. This.

Her body responded instantly. It always had. She buried her fingers in his hair, pressing herself against him. His tongue slid into her mouth, picking up the old dance as if it had been only yesterday.

Jazz moaned as he pushed her back against the wall, his hands sliding down past her hips to grab her thighs and lift her from the ground. She locked her ankles behind his waist. He was already hard, grinding against her, turning the heat building between her legs into a firestorm.

In the back of her mind, she recognized the pattern. Extreme emotion of any sort always led to sex. Whether it was an argument or… Okay, usually it was an argument.

She knew she needed to hold on to some semblance of self-control, but at the moment, she couldn't even think. All she could do was feel. And she wanted more.

"Psst! Guys!" Daphne's voice cut through the euphoria of Finn's kiss.

Jazz was panting when he pulled away. He kept staring into her eyes for a long time. Daphne stalked up to them and started pointing toward the kitchen.

Finn turned to her and hissed, "Do you mind?"

Daphne pointed at the wall next to Tommy's door. "Paper thin, remember? You want to have sex with your girlfriend, fine. Just do it in your room and be quiet about it."

"I'm not his girlfriend," Jazz said.

At the same moment, Finn said, "She's not my girlfriend."

She tried not to scowl at him when he looked back at her. Good to have that clear.

"I don't *care*," Daphne said. "Just move."

The last of Jazz's jealousy vanished. Daphne had taken on the role of mother-hen for the Connellys—and now Jazz too, from the look of it. Jazz hadn't been replaced after all.

Finn let Jazz's legs slide to the floor. He kept his hand on her back as they walked into the kitchen area of the apartment. It annoyed her. She still didn't want him to stop.

"Downstairs." Daphne pointed and Finn and Jazz obeyed.

Once they were back in the bar, they could speak in normal tones. Jazz had been there enough to know that the ceiling at least was sound-proofed well.

Daphne was glaring at them. Jazz almost wanted to laugh. Yet again, she'd been caught in a compromising position. A tiny glimmer of hope stirred deep in her soul. The last time she'd felt this way was when she and Finn first made the leap from working together to being lovers.

That was a long time ago. He was probably just reacting because of the stress. It was part of his nature. He was impulsive, passionate. She was still tingling from that kiss—and everything that went along with it.

The timing was horrible to rekindle anything, even if Finn was interested. She shouldn't be thinking about it at all right now. Or ever. Finn had trampled her heart. He would probably end up leaving her again. He had been just as quick to correct Daphne when she called Jazz his girlfriend.

Ardor effectively dampened.

Daphne didn't light into them. Instead she said, "I'll stay with him while you work the case."

"I can't go," Finn said. "Not until I know he's okay."

"I took care of my mom for years before she passed. I know how to look after people."

Daphne walked over to Finn and rested her hand on his arm. No, she left it hovering an inch away, not touching his skin. She really did know how to take care of people.

"What he needs are answers," she said. "And what you need is to run this down. It's what your sister needs too. If she's hanging around and so upset that her presence is messing up your powers, you need to find a way to help her."

Damn. Daphne knew them well.

"I know where to start," Jazz said.

Finn turned to look at her. "Where?"

"Michael's house. Remember, I was there right after everything went to hell. I know where Michael lived. I also know that the police have pretty much finished with the place."

Finn nodded, his gaze becoming unfocused as he thought things through. "So no one will be there right now."

"Go." Daphne stepped back. "I'll take care of things here. You just take care of each other, okay?"

Finn glanced at Jazz, but quickly looked away. He nodded again. "Thanks, Daphne."

Daphne smiled and almost slipped and patted his shoulder. She looked puzzled about what to do for a moment, then patted the air above it. Finn let out a tiny chuckle. It was such a sweet gesture and had helped ease his pain, even a little.

"I know the shirt is supposed to help, but I don't want to take any chances," Daphne said.

Jazz felt a lump forming in her throat. She coughed to clear it.

"Let's go." She headed to the door and unlocked it, then held it for Finn. "Lock up after us."

"Of course." Daphne was already headed for the door.

Jazz waited for her to be close before murmuring, "Thanks for taking such good care of them."

Daphne smiled and Jazz felt a little tug on her heart. Yeah. Jazz was pretty sure she loved Daphne now. She tried to figure out how that would work as she unlocked the SUV and climbed into the driver's seat.

She would have to keep Daphne separate from her other friends. If she introduced her to Elsa and Rachel, there was no way Jazz could keep her relationship with Finn a secret. Daphne was too open. Then there would be endless questions and all the angst and drama of explaining why Jazz hadn't told anyone and why things hadn't worked out.

Jazz didn't have the stomach for it.

"Why didn't I tell you? Because he was mine. I didn't want to share him."

And the deeper truth.

"Because I loved him so much, I was afraid if I let anyone know, Fate would take him away from me."

It wouldn't have been the first time. Not by a long shot.

She had lost Finn anyway. But now he was back in her life and he needed her. He was letting her actually help him with something. No matter what came of it, she couldn't let the opportunity pass.

Being with Finn and Tommy had felt like Fate's reward for all the crap Jazz had gone through. Like being repaid for every loss she'd suffered. Their home was her oasis— the one place she could show Finn how she felt, even if she still didn't dare to say anything out loud.

Maybe this was her chance to even out the scales a bit and pay him back for everything he'd shared with her, everything he'd offered and she'd been too afraid to accept.

She pulled away from the curb, heading toward Michael's house. Finn didn't say a word.

"You okay over there?" she asked.

Finn was staring out the window. He glanced over at her and shook his head.

"Just trying to sort things out. I can't believe I had a sister. All this time and Dad never told me."

"I'm sure he had his reasons."

Finn snorted. "No wonder you two got on so well. You love your secrets."

Her grip on the wheel tightened.

He sighed. "I'm sorry. That was a shitty thing to say."

Whoa. Another apology. He sure was doing that a lot. She couldn't remember him doing it much before.

"When did you become so self-aware?" That sounded better in her mind. "I didn't mean that to be catty."

He laughed a little. Just a tiny fast exhale. But it made her smile, warmed her up inside. She wanted to help him feel better.

"You know, I think we've talked more in the last few hours than the last few weeks of us dating." He looked over at her and grinned.

God, that smile. The streetlights caught and reflected in his pale eyes, gleamed on his straight teeth.

"As I recall, we were busy doing other things toward the end," she said.

His smile faded and he turned back to the window. How had that killed the mood? It was true, anyway. At the end, all they did was argue and have angry make-up sex.

Amazing angry make-up sex.

Her skin tingled as she remembered some of the more spectacular encounters. The argument was always the same by that point. He wanted to come out about their relationship. She didn't.

Going out meant being seen. Summer Park wasn't a big enough town to avoid the grapevine. Their friends would find out. Then the playful banter would start.

"When are you going to get married? How many kids do you want? What breed of dog? What's your retirement plan?"

Hell, even strangers felt they had the right to weigh in on her personal life. Just the other day, the sandwich shop owner where Jazz often picked up lunch asked her when she was going to meet a nice man and settle down.

Right, I need to find a new lunch place.

Her sister Mei complained that after the first kid, people would ask when she would have her second. And after her second, they asked about her third. It never ended.

Okay, after three kids, Mei had stopped mentioning it. Then again, she'd pretty much stopped talking to Jazz. The girls kept her busy.

Jazz missed her family, but Kansas City held too many memories of her father. She hadn't been back since the funeral. Mei and her family had come to Florida every other year for a while, along with their mom. They had visited various state attractions and Jazz had driven up for a day or two to visit.

It had been a long time since they'd made the trip. Not since just before her break-up with Finn.

She hadn't told him they were visiting. Her family was in the same state, and she didn't even tell him, let alone introduce him. Meanwhile, he had opened his home, his family, his heart to her.

Yeah. She had messed things up with Finn big-time. Trying to keep him compartmentalized. Trying to keep herself from bragging about her amazing boyfriend and letting anyone know how happy she was. The crashes always came when she was at her happiest.

The first one was literal. When she was a kid, her puppy had been hit by a car and killed while she had been walking it to a friend's house to show off. She shuddered at the memory.

She had bragged about a scholarship to a prestigious performance academy. The teacher she was supposed to study with had fallen ill right after Jazz told everyone at school about it. She could think of half a dozen times she'd been over the moon about something and told everyone about it, only to have it snatched away.

It took her too long to learn her lesson. Right before graduation, she had talked to her father about her fear— had even shared her suspicion that it was a curse. She told him she was afraid to be happy that things were going so well. Agents had already contacted her, wanting to represent her. She hadn't told anyone, because she was afraid something would happen to them.

He had laughed and told her not to be afraid. He encouraged her to enjoy this part of her life and said that whatever Fate had in store for anyone, she couldn't change it, especially just by being happy. He told her the universe wasn't cruel and to lay down her fear.

She had bragged to her friends after that. Not about the offers, but about him. What a wonderful father he was. How supportive. How he believed in her ability to make it as a singer.

The entire month before graduation, she wouldn't shut up about him. She told all her friends how much they were going to love him and how great he was and didn't they wish they had a father like hers.

She hadn't sung a note since her final performance in college. Not at birthdays, not lullabies to her nieces, not even alone in the shower.

She had thought her family was in the audience. They hadn't even made it to the state.

Jazz had never admitted that she loved anyone out loud again. She was cautious every time she was with the people she cared about, trying to hide how she felt. Trying to stifle her feelings.

It was suffocating.

Now she was wondering if other people were falling to her curse. She hadn't said anything about how happy she was for Elsa and Dante when they found each other, but she'd thrown that party. In her heart, she'd known it was to celebrate them getting together.

She'd worked with Dante behind Elsa's back to help him set up a life for himself, knowing her best friend wouldn't be able to relax and really enjoy being with him until she knew Dante was self-sufficient.

Then Michael happened.

What if it had somehow been Jazz's fault? She'd had way more than her share of bad luck in her life, and was convinced there were powers working behind the scenes—scales that insisted on being balanced, energies that influenced the course of human events. Beyond the obvious, mundane precipitator—Jazz was the one who had fucking introduced Michael to everyone.

Goddammit, Jazz. Get your head out of your ass and back in the game.

She could feel sorry for herself later. Finn needed her now.

Michael had lived outside of town in a small house built near the edge of swampland. Jazz hadn't been back since Rachel's rescue. Thinking about that night was just what Jazz needed to renew her focus.

Michael's house was haunted with her own memories. She would keep Finn away from the garage—that was certain. Even still, how could they sort through Michael's memories safely? She didn't want to see Finn get lost in a vision again, especially now that they knew Michael had killed Finn's sister.

Jazz was tempted to call Rachel and ask for help. If Siobhan was hanging around and somehow messing with Finn's powers, Rachel would be able to help them figure out what they needed to do. Siobhan could just tell her.

But Rachel was dealing with her own issues. Jazz had to try to sort this out herself first. She didn't want to drag Rachel into it. Not unless it became absolutely necessary. They would try Michael's house first and see what they could find.

Jazz turned onto the gravel driveway, her lights flashing across the windows of Michael's brown and tan single-story house.

"We're here."

Chapter Ten

The house looked ordinary. Finn could hardly believe so many terrible things had happened inside. At the same time, he could feel a chilling energy creeping out from it, even from inside the SUV. Jazz had her door open already, letting in the muggy night air.

"You ready for this?" Jazz asked.

"Yeah. I think so." He reached for her hand on instinct. Having her near him... Well, he wasn't sure how well he'd be coping without her.

She pulled away. It was standard procedure for her, but every time it felt like she kicked him in the chest.

"Cut me some slack," he said. "I wasn't trying to start something."

Not this time, anyway.

That moment in the hallway had been intense. He hadn't been able to stop himself from reaching for her. And yeah, it was instinct again that made him want to hold her hand, to touch her. It wouldn't have escalated, though. Probably.

"That isn't why..." She sighed and slid from her seat, her boots crunching as she hit the gravel. She slammed the door shut.

That was not-so-standard.

He followed her out, closing his door a bit more gently. He was walking on her heels. When she stopped abruptly, he almost ran into her.

"I was trying to protect you, you ass," she said. "I didn't want you to be flooded with my thoughts."

"Oh."

Damn. That was the first time he could remember her unloading on him like that. Now that he knew why she pulled back, it was well deserved.

He'd always felt alone in their fights, like he was talking to a wall. She never yelled back. She always stayed so calm. It made him wonder if she cared about him at all. Eventually, he'd start shouting, trying to be heard. They always ended up in bed, his last resort to establish some form of connection.

"It's okay if you touch me," he said. "I still can't read you, even with my powers messing up."

"Oh."

He shook his head and smiled. "Didn't you notice before when we made out in the hallway?"

"I wasn't *thinking* then." She was quiet for a moment, then said, "Wipe that grin off your face."

"How do you know I'm grinning? It's pitch black out here."

"I don't need to see you to know you're smiling."

"I guess you just have that effect on me."

Her breath hitched and she turned away, walking toward the house fast enough that he had to trot to catch up. What had he stepped in this time? Talking to her had often been challenging, but this was like walking through a minefield. She hadn't been volatile before.

She had actually once told him, "I suck at talking. Can't we just have sex instead?"

It had sounded great at the time. With how anxious he was, it sounded great at the moment too. It had always comforted him, made him feel grounded.

Remembering their time in bed wasn't a good way to keep his focus, especially with the recent reminder of how well they fit together. Talk about losing control. But in that moment, when she asked what he needed, all he could think about was being closer to her, holding her.

She had always been the one person that he could touch without worrying about reading her thoughts. Now she was the only person he knew he wouldn't lose himself in.

At least, not his mind. His heart was another matter.

She pulled out her phone and turned on the flashlight as they walked to the side of the house. Windows lined a door tucked behind some bougainvilleas. One of the panes had been broken out and was taped over.

"I don't suppose you brought along your gloves?" Jazz asked.

"They're back home on the kitchen table."

"Forget it," she said. "I've got this."

She hit the tape with her elbow a couple of times until it gave way, then snaked her arm through the gap and opened the door. Holding her phone up, she led the way into the house. The door opened into a narrow laundry room.

"Is the AC on?"

The house felt at least twenty degrees cooler than outside. The night air was stagnant and oppressively hot, even in the pre-dawn hours they were approaching. The house was an ice box in comparison.

"I don't know. I think they shut off the utilities, so probably not." She ran her light over the washer and dryer. "It is cold in here."

Cold and creepy as hell. Finn's skin was crawling and he hadn't even touched anything.

"Tell me again how this is less visceral than reading the walls of the gallery?"

"I'm not going to have you read the garage or anything."

"The garage?"

Jazz was silent for a moment. "That's where he kept them."

"Oh." Finn had never been able to see past the workbenches in his dreams. Shelves and tables blocked his view.

He shivered, walking a little closer as they made their

way into the kitchen. A small square table was tucked against a wall. Two chairs. Michael must not have entertained often. The counters were mostly bare.

"Maybe we should start in here." Jazz moved the light over the cabinets and counters. "I don't know where he kept his empty jars. Let's avoid the cabinets."

Jars? Oh right. To hold the blood. Finn would avoid the cabinets unless absolutely necessary.

"How about the table?" he asked.

She turned around and flashed the light across its surface. It seemed innocuous enough. Then again, the whole house did. On the surface, anyway. The longer he was in the dwelling, the more he sensed the malice lurking there, as if it had soaked into the walls, the ceiling, the floors.

"That's a good idea. Rachel said Michael brought her here after a date to capture her. He might have sat with his other victims before…" Jazz shook her head and stepped closer to him. "Maybe start with the chairs?"

"Okay." Finn scooted one of the chairs away from the table with his foot. Jazz grabbed his arm before he could sit down.

"Don't sit. I'll need to be able to break your contact if something goes wrong. It'll be easier if you're standing."

He hesitated, wanting to keep feeling her hand on his arm, the softness of her touch. He loved having her with him, knowing she was thinking about him, that she cared what happened.

That was as far as they'd ever gone conversationally. She admitted she cared about him.

Now is not the time, Finn.

He tried to keep things light. He laughed and said, "Easier for you, maybe. My knee still hurts from the gallery."

Her voice softened. "I didn't know it was you."

"It's okay. I'm glad you didn't forget everything I taught you. That was a pretty good takedown."

She hadn't wanted to learn self-defense at all. She said words were her best weapon and that she always had her phone handy for calling the police. He had kept after her about it. She worked such late hours at the gallery— usually alone, on the nights he wasn't with her.

When she'd asked him to hang around more, acting as her bodyguard, she could tell it set him off. They never talked about it, but he thought maybe she had agreed to the lessons to sort of make it up to him.

Acting as her bodyguard was another form of working for her. He didn't mind playing the part on occasion, but he wasn't interested in her being his boss. That was another reason he didn't want her helping him. She'd take over, ordering him around, running everything.

Yeah, he was proud and didn't like asking for help. He knew that. But he especially didn't like asking for help from someone he saw as a partner but who treated him like a minion.

And on that cheery note...

He turned back to the chair.

The wood was old and the paint worn and peeling. Finn would have thought someone who called themselves a painter would be more particular about that. Then again, when Finn thought about what Michael used for paint... Definitely a good thing the chairs hadn't been redone.

Get it over with.

He grabbed the back of the chair with one hand, keeping his weight a little off-balance. If Jazz needed to push him loose, it would help her out.

The room lightened as if the sun was rising in fast-forward. Illuminated, it looked less creepy and more normal. Homey, even. The eerie atmosphere was gone.

Finn didn't feel like he was floating. Instead, he was sitting at the table across from Michael.

Finn felt his hands curl into fists. He wanted to punch Michael in the face. Wanted to make him hurt for all the pain he had heaped on others.

This is the bastard who killed my sister. I'll never get a chance to know her because of him.

Michael was smiling as he leaned back in his chair and spoke. "This next piece will be spectacular. Not one, but *two* subjects. I don't know why I didn't think to try this sooner."

He was staring at the ceiling, a dreamy look on his face.

He interlaced his fingers and put his hands behind his head, stretching out his legs. He looked relaxed. As if he hadn't a care in the world.

"The canvas is prepared. I just need to gather the materials. They're already selected. Both subjects are friends of the gallery owner. I'm hoping to be able to display the piece in an exhibit there. Can you imagine?"

Michael laughed. He actually laughed.

Sick psychopathic bastard...

"She keeps me on my toes, that one. Always trying to see through me. It's too bad she's not a match for my needs. Perhaps someday I'll expand my subject matter and the little gallery owner can grace her own wall."

Michael's gaze became unfocused as he stared at the ceiling again, casually contemplating *killing Jazz.*

Finn wanted to leap across the table and—

"Stop looking at me like that."

He felt a chill sweep through him. Holy shit. Michael couldn't see Finn, right? Now that he knew time travel was possible, he wasn't as sure.

"Pig! Stop looking at me."

Finn's gaze dropped, as if he had lowered his head to look at the floor. Except he wasn't looking at the floor. He was looking at somebody's lap.

"Did you take care of it?" Michael asked.

Finn's view bobbed up and down, as if he was seeing through someone else's perspective and they were nodding. At least he was holding on to his sense of self. Whoever this was, Finn was just along for the ride.

Michael nodded. "Good. The alligators near Auntie's house are getting fat helping us clean up after my work. I hope they're hungry for what's next."

Alligators...

Finn felt sick. He wanted to leave the memory, but couldn't. Michael stood and walked to the sink. Whoever Finn was seeing through watched out of the corner of his eye. When Michael turned back, the person quickly looked back at their lap.

While Finn was stuck there, he might as well do some good. He looked for details that might help him ID the person he was occupying.

The man's hands were bony, calloused and leathery—and curled into tight fists. His arms were emaciated. Judging by the length of his legs, he was pushing six-feet in height. His pants ballooned around his body. He couldn't weigh more than one-hundred-thirty, one-hundred-forty pounds. Tan skin. Mud stains on worn boots. A bit of sphagnum moss stuck to the side.

Michael walked back to the table.

"Poor piggy. Are you hungry too?"

Finn felt the man's chest catch, saw his fists tighten further. He looked up, but before he could say anything, Michael's lips pulled back in a snarl and he flat-out punched the guy. The blow sent him reeling, the room spinning in Finn's view until his face hit the floor.

"Finn!"

Finn sucked in a huge breath. He felt like he was drowning. The cold linoleum pressed against his cheek. Warmer hands were on his shoulders.

Jazz helped him sit up, pulling him against her chest and wrapping her arms around him. Finn's body was shaking violently. But it was *his* body. He'd made it back.

"That was so not-okay." His teeth were chattering and he felt...weird. Oddly disconnected. He focused on the soft feel of Jazz's body behind his, closing his eyes and trying to take deep breaths. Something thick and wet was interfering.

"You're bleeding."

"What?"

He lifted his hand to his nose. When he pulled it away, he could see red on his fingertips from the dim light of her phone, which was sitting on the floor next to them.

"I must have hit my head when I fell."

"You didn't. I caught you. Well, I tried to anyway. You're heavy."

Finn let out a chuckle. It sounded a little hysterical to him. Nothing felt real.

Auntie's house...

"What do you know about Michael's family?" he asked.

"Nothing. We didn't talk about anything but art and the gallery."

"But you knew his body was cremated."

"Rachel told me."

If Michael had any family, they probably weren't too eager to come forward and claim his remains. The state would have taken care of the matter. But just because no family came forward, that didn't mean they didn't exist.

He pulled a handkerchief from his back pocket and wiped his nose, then picked up her phone and stood. He ran the light over the floor, table, and chair to make sure he hadn't bled anywhere. They needed to leave behind as little evidence of their visit as possible.

Jazz rose and crossed her arms, glaring at him. "What did you see?"

No way was he filling her in on all the details. He still felt half-sick from what he had learned, what he knew in his gut to be true. He stuck with the basics. What she needed to know.

And that knowledge was chilling.

"Michael has a cousin who helped him. He wasn't working alone."

Chapter Eleven

Jazz couldn't believe that Michael had an accomplice. Someone who had taken part in his crimes was walking around free. That part of this awful situation was supposed to be over. Justice had been served. Right?

"The police would have caught that," she said.

"The police might have talked to the guy and not realized his role in it. From what I saw, he was cleanup."

"Cleanup?"

The light from her phone was enough for her to see how Finn grimaced. He didn't want to tell her what he knew.

"I need to know. I'll deal with it."

Finn let out a tired laugh. "I've never heard you use that phrase on yourself. I thought you only used it on other people."

"Finn…"

He sighed. "Michael's cousin helped him get rid of the bodies. I only got a nickname, but I could tell enough about what the guy looks like to give me a good lead. Once I track down Michael's hometown, I should be able to find him."

"Don't you mean *we*?"

Finn shook his head. "I was only okay with you coming along when I thought the killer was dead and you'd be safe. If this other guy was working with Michael, we have no idea what he's capable of."

She bristled. Finn was *not* benching her. He was not leaving her behind again.

"Well, you know what *I'm* capable of. Or does your knee need a reminder?"

"Jazz…"

"And we know what you're *in*capable of. You can't control your powers. You need me." At least for this.

"I can't risk you being hurt."

She let out a laugh. That was just too rich. No one had ever hurt her like Finn had. Her heart had never healed, never moved past him. She still felt butterflies in her stomach when they were close, still wished things could have been different—that he hadn't chosen to walk away.

"You're forgetting that I drove," she said. "Unless you're walking back to town to pick up your car, you're stuck with me. Deal with it."

His jaw was tight and he was frowning so hard deep grooves were shadowed on his face.

"Don't ever say that to me again." He bit out each word, clipped and tense.

"What? Walk back to Summer Park?"

"*Deal with it.* Do you even know what you're really

saying? What that means? 'I don't give a shit about what you feel. Sort it out yourself.' I don't *ever* want to hear that phrase again."

She felt like the floor had dropped out from under her. That was her catchphrase. She used it all the time with everybody. No one had ever complained. She had never thought it could be taken that way. But…he had a point.

If he hated that expression, she must have upset him dozens of times while they were together. He never mentioned it.

Talking was something they had never excelled at.

"Finn, I'm—"

"Just forget it. We have a job to do."

What the hell? She had been about to apologize—something she *never* did. Her skin prickled as rage surged up. He shouldn't rock someone's foundation and then walk away.

But that was what he did with her. Turned her world upside-down, then walked away.

Not this time.

She grabbed her phone from his hand, then turned around and headed for the laundry room. He fell in step just behind her.

"Where are you going?"

"Back to the SUV. Unless you think you can safely read something else in here to find out where this cousin lives, we're probably better off searching for him on the

Internet."

She opened the door and held it, staring at Finn expectantly. He only hesitated a moment before walking back into the steamy night air.

After the chill of Michael's house, it felt good. The moisture carried the heat right into her bones. She couldn't wait for the sun to come up and chase away...everything from this night.

Not everything.

She had reconnected with Tommy. She was even happy to be with Finn, even though he was driving her crazy. She was so scared he was going to leave. Watching him walk out of her life again was something she couldn't bear to think about. But she was more afraid he'd try to do this alone and get hurt.

Once they were back in the SUV, she said, "Wherever Michael is from, there are bound to be other people around. It won't be too dangerous. And you need me to back you up, whether you'll admit it or not."

He sighed, but then pulled out his phone and started searching the Internet. That was a good sign. She thought over what she knew while she waited for him to find something. She needed to be as useful as possible so Finn would admit that he needed her.

Things were starting to make more sense.

Someone was out there who played a part in the deaths of those women. Someone who needed to pay. Finn's sister was using the only connection she had to help get herself—and hopefully the other victims—some peace about what happened to them. Jazz would do everything in her power to make that happen.

"Clearview. Michael was from Clearview." Finn put his phone in the cup holder and pulled on his seat belt. "It's a small town a few hours to the northwest."

Jazz picked up his phone and looked at the map he had brought up. She memorized the highways and turns.

One of the best parts of living where they did was that not many roads passed through. The cities were small oases in the middle of sand and swamp. It was a fairly straight shot to Clearview. They could be there shortly after dawn.

She handed him his phone and buckled up, then started the engine. Finn put his hand over hers as she gripped the gearshift to kick it into reverse. They stared at each other for a few long moments. She resisted the urge to flip her hand over and lace their fingers together.

"Are you sure about this?" he asked. "We can head back to town so I can pick up my car. You don't have to come."

She did. She would never find peace with herself if she didn't help Finn's sister find her own.

"I'm coming with you. Deal—"

She sucked in a breath, stopping mid-sentence. Turning to look through the back windshield, she put the car in reverse, then pulled her hand out from under his and hit the gas. "You're not getting rid of me this time."

They were well away from Michael's when Finn spoke again.

"I never wanted to get rid of you."

She let out a laugh. Was he really going to go there? Fine. She'd play along.

"That's funny. As I remember it, you're the one who jumped out of the limo. I'm surprised you waited for it to stop, you were so eager to get away from me."

He shook his head. "There was so much wrong with that moment."

She shrugged. "You wanted out."

"No, Jazz. I wanted *in*. That's all I ever wanted with you. But you always kept me at arm's length. Hell, not even arm's length. It was more like a ten-foot pole. Like you kept yourself in a fucking castle surrounded by a moat filled with..." He shook his head and looked out the window.

Was he kidding? She had never let anyone get closer to her than Finn. She told him about her dreams for the gallery, funny stories about her clients. She shared every moment of her life with him.

Unless they involved Elsa. Or her family.

That had always been her boundary. Her line in the sand. But Jazz didn't talk to *anyone* about her loved ones. It wasn't safe. The only reason she talked about Elsa with

Garrett and Rachel was that they all knew each other. Even then, Jazz was careful to keep it low-key and not give away how much she loved them all.

Finn had barely grazed the outskirts of her social circle, which was what Jazz wanted. There was no way she could hide how much she loved Finn if they were all hanging out. No way she could avoid talking about it.

He was Garrett's best friend, but he'd only met Elsa in passing and Jazz didn't think he'd even been in the same room as Rachel. Yeah, she didn't tell Finn stories about her friends, but he still knew how much she cared about them all. Her friends knew *nothing* about Jazz and Finn. Their relationship was sacred.

If she had told the others, they would have insisted on meeting him. Rachel would have started pressuring Jazz about a wedding, wanting to plan it and design a dress. Elsa wouldn't say anything, but she was a romance novelist. Who knew what sort of daydreams she'd create. And Garrett...

Garrett would be over the moon about it. He'd insist on double dates, even though he wasn't dating anyone— hadn't dated anyone since Jazz tried to hook him up with Elsa. And it would be awkward all around. Awkward and dangerous.

The more people who knew about Jazz and Finn, the worse it would be when something finally happened to him, especially with how much she loved him. That was how the curse worked. She loved him too much to risk it.

Curse aside, she didn't want to deal with the inevitable pressure her friends would heap on her with their well-meaning comments, building up dreams for how they wanted her life to be. Settle down. Get married. Have kids. People loved pairs and spawning.

Even Jazz had fallen into that mindset. She kept trying to set up her friends. Then again, she *knew* they wanted families and partners. They'd told her as much during uncomfortable conversations where Jazz had to work to keep the focus off of herself.

She sucked at matchmaking anyway. Rachel and Garrett had seemed a natural fit, but something had kept them from ever connecting, even when it seemed like Fate kept bringing them together over and over again. He and Elsa hadn't worked out either. But they became great friends after Jazz introduced them. They all had.

Jazz had known they would get along. She didn't know what she had been thinking when she sent Elsa on a blind date with Michael.

I wanted her to have a chance to find the happiness I had lost.

Okay. Maybe she did know.

Chloe had once told Jazz that she was a "nexus". It was just another way of calling her Fate's tool. Supposedly, Jazz had an energy that brought the right people together at the right time. But she was the one who had brought

Michael into everyone's lives. How the hell could anything be right about that?

At least Elsa had Dante now. Jazz was so happy for her —for them both. She was so grateful they had…survived. Dante would heal. Rachel was already doing much better. And Finn…

His forehead rested against the window and his eyes were closed. Either he was asleep or trying to avoid conversation. Jazz let him be. She wouldn't know what to say even if she tried. She *hoped* he was sleeping and did her best to keep the ride smooth for him.

The miles rolled by, dark scenery turning to slate gray as dawn approached. The sky brightened to a cloudless blue. They were nearing the coast. It would be a hot and humid day.

Finn lurched forward in his chair shouting, "No!"

Jazz jerked on the wheel. The SUV shimmied as she tried to regain control. She barely kept it from rolling.

"What the hell, Finn?" Her heart was pounding and her mouth had gone completely dry. She glanced over at him.

He was clutching the dashboard, his chest heaving and eyes wide. He swallowed a few times and pressed his head back against the headrest.

"Are you okay?"

"Yeah… Yeah."

She was not buying it. It must have been one of the nightmares he talked about. His eyes were haunted.

"How bad was it?" she asked.

"What? It wasn't..." He shook his head, then ran his hands over his face. "I don't want to talk about it."

"Fine."

She could hear his heavy breaths, and they weren't slowing down. Glancing over, his eyes were still wide.

"You doing okay?"

"Yeah."

"Bullshit."

"Jazz, please just leave it." He closed his eyes and shook his head.

"Okay." Whatever he had seen in the dream must have been horrible. She let him be for a while, trying to figure out what to say. "You had quite a night."

Lame.

He laughed. "That's an understatement. Not all of it was bad though."

"Really?" What could he have enjoyed?

He shrugged and grinned at her. "That part in the hallway was kinda fun."

She snorted. "Only kind of? I must be losing my touch."

"I wouldn't say that."

"That was always our strongest suit. Touching."

"Yeah. Too bad we sucked at the rest of it."

"We had some good times out of the bedroom. Didn't we?"

She hated how small her voice sounded. Hesitant. But she wasn't sure if she wanted to know the answer. Had he really wanted her to be part of his family? Had he enjoyed those times together?

"In the bar. Upstairs."

The bitter edge to his tone cut deep. He'd wanted to tell Garrett and everybody about their relationship. Jazz kept saying she wanted her privacy. It was nobody's business if they were dating.

When they were at the bar, just the two of them or with Tommy around, Jazz could let herself be happy. Somehow, she felt like it was the one place Fate wouldn't peek, the one concession to Jazz's calling as a *nexus*. If they had ever gone out, she would have constantly been on guard, trying to make sure no one realized how much she cared for Finn. The few times Garrett had seen them together, Jazz had scowled so much that Finn later told her Garrett thought she hated him.

Why couldn't Finn have been as happy as she was to carve out a corner of the world where they could be together? A place they could retreat to and be safe. She hadn't been able to risk losing him and because of it he had left.

Maybe Fate found out anyway.

For their last date, Jazz thought she had come up with the perfect compromise. Rent a limo for the night and drive around town. She had arranged for take-out from an upscale restaurant to celebrate their two-month anniversary, which was no small feat in itself. The chef had been offended when she first approached him with the idea, but she turned it around.

The back of the limo was spacious enough for them to have a nice dinner and even a good time, if he'd been up for it. She had dressed to the nines, spent hours preparing for the evening, trying to make it perfect—trying to make him happy and keep him safe.

Finn had been uncomfortable from the beginning. When she explained the evening she had planned, he pounded on the glass partition hard enough she was afraid it would break. The driver opened it to see what he needed, and Finn demanded they pull over.

He hit the curb the moment the limo came to a stop.

She tried to talk to him afterward, and he told her he was done. She remembered the moment with crystalline clarity.

"I want to really be with you. To start a life with you. Not this sneaking-around crap. I used to work divorce cases. This isn't a relationship—it's an affair. I won't be 'the other man'. That isn't what I want for us. If you're not all-in, I'm out."

But she *couldn't* be all-in. Not with anyone. Beyond the supernatural obstacles, it wasn't what she wanted, what she was meant for. It just wasn't who she was. She didn't want to treat their relationship like an affair, but the alternative…

If he had asked again to tell their friends, she might have considered it. If he wanted to go out that badly, she would have managed. But what he was asking… It was something she couldn't give.

Would it have been so bad to marry him?

She felt like she had asked herself that question a thousand times since he left. Along with wishing they had talked about the entire situation more. She thought they would have more time—like she always did right before Fate took someone from her.

If he really needed the traditional lifestyle, they could have adopted some kids, picked up a dog somewhere, bought a house in the suburbs…and lived a lie. Had children she loved but would never connect to the way a mother should.

She didn't want to be a mother or a wife. She just wanted to be *Jazz*.

Apparently, that wasn't enough for him.

Chapter Twelve

"This is the turn."

Finn pointed at the exit. A rusted sign with a few bullet holes read *Clearview*.

Jazz didn't say anything. Just turned the SUV and headed to the town. She hadn't said anything since he'd brought up how their relationship ended.

Great idea there. Really good form.

He knew he was still raw over it. He didn't expect her to be after so many years.

Isn't it right that she's suffering as I am?

Wait… What?

No. Absolutely not. Finn didn't want her to suffer. He didn't want either of them to. He would honestly have been glad to find that she'd moved on and was happily having a purely physical relationship with someone else.

Okay, maybe not *glad*. But it would have helped him move on to see that he was right all along about what she was looking for from him. Knowing she was still upset about the breakup made him question things.

Including his decision to end their relationship in the first place.

If he was being honest with himself, they hadn't only clicked in the bedroom. She had been part of his family. She and his dad got on so well, sometimes Finn wondered if Dad liked her better than him. Finn used to tease them both about it all the time.

Finn and Jazz would have been great together—if she'd let them actually make a life together instead of hiding their relationship. He knew Jazz hadn't been involved with anyone else, but it still drove him crazy that she acted like Finn was *the other man.*

After the initial phase of pretty much constant sex, he'd spent all his energy trying to get them out of the damned house. When they should have been talking about what they wanted out of their relationship and where they were headed, he was busy trying to understand why she wouldn't let their friends know they were involved.

It seemed a necessary first step before getting into the heavier conversations, like kids and marriage—and why Finn wasn't interested in either. That didn't mean he didn't want a long-term commitment from her. It didn't mean he didn't love her.

She had kept herself so guarded. Never once—not a single time—had she ever told Finn she loved him. Even after he said it. She just sat up in the bed and walked away. Said she wasn't comfortable talking about feelings.

He might have jumped the gun, telling her how he felt after only a month, but he'd thought they were on the same page. He hadn't brought it up again. He hadn't had a chance to.

Now she was back in his life and it was messing with his head. He was losing his focus. Not that he'd had much of that lately, either. At least she'd be there to pull him out if he became trapped in a memory again.

"Where are we heading?" Her question snapped him out of his spiraling thoughts, thankfully.

"Let's take a pass through town. See what's off the main strip."

"We're going to be conspicuous. All I'm seeing are old trucks and rusted-out compacts." She smiled at him briefly. "Maybe we *should* have gone back to Summer Park to pick up your car."

He bristled. "I junked it."

"No way."

"It might have fit in here, but I was sticking out like a sore thumb in Summer Park. I had to upgrade for stakeouts."

Of course, he had bought his new car—topping out his budget—just a few months before Dad's hospital stay. Dad insisted he keep it, and Finn couldn't argue. It really was helping with stakeouts. He and his dad were doing okay so far with their savings and what the bar brought in, but Finn needed to get this squared away so he could get back to work.

"I liked that car," Jazz said.

"Seriously?"

She shrugged and glanced over at him. "It had character."

"That's one word for it."

Maybe the car was a happy reminder that she was above me.

What the fuck? Where were these thoughts coming from? He shifted in his seat, staring out the window at the few buildings they passed.

The thought was an unwelcome reminder of one of the main doubts that plagued him through their relationship. He had wondered the whole time they were together what Jazz saw in him. She was self-made, well off, and *owned* herself. Finn tended to fly off the handle. Jazz was always in control. What could she want with a private eye living above a bar with his dad?

Then he'd look in the mirror and remember.

Finn never had trouble getting a date before her and he doubted he'd find it challenging if he decided to put himself out there again. Jazz had made no secret of enjoying his body. She even made jokes that she could display him in the gallery if she didn't want to keep him all to herself.

If she was only into him physically, how could he keep her interest over time? He wanted to grow old with her. He didn't want to constantly be checking his physique, wondering if she was getting bored or looking to trade up.

No matter what she said, her secretiveness kept reminding him of too many cases he'd worked.

Switching to investigating insurance fraud had helped him move away from seedy hotels and some truly disturbing moments gathering evidence that he wished he could forget. He was gaining a reputation with his new cases as someone who could crack seemingly impossible mysteries.

People had already started asking him what his secret was. He had to be careful.

If anybody figured out that he was using his powers to read objects—and people—involved in the cases… He'd lose all his business in a heartbeat. No one would believe what he did was real. He'd become a joke.

Dad disapproved of what he did. They weren't supposed to use their powers to make money. Their gifts were meant to help people. That was what his granddad passed on when teaching Dad about his powers.

But Finn *did* help others with what he could do. He just also helped himself and his family.

"You're walking a gray line, Finn." Dad always let Finn know when he was about to take on a case that would cross the line, no matter how big the payout. Finn was grateful. He'd been tempted a time or two, but his dad always kept him on track.

Now he had Jazz to help him.

They passed the last building, the scenery reverting to

thick foliage crowding between palm trees and pines. Damn, Clearview was tiny. Most of the buildings had busted-out windows and peeling paint.

"That was one shitty town," Jazz said.

He couldn't disagree. People were struggling here. He could feel it.

"I saw a bar that wasn't boarded up," he said. "That's our best bet."

"Let's hope Michael's cousin is a drinker then."

From what Finn had seen, he wouldn't doubt it. Not much of an eater, though. That nickname Michael kept using was just cruel. Finn almost felt sorry for the guy.

Almost.

She turned the SUV around using a side street, then headed back the way they had come. The parking lot for the bar had tons of potholes filled with sand and gravel. The SUV bounced as if they were driving off-road.

"Pull around so you're facing the street." He scanned the area, looking for the best place to park. "There. Park there. If we need to, we'll be able to get out fast and it'd take several trucks to block us in."

She raised her eyebrows and glanced at him, but did as he said. "You get to think about fun stuff in your line of work."

He shrugged. "Things happen. I don't like repeating mistakes."

Like being with you.

What the fuck. He was seriously about to reach into his head and punch his brain. The lack of sleep must be getting to him more than he thought. Or the nightmares.

The most recent one… It was different. He suppressed a shudder.

Dreaming from his sister's perspective made a lot of sense now that he knew their relationship. He'd researched psychic powers enough to know about the twin bond. Even non-psychic twins had heightened connections.

Experiencing what happened to her was horrible, but he understood it. What he didn't understand was the dream on the way to Clearview—the nightmare from *Michael's* point of view.

Finn had seen Siobhan's memories so many times. Maybe his brain had decided to mix things up a bit. It was sure doing its own thing with the extremely unwelcome thoughts that kept popping into his head.

Yeah, he was bitter. But when had he become an asshole?

"Are we going to go in or just sit in the parking lot all day?"

He didn't bother responding. Just scowled at her and opened the door. She fell in step beside him, keys in hand.

"Wait." Finn grabbed her arm before she could lock the doors. God, he missed touching her.

She stared into his face. Didn't ask. Didn't say anything. Just waited for him to make a move.

He cleared his throat. "I don't want them to hear the car arming itself and look out the window. We need to keep a low profile."

She nodded. "I can lock it without it making a sound."

He felt the muscles in her arm shift as she pressed the button to lock the door. He couldn't bring himself to let go of her, even while she put the keys in her pocket.

He wanted to kiss her again. That was a bad idea. Whether she went along with it or not, he was certain the results would gather attention. He finally let go of her and turned back to the bar.

Trees lined the parking lot. There were too many places people could be hiding and watching them. He headed for the bar at a brisk pace. At the door, Jazz ducked ahead of him and opened it so he didn't have to touch the handle.

"Thanks."

She actually smiled at him. "No problem."

The bar was busier than Finn expected. The smell of grease and eggs explained that. It was quite possible that they were in the only restaurant in town, unless there were others tucked away down a side street. A wiry woman stood behind the bar, wiping the counter. She was maybe in her late thirties and looked pissed as hell.

Tread carefully, Finn.

He walked to the bar, making sure Jazz stayed close as he kept track of the patrons. A table of four guys with full plates. They'd be busy for a while. The pitcher at their table was full of beer instead of orange juice, though. That was an early start and a bad sign, especially since their glasses were still half-full from a previous pitcher.

Two other tables had guys sitting at them, but they were solo and focused on their food. Finn wasn't as concerned about them. Numbers gave people false courage. Drinking would make matters worse.

He turned his attention back to the bartender. Flirting was out. He didn't need his powers to detect the "do not fuck with me" mojo she was putting off. He'd need to be direct, but not give too much away.

This will be fun.

Finally, something he and his brain could agree on. Unless he wasn't being sarcastic…while he was thinking to himself.

I'm worse off than I thought.

He brought his mind back to task and smiled as the woman made eye contact. He waited to speak until they were close and he could keep his voice down while being heard.

"Good morning."

She nodded. "Morning."

The rag on her shoulder had what looked like raw egg yolk on it. She was probably also the cook. He kept that in mind while figuring out how to get information from her. Using his powers to read her mind was out. He was pretty sure she'd cut off his hand if he tried to touch her.

At the very least.

Shut up, brain.

He sat on a stool, careful not to touch the counter. "Could we get two plates of eggs and toast with some orange juice?"

"Just some bottled water for me." Jazz was glancing around with a grimace on her face. She looked revolted— like she didn't want to touch anything herself.

The bartender snorted. "I can pour some from the tap into an empty. That work for you?"

Finn was sure Jazz was about to say something impolite in response. He reached over and touched her arm, giving her a pointed look. She seemed to get the message. He turned back to the bartender and smiled.

"Orange juice is fine," Jazz said.

"I'll have it right out."

As soon as the bartender left Finn whispered, "What the hell was that?"

Jazz stood near the bar, but didn't sit. "What do you mean? You're going to get rabies eating the food here."

"Come on."

She leaned closer and pointed to the door that led to the kitchen. A possum was hanging right above it. It didn't move as he stared at it. After a moment, he realized it was stuffed.

Great décor…

"At least it's not going anywhere," she murmured,

crossing her arms.

"I don't plan to eat anything." Especially after seeing that. It would be a while before his appetite returned. "I just wanted to buy something so that I can overpay when I ask my questions."

"Oh. So that's how you do it."

"Would you please sit down?"

"No thanks." Jazz eyed the barstool. "I'm having enough trouble thinking of you sitting in my SUV in those pants."

She shifted closer, scanning the room. Her arm brushed his shoulder.

"I could always take them off first."

Dammit, he couldn't keep himself from flirting with her, even now. Especially now, with her standing close, being there for him when he needed her. She had dropped everything to help him. He only just realized that.

She smiled at him and he felt it reflected on his face. He had forgotten that smile. How could he have forgotten it? It made him feel like he was the center of her universe. Her eyes softened, her lips parted, and…

He was already leaning in when she snapped out of it and pulled away. Damn good thing one of them was keeping a level head.

"Sorry," he said.

"Forget it."

She crossed her arms and looked at the bottles lining

the shelves in front of them. Most were fairly empty.

The bartender returned and set two plates with wet eggs and burned toast in front of them. There was nothing floating in the orange juice, but Finn didn't actually want to chance it.

He pulled four twenties from his wallet and set them on the counter. "Thanks."

She didn't reach for the cash as he'd expected. Instead, her eyes narrowed. She put her hands on the counter and leaned forward in an aggressive stance.

"What do you want?" she asked.

"My friend and I are just passing through town."

"Good for you. Get on with it."

Finn smiled at her, turning up the charm. Her lips pressed together more tightly. Perfect. She might be resisting him, but that meant he was at least affecting her.

"We're hoping you can settle something for us." He glanced at Jazz, then said, "I was telling my friend that this is the town where that serial killer grew up. You know..." He lowered his voice to a whisper and leaned forward. "Michael Angelo."

"Get the hell out of my bar."

Jazz jumped in. "I told you this isn't the town. If it was, they'd be cashing in on the publicity."

The bartender snorted again. "Right. Cops and reporters hassling your regulars is great for business. They didn't find anything here for them and neither will you."

Her gaze lingered on a seat a few spots to Finn's right.

"I'm not talking regulars," Jazz said. "I meant tourists. Florida is already full of them. If Clearview is where that guy grew up, you could advertise it and draw in more business. Charge an admission fee just to get into the place for special events."

"Events?"

Jazz had the woman hooked. Damn, she was a natural at this. He should have known, with the way she ran her gallery.

"His birthday. Halloween. You could make a whole show of it. Cash in on the creep factor."

The bartender leaned back, considering. Jazz kept on, pressing her advantage.

"Of course, you might catch some flak from his family. Does he have any in the area?"

The woman's gaze flicked back to that seat. Finn was able to track it better this time. Three stools over.

"You leave him alone. Travis is a good man."

Perfect. Now we have a name.

Finn leaned forward, keeping his elbows on his knees so he didn't touch the counter. "She didn't mean anything, Nell."

The woman and Jazz both stared at Finn. He wasn't sure why.

"What?" he asked.

Nell lowered her voice to a very menacing register.

"How do you know my name?"

Shit. Did he? He hadn't even touched anything. How could he have picked that up? His mind spun, trying to come up with an explanation. He needed to keep it together. He needed to get her off their case for long enough to read Travis's spot.

"Okay, you caught us," Finn said. "We had this idea for building a tourist trap in Clearview. My friend here is a marketing genius. We thought maybe we'd scope the place out. See if there's partnership potential."

"There's not," Nell said. "So you keep on moving out of town."

"Okay, okay. We get it." He held up his hands and nodded. He gave her his best smile and said, "Can I at least finish my eggs?"

She snorted, then snatched up his money and stalked away.

Chapter Thirteen

Jazz was ready to leave. She wanted to head back to Summer Park, burn their clothes, bleach the inside of her SUV, and spend three days in the shower. Maybe she could convince Finn to join her.

As soon as the bartender went back into the kitchen, Finn stood up. He didn't head for the exit as Jazz had hoped. Instead, he walked to a different barstool and sat.

"What are you doing?" she asked.

"This is where Travis always sits. I need to read the spot."

"That's a terrible idea."

They were in a public place. He could get lost in the memory. He could get a horrible disease from touching something in the bar. Jazz had looked at the floor once since coming in. Things were…moving.

"We need to know more about him. Who he is, where he lives. Scoot my plate over here, will you? It'll be less conspicuous."

She glanced at the plate. The eggs were half-liquid. It was one thing to have a ratty place, but the bartender—*Nell*—could have at least cooked the eggs properly.

"How did you know the bartender's name?"

"I must have picked it up somehow."

"What, by reading the seat through your ass?"

He busted out laughing, then shook his head. Part of her delighted in hearing him laugh. Most of her was terrified.

"This is serious. Have your powers gone airborne or something?" she asked.

If they did, she would have to get him away from people, away from civilization. It would be the only way to keep him sane.

"No. It must have been something I picked up from reading Michael's memories earlier. Or maybe from Travis."

She wasn't buying it. Something about the whole thing felt wrong—beyond his powers being whacked out.

"Jazz, please. You've been so keen on helping me. I need you now."

Dammit.

She pushed the plate over to him, then set up her dishes at the seat next to it. She still couldn't bring herself to sit down.

"I'll be right here."

"Give me ten minutes tops. If I'm not done, shake me out of it anyway."

"Okay."

She didn't like it. She didn't like anything about this. Her stomach was still in knots from giving that woman ideas for ways to use Michael Angelo as a *marketing tool.* Jazz hadn't known what else to do. If she ever found out this place was acting on those suggestions, she wouldn't forgive herself.

But they had made progress. They had a name for Michael's cousin. And if this worked out, they would know even more.

Finn put his hands on the counter. No more time for self-recrimination. She needed to keep her attention on him.

His eyes became blank. Maybe that was a good sign? At least he wasn't talking to himself. If she needed to snap him out of it, she could kick the barstool out from under him. Comforted by her plan, she crossed her arms and watched him work.

He was handling everything remarkably well. Yeah, he kept making snarky comments and he had yelled a few times, but he had flown off the handle on a regular basis when they were a couple. Either time or this had calmed him down. She hoped it helped him find happiness. With someone else.

Enough with the maudlin self-pity.

She was tired. She hadn't slept in over twenty-four hours and had no idea when she'd sleep again. But she was with Finn, and he kept looking at her with those soulful eyes, holding on to her longer than was necessary.

She wanted to put her hand on his back. Run her fingers

through his hair. Okay, she wanted to pull off his tank top and see if he really was in just as good of shape as the last time she'd seen him shirtless.

She wanted to do much more than that. She wanted to hold on to him and never let go.

One touch. One tiny touch…

But she had no idea how that would affect him. She kept her hands to herself.

"Look at that."

The hair on the back of her neck stood on end at the voice that was too close for comfort. She turned around slowly, uncrossing her arms and shifting her weight to put herself between Finn and the four guys blocking the door to the bar.

They reeked of beer, and the smell wasn't just coming from the pitcher in the front man's hand. Each was smaller than Finn, but there were four of them. Jazz wished she had let Finn teach her more about fighting.

"You lost, little lady?"

"I'm fine, thanks."

How much time did Finn need? How much time was left before she was supposed to snap him out of it?

"I heard you talking to Nell about trying to bring in some tourists. I think that's a fine idea."

"Great. Take it up with your local Chamber of Commerce."

They all laughed and the three men behind him said,

"Woooo."

"Sounds to me like you've already got it all worked out. We were just saying we can take you around. Show you what Clearview's got to offer."

"*My friend* and I are fine on our own, thanks."

She didn't want to call their attention to Finn, but needed them to know she wasn't alone. And at the same time, she kind of wanted to start screaming for help. She doubted there were any police nearby. To make things worse, the last solitary customer stood and half ran out of the place, as if he was scared.

Shit. What did he know that she didn't?

She focused on the four men in front of her, took in the way they were looking at her, and panicked. She pushed it down.

Where was the bartender?

"Your friend over there seems more messed up than us. When did he start in, anyway?"

The three guys laughed while the ringleader just smiled at her.

"He really likes eggs," she said.

"I'd be paying more attention to you. I bet he spends more time with that shiny SUV outside. That thing's barely got a speck of dirt on it."

She hadn't noticed the guy leave or come back. It unnerved her to imagine him eyeing her car while thinking about her and Finn.

"A man shouldn't spend more time on his ride than his woman. Unless of course—"

She refused to let him finish his lewd comment. "Actually, the SUV is mine."

"Is it now? I do like a woman with fine taste. Why don't you let your friend there finish his eggs and we can all go for a ride in that fancy car of yours. We can show you those sights and maybe talk about those plans you got."

"My only plan is to stay here."

"Come on. I heard your friend say you're a genius. You gotta have a few more ideas for bringing people to the bar in that gorgeous head of yours."

How the hell did this guy have such good hearing?

One of the guys behind him laughed. "I have one. Wet T-shirt contest."

He grabbed the front guy's arm and flung the pitcher of beer at Jazz. Her shirt was doused and she stumbled back into Finn, knocking him off the stool.

"What the fuck?" she shouted.

The men started to laugh. Jazz felt her shirt plastered to her front. She didn't bother crossing her arms to cover herself. They probably wanted her to feel cowed, and she refused to give them the satisfaction. Also, she was wearing a bikini top under her shirt—she always wore bikinis under her clothes so she could hit the pool the moment she went home at night. They weren't getting the view they were after.

Mostly, she wanted her hands free so she could grab some bottles from behind the counter and smash them over these guys' heads.

She felt strong hands clasp her arms and lifted her foot to stomp on the guy's instep. She realized it was Finn just in time. Before anyone could say anything else, the bartender stormed out of the kitchen. With a shotgun.

"What the hell is going on out here?" she shouted.

"Hey, Nell." The front guy—all of them—acted contrite. He pointed at Jazz and said, "We were just welcoming these two strangers to Clearview."

"And flinging my good beer all over the place for me to clean up."

"If she'd been a little friendlier—"

Nell shook her head. "I don't want to hear it. You're all banned for a week. If I see you in here before then, I'll call the sheriff."

"A week? You can't—"

"I can and I did. Now go home and sleep it off. Unless you'd rather spend the rest of the day in the drunk tank. Again."

As the men filed out, the glares they cast at Jazz made her skin crawl. It took all her strength not to lean back into Finn.

The bartender was Jazz's new hero. Nell walked over to them and threw her rag on the floor in the center of the beer that hadn't soaked into Jazz's clothes.

"Thank you," Jazz said.

"Thank me? You just cost me four of my best customers for a week. Do you even know what that's going to mean for my business?"

She didn't, but from the looks of things, the bar was barely making ends meet.

"I can make up for it," Jazz said. "I have money."

"Keep your goddamned money. Just get the *fuck* out of my bar and don't come back."

Finn gripped Jazz's arm more tightly and led her to the door.

"Finn—"

"I know. Just keep walking."

The men from the bar were clustered around a truck parked in the back corner of the lot. Jazz unlocked her doors quickly, her heart pounding.

When they were in the car, she said, "Is Nell going to be okay?"

"They won't take this out on her. She's their source for a bar. We're a different matter, though. We need to leave. Now."

Jazz started the car and kicked it into gear, trying not to seem too much in a hurry. She wanted to floor it. She wanted to go back to the parking lot and run them over.

"What the hell was wrong with those people? Who throws beer? Seriously! And the whole, 'Hey baby, let's all go for a ride in your SUV.' Give me a fucking break."

"They tried to get you to leave with them?"

Finn's voice was quiet. Disturbingly so.

"It was no big deal."

"You should have snapped me out of it."

"You were busy."

"Jazz, don't dismiss this. Guys like that can do a hell of a lot worse than douse you in beer."

"They didn't make a move. I was ready to scream for help."

"And who would have come to your rescue?" He let out a deep sigh. "Some small towns, even down on their luck, the people pull together and help each other. Others go bad. This one is about the worst I've ever felt. In a town like this, you keep your head down and your mouth shut. You don't look too close at what other people are doing."

"I handled it. Deal—" She stopped herself again, clamping her mouth shut.

Finn shook his head. "This is why I didn't want you coming along. You're too cocky. You're going to get hurt. We should turn around and head back to Summer Park."

"I can take care of myself."

"Against four guys? Come on."

"I had you to back me up."

"Four guys, Jazz. I would have gotten my ass kicked if it wasn't for Nell."

The thought of Finn trying to fight them off—and

failing—sent ice shooting through Jazz's veins. Her imagination painted a scene with him on the ground, them surrounding him…

"And they wouldn't have been finished after me. Do you even realize how dangerous that situation was?"

Yes. She did. She just didn't want to think about it. That had honestly been one of the scariest moments of her life. She didn't need to be psychic to see what the ringleader at least had in mind.

She wanted to have the courage to help Finn, to keep moving forward with him. *Nothing* would stop her.

"If something happened to you…" he said.

Her heart was still pounding, but suddenly for a different reason. She wanted him to finish his sentence. Wanted to hear him say he still cared.

"If something happened to me what?"

"Forget it." He shook his head. "I know who we're looking for. I have a good idea of where he lives. Head back to Summer Park. I'll pick up my car and take it from here."

"What about your powers malfunctioning? You need me."

"They worked fine back in the bar. Maybe now that I'm on the case, Siobhan's spirit is taking it easy on me. Hell, maybe she'll even help."

Replaced by a ghost. Harsh.

"What if you're wrong?"

"As you so often say—I'll deal with it."

And that was it. No more chances to fix things between them. Maybe they'd never be a couple again, but she had missed him. His absence in her life left a gaping hole. She wanted them to at least be friends.

She hadn't even realized that hope had bloomed in her until he stamped it out. End of opportunity.

Except she didn't want it to be. She didn't want things to be over. The thought of Finn lost in a serial killer's memory while an accomplice crept up on him sent a chill through her. She needed time to change his mind.

She needed to change.

"I stink," she said.

Finn turned back to her.

"I stink like cheap beer. I don't want the smell getting stuck in the upholstery. Summer Park is hours away. Let's find a place to clean up first. Okay?"

He sighed, but nodded. "Okay."

Chapter Fourteen

An hour later, Finn was standing in a shower stall in a cheap, relatively clean hotel room that he had paid for in cash under an assumed name. They had wolfed down some power bars and bottles of water he grabbed from the office. The SUV was parked around back to keep it out of sight from people cruising down the highway. He hoped that would be enough.

He had called to check in on his dad, and Daphne had answered. She said Dad was sleeping, but seemed okay when he was awake earlier. Withdrawn and devastated, sure. But physically she didn't think he was in danger. That was enough to help Finn keep going. Daphne would update Dad next time he woke up and Finn would keep his focus on the case.

Jazz had showered first and borrowed his shirt to wear while her T-shirt and pants dried. She had definitely taken the brunt of the pitcher of beer, blocking it with her body as she'd fallen into him.

If she hadn't knocked him off his stool, he might have stayed lost in that memory too long to help her. When he came out of it, she might have been gone.

He was certain those guys were capable of…things he didn't want to think about. He wasn't sure how he knew. Just like he wasn't sure how he knew Nell's name before reading anything.

He didn't want to think about that either.

His focus needed to be on getting Jazz back to Summer Park. Once he knew she was safe, he could track down the guy who helped kill his sister. His twin.

A pang shot through his chest as he thought of Siobhan again. How could he miss her when he'd never even met her? He was having a hard enough time keeping it together as it was.

His thoughts kept running on bizarre tangents that just weren't him. No matter where they were, he felt like he was being watched. The case was getting under his skin. He needed to regroup as much as he needed to get Jazz out of harm's way. Focusing on the warm water pouring over his shoulders helped.

Last he had seen of her, she was sitting on the queen bed, bare legs stretched out and crossed at the ankles. She had one arm bent behind her neck and was leaning back as if staring at the ceiling, but her eyes were closed. He'd taken off the comforter for her and folded it on top of the dresser. The bar had reminded him that she wasn't used to dives.

His shirt looked so damned good on her. She left the top few buttons undone. The sleeves dangled past her elbows. He wondered if she had put her swimsuit back on underneath.

The first time he had seen her had been at her condo's pool. He had stopped by to introduce himself after Garrett had recommended Finn for a case involving one of the exhibits at her gallery. It had been late and she had been alone, standing on the other side of the clear water. While he watched, she'd peeled off her shirt and pants. He hadn't known she wore swimsuits under her clothes.

His brain had sort of stalled out before letting him realize what was happening. By then, it had been too late. His dick was already at full attention. He had planned to introduce himself and try to score her number before he'd found out she was his new client. It had been an awkward moment.

He never mixed business and pleasure, but had still hoped to make a move after the case was finished. They were definitely on the same track there—like two trains heading for each other.

He shouldn't be thinking about this. Even the memory of her sleek body cutting through the water was enough to get him hard. He turned the temperature on the shower down a notch, then braced his arms against the tile and closed his eyes as the cooler water washed over his body.

He felt her hands on his shoulders.

Shit. This isn't happening.

At the same time, it felt inevitable. The two of them

trapped together, with their history and all that was unresolved between them... Okay. Yeah, it was happening.

Her fingers glided down his back, playing with the planes and valleys of his muscles. She always said she loved his back. Then again, she'd been a fan of everything about him—physically, at least.

She slid her palms over his hips. One traveled up along his abs while the other went straight for the prize. He groaned as she wrapped her slender fingers around him and squeezed, then started slow, rhythmic strokes.

"Jazz..."

She shifted so she was kneeling in front of him. He could feel her moving around him and clenched his eyes shut tighter. If their gazes locked, she would see the conflict in him and this would be over. And if this was all he had left of them right now, dammit, he would take it.

Her lips slid over his dick, pulling him deep into her mouth. Her tongue joined in the stroking, her hand still working the base of his shaft. Damn, he had missed this. The heat, the energy.

His body relaxed under her touch, his tension and unease vanishing as he fell into the familiar rhythm. His hips rocked against her. He wanted to fuck her so bad, but she didn't seem ready to stop what she was doing. He sure as hell wasn't ready to stop her. Maybe she'd missed this as much as he had.

There's no possible way.

Finally, she slid up his chest, wrapping her arms around his neck, jumping up to lock her legs around his waist. She nipped at his neck and pressed her chest against his.

Somehow, he could still feel the water from the shower running along his skin. That wasn't right.

He opened his eyes.

Jazz wasn't there. No one was. He was standing in the shower alone, hard as he'd ever been, water pouring over his chest—and he could still feel her all over him.

Her thighs were tight against his hips, calves gripping his back. Her arms distributed her slight weight across his shoulders. He felt the softness of her skin, the heat of her body, the slickness of her core as she lined herself up.

But she wasn't there.

He lurched back and she went with him. At least, the sensation of her. He reached for her instinctively to keep her from falling. He felt the warm skin of her back—dry, not wet—felt her tense for a split-second, then the... whatever the hell it was...vanished.

Moments later, Jazz flung the door to the shower open. Cool air from the AC flooded the tiny space.

"What the hell was that?" she shouted.

He tried to cover himself, but basically ended up just holding his dick against his stomach.

"What are you talking about? And do you mind?"

"Yeah, I do! You used your powers on me."

Oh shit.

He fumbled for the knobs to turn off the water, panicking. Stepping from the shower, he grabbed a towel and wrapped it around his waist.

"Jazz—"

"I felt your hands on my back."

"Wait... Just your back?"

"Yeah. What the hell difference does it make?"

Relief rushed through him. He had thought she felt the whole thing—that his imagination was somehow manifesting on her body. He would never touch Jazz—or anyone—like that unless they wanted him to, through his powers or otherwise.

Wait a minute...

"You only felt my hands on your back?" He had to be sure.

She crossed her arms and shifted her weight, raising one eyebrow and glaring at him. "Yeah. So?"

"Because I felt a hell of a lot more than that. For the last five minutes at least. What have you been doing out there?"

Her mouth dropped open. She snapped it shut, then turned on her heel and stalked out of the room.

Yeah, his powers were acting up again, but *she* had prompted it. He could tell from the look on her face, the way her cheeks and the skin of her neck and chest were flushed.

She was thinking about him, imagining or remembering

what they had experienced together. And he had felt every moment.

He still wanted her. Of course he did. But now he knew she wanted him too. Damn, did she want him.

He followed her into the bedroom. "We need to talk."

"You're right." Jazz stopped on the far side of the bed, crossing her arms again. "I'm not going back to Summer Park."

"What? That's not what I meant." He would save that argument for later. And it *would* be an argument. "We need to talk about what just happened."

"No we don't. Your powers are malfunctioning. End of story."

"That's not... Do you even listen to yourself? You can't put this all on me."

She let out a snort. "Pardon me for not being more careful with my thoughts around a telepath who told me he can only read people when touching them—and that I was immune to his powers. Anything else I should know?"

"What the fuck, Jazz. Are you kidding me? I didn't try to read you. My powers have never done anything like that before."

"I get it. It's not your fault. I don't get why we have to talk about it."

"Because it shouldn't have happened. On so many levels, it shouldn't have happened."

"Well it did and it's done. You're dripping on the

carpet. Go dry off."

Seriously? That was her diversionary tactic?

He'd had enough.

He pulled the towel from his waist and roughly dried his chest and arms, then his legs. He glared at her the whole time. Well, at first, anyway.

The more she stared back, the less angry she looked. He started to forget what they were fighting about. Her lips parted and her arms dropped to her sides.

He ran the towel over his back and scrubbed his hair, then ran his fingers through it. When he was done, he threw the towel over the back of a chair and just stood there. One of them had to make a move, a gesture, anything to break the icy silence between them. He couldn't stand being so close to her without touching her.

And that was always the problem.

"Jazz…"

She didn't give him a chance to finish. She ran across the room and grabbed him. Her arms locked behind his neck, pulling her up so she could crush her lips against his. Her tongue slid into his mouth, not so much demanding as starved.

He pressed her against his body—thrumming as anticipation built. He let his hands slide down to her ass, lifting her off her feet. She wrapped her legs around his waist, deepening the kiss as her weight was taken off her arms.

God, he had missed this.

He walked them to the bed, then laid her down and covered her with his body. She ran her legs along his thighs, the softness of her skin making him want to just plunge into her. He couldn't risk hurting her, though. He had to be sure she was ready.

Sliding a hand between them, he let his fingers follow a familiar path through the soft curls at the apex of her legs. She was already slick. Maybe she wouldn't need as much warming up as he thought. He ran his fingers through her wetness, then drove two in deep.

She gasped against his mouth, back arcing as he started moving within her, steady thrusts, thumb circling her clit. She melted back into the mattress. The more she relaxed, the more worked up he became. His dick was so hard he could probably cut glass with it. It would be so easy to sink into her.

He felt her shift beneath him. He didn't want to break the kiss. He was afraid of what would happen when they made eye contact.

Would she pull away? Freak out? Say something that made his heart reach for her or shrivel up in his chest?

He forced himself to pull back. She didn't even look at him. Just reached for the bedside table—and her wallet. She pulled out a condom, then flung the wallet back on the table.

Practical, as always.

He tried not to care—tried not to let it get under his skin—but who was he kidding? She lived under his skin. Had since the beginning.

He sat on his knees, waiting for her to do her thing. She'd probably want to be on top and run the show. He never really minded. Hell, it was great to be with someone who told him what she wanted instead of making him figure things out on his own.

Other guys probably thought Finn was lucky to be able to read people's thoughts through touch. He always knew what his partner enjoyed or didn't enjoy. But the running commentary wasn't what it was cracked up to be.

It didn't usually take him long to realize that most of his lovers were so smitten with his looks that they didn't care at all about who he was as a person. Others compared him with previous lovers, which was almost worse. The result was that his experience outside of Jazz was actually pretty limited. Sex was too complicated when he could read people's thoughts.

Jazz opened the wrapper and slid the thin plastic over him without missing a beat. Her skill set didn't seem rusty at all. A surge of jealousy hit him in the chest. Dammit, now was not the time to be thinking about that—or anything. This could very well be his last chance to be with her like this. He wanted to enjoy it.

She kissed him again, slow and deep. Then she knelt next to him and unbuttoned the shirt she was wearing. She let it slide down her arms before tossing it away. Instead of pushing him down on the bed, she wrapped her arms around his neck, gently pulling him toward her as she lay back.

That was new.

He'd take it. He'd take her any way he could get her. He nestled himself between her thighs, perched right at her entrance, trying to hold on to the moment, to remember every touch, every look.

And the way she was looking at him…

It was unguarded. She actually looked vulnerable.

"Jazz—"

She shook her head and wrapped her legs around the backs of his thighs. "No words. Just this."

Then she pulled him home.

Chapter Fifteen

Jazz felt Finn enter her as a cascade of bliss flowing along all her senses. He slid his hands beneath her back, embracing her as he slowly thrust in and pulled out, over and over again.

Wrapping her arms around him, she held him as close as she could, nuzzling his neck and pressing kisses along his warm skin. She let her legs glide up along the backs of his thighs, then locked her ankles so he could land deeper.

He made a little grunting noise and his fingers tightened against her back. He was trying to hold on to the moment, to make this union last. She couldn't blame him.

She didn't know what would happen when it was over.

He buried his face in her hair, his stubble tickling her ear. "I missed you."

"I missed you too."

He pushed himself up on his elbows and stared down at her, his hips still making languid thrusts into her body. She didn't want to talk, didn't want to think. She only wanted to feel.

She lifted her lips to his. He kissed her, pressing her back against the pillows. She nipped at him, urging him on. She met his tongue as it slid into her mouth. He was still drawing his shaft out slowly, letting them savor the friction, the building heat. But then he'd drive himself back in quickly, as if he couldn't stand being apart from her.

The pace of his thrusts increased, his kiss deepened. She distracted herself from the pressure building within her by tracing the muscles of his back as he moved above her, exploring the valley of his spine just above his waist. She dropped her legs to the side so she could spread her fingers over his ass and feel them flex.

They should have done this more often. She had taken the lead most times when they had sex. It might not be safe to tell him how she felt, but she had always thought she could at least show him. She could give him as much as he gave her.

At the moment, she needed to feel as much of him as possible. She wrapped her legs around his, pulling against his thighs as he buried himself in her over and over again. The rough hair of his legs prickled against her skin.

He shifted his mouth to her neck, sucking and nipping. His weight pressed her into the mattress, his heat surrounding her, filling her. Every time he buried himself in her, he ground against her most sensitive spot. He was moving faster, each pump increasing the pressure she felt deep in her belly, sending tendrils of pleasure out through her body.

He pushed himself up on his arms, letting the cold air from the AC flow over her. His pace quickened, the pull against her skin, the grinding of his thrusts, setting off an avalanche along her senses. The tension he had built shattered as waves of pleasure pulsed through her body from where they were joined.

She wanted to pull him in even deeper, but he wasn't done. Gasping as she caught her breath, she looked up at him. His eyes were shut tightly, his lips parted as he started pumping into her even faster. She wrapped her legs around his waist again, running her fingernails lightly along his back as he landed hard and deep.

Finally, he threw his head back and groaned, burying himself as deep as he could, pinning her to the bed. She felt him pulsing within her, spending himself. With a last shuddering breath, he lowered himself so their chests were pressed together again. He wrapped his arms around her back, embracing her without crushing her.

"That was…amazing," he said.

There was a lump in her throat blocking her words. She ran her hands gently down his back instead of trying to talk.

Panic started to set in.

He was going to pull out soon. She felt him softening. Then they would go back to being…what? Friends? Ex-lovers? Friends with benefits? She had no idea.

They couldn't pick up where they left off. She didn't

want to be the couple who always fought. How long could they really be together anyway? She couldn't give him a family, didn't want to settle down. She didn't even want to live with anyone. She wanted her own place to retreat to. She needed her space.

But she wanted Finn. She wanted to be with him.

She felt him slide from her body. He rolled over, taking her with him, then reached to the nightstand and grabbed a handful of tissues. He managed to take off the condom and bundle it up with one hand before tossing the whole thing in the trash.

She wrapped her arms around his chest and willed her body to relax. He wouldn't need his powers to detect her tension at this rate. The longer she could put off talking, the longer she could stay in this moment, this fantasy of them being together.

Everyone always thought of her as brave. Her friends had outright said it on many occasions. But labeling her as brave was dismissive. She was human. She felt fear. They only thought Jazz was brave because she never let them see it. She was terrified of losing all of them, just like she'd lost Finn.

Now he was back in her life and she wanted to keep him there. If she was honest with herself about it, she was desperate to.

She knew that he would never have had sex with her if he was involved or even interested in someone else.

Adultery was one of his triggers. She had witnessed that enough times when he flipped out about her keeping their relationship secret.

Back then, she had felt like she was protecting them— *keeping* them together. If they told people, Jazz had been sure something would happen to tear them apart. Instead, their relationship had deteriorated.

What if this was a second chance? What if Fate was cutting her some slack at last, *giving* her someone instead of taking him away? What if her curse was finally breaking?

They both seemed to have changed. Jazz wasn't sure if she'd changed enough. But she could try. She *would* try. If Fate was giving them the opportunity to see if they could work out, Jazz wouldn't waste it.

And if Fate was messing with her...Jazz wouldn't tolerate it. She'd done everything she could to help people along their paths, to be Fate's implement. It was her turn to guide her own life. And she wanted a life with Finn. She would *make* that her destiny.

The trouble was, she had no idea how to go about it.

No, she had one. She needed to talk to him. She needed to tell him how she felt. Even though the thought of it scared the crap out of her. She would find a way to keep him safe, even if she had to go up against Fate to do so.

His breath had evened out and his eyes were closed. She felt her own exhaustion catching up with her.

Eventually, his steady heartbeat lulled her to sleep.

Chapter Sixteen

Finn was walking through a swamp. He felt the weight of...something in his right hand. He looked down to see that he was holding a machete.

Why was it in his right hand? He was left-handed. Wasn't he?

He stared at the ground. Some kind of animal trap had been sprung by a squirrel. The poor thing had been snapped in half. Finn poked at it with the end of the blade. He tried to stop himself, but couldn't.

"Leave it, Mikey!"

Finn turned as a gangly teen ran up to him. The boy's clothes were worn and dated. He had short-cropped brown hair and bright blue eyes. He was taller than Finn, which didn't seem right. The kid was maybe five-six, but Finn was looking up at him.

Finn turned back to the squirrel, noticing that the hand holding the machete—his hand—was smaller than it should be. His feet were bare and crusted with sand. It looked like he was about the same age as the other kid. Maybe a little younger.

"You're going about it all wrong, Travis." The words

came out of Finn's mouth, but he didn't recognize his voice. "If you want the pelts, you have to use live traps. Oh, right. I forgot. You're too much of a coward to kill anything yourself."

Travis... The gangly kid was Travis? Finn tried to commit the boy's face to memory, updating it with time. Finn was surprised at how healthy he looked. He was thin, but not gaunt.

"They don't all get hit like this one." Travis knelt down and dug a length of chain out from the sand. He pulled it, and the trap and squirrel came with it. He stood and said, "If the pelts won't work for practice, the meat's still fine for dinner."

Finn felt his mouth open again, his voice young and strange. "Is food all you ever think about? Ma isn't that good of a cook."

Travis grabbed the collar of Finn's shirt and jerked him forward. "She's not your mom."

Finn laughed. "It doesn't matter. She still likes me best."

Travis looked like he was about to punch Finn. Finn wouldn't blame him. Instead, Travis shoved Finn in the chest. He stumbled back, the machete slipping from his hand.

"Mikey!"

Travis dropped the trap and grabbed Finn's arm, his face horror-stricken. Finn looked at the ground, at the *crimson spreading from his foot, at the digit lying in the sand next to the blade.*

He started to laugh.

Finn jolted awake. He sat up, frantically searching the room for... He didn't know what. He was alone.

"Jazz?" he called.

"Just a minute." Her muffled voice came from the bathroom. He could hear water running.

He was cold. How low was the AC set? Finn threw his legs over the side of the bed and stood. The room spun around him. Had he always been this tall? He felt kind of drunk.

His clothes were draped over a nearby chair. He stumbled to it and pulled on his jeans and tank top. Jazz must still have his shirt. He slid his feet into his shoes, then ran his hands over his face, trying to shake off the dream's effects while remembering what had happened.

Travis. Finn had dreamt about Travis. But when they were both younger. No, not him. Michael. In the dream, Finn had seen everything from Michael's point of view again. It was visceral. He had actually been *in* Michael's body.

Why did he keep dreaming he was Michael?

Pushing that...admittedly terrifying thought away. What did you learn?

They were in a swamp. Their house was close. Finn wasn't sure how he knew, but there it was. Travis was trapping animals for practice. He wanted the pelts.

Finn remembered the stuffed possum at the bar and Nell's instant defense of Travis. Taxidermy. As if this wasn't all creepy enough as it was.

Finn scoffed. *He actually thought those ugly little pets of his were art.*

Wait... Where had that thought come from? That laugh? Finn shook his head again. The room was still spinning.

"These are ruined."

Finn jumped at the sound of Jazz's voice behind him. He could feel his heartbeat in his throat, making it difficult to swallow. She was holding her leather pants and staring at him.

"You okay?" she asked.

"Yeah, I'm fine."

He and "fine" weren't on the same continent.

She tossed her pants on a chair. She was wearing her bikini with his shirt, which was completely unbuttoned. The swimsuit was wine-red and more string than fabric. The dark blue silk of his shirt flowed around her body as she walked.

Finn had always thought she moved like she'd been trained for the stage. He asked her about it once, but it brought on their first big freeze-out. Watching her now, though… The room seemed to warm as he looked at her.

Her T-shirt was wadded up in her hand. She sniffed it, then curled her nose and tossed it on the chair after her pants.

"Do you mind if I keep wearing your shirt for a while? I'm not up to trying to shimmy into that leather, and the whole outfit reeks."

"You can walk around in a bikini and one of my shirts for the rest of my life, as far as I'm concerned."

She smiled at him. Honest-to-God smiled. He felt himself calm down, the last chill from the dream receding. Good thing she didn't throw her smelly clothes on the bed. He had other plans for it. But no condoms.

Dammit.

He hadn't needed any in so long, he didn't bother carrying them anymore. He hadn't been with anyone since Jazz and he knew he couldn't get her pregnant. Depending on how active her social life had been, maybe they could go without. The idea of sliding into her heat, feeling her skin-to-skin in the most intimate way possible…

He wanted her again. And again and again. The room was paid up through the next morning. They could rest, recover, and reconnect. But first he needed to find out if she was on board.

She'd brought up the subject of kids once. Finn had panicked, his mouth running off about how much he loved them—which was true. Up to a point.

He was worried if she found out he'd already made the decision not to have kids and taken steps to make sure it didn't happen that she would freak out or something. He'd never been with anyone long enough for the topic to come up and didn't really know how to handle it. He wasn't sure how she'd react now.

"We should talk."

Her smile faltered. "Okay."

She walked to the empty chair and sat, pulling her slender legs up and hugging her knees. The curve of her hips against the lines of her legs... It was not conducive to a coherent conversation. Finn would make it work somehow, though. He was enjoying the view too much to ask her to move.

"What do you want to talk about?"

She looked like she was bracing herself for something, her lips pulled in a frown and her gaze laser-focused. Preemptive freeze-out.

Great. Even the room seemed to drop in temperature.

"Cut me some slack, Jazz. This isn't an interrogation."

"I know. I'm just..." She shook her head. "You said you wanted to talk."

Finn felt his fatigue hit him again. He was suddenly bone-weary. He sat on the edge of the bed and leaned forward on his elbows.

Go ahead and offer her your heart again. Watch her laugh as she crushes it beneath her feet.

Man, he was being hard on himself today. He was too tired to even fight back.

"Do you ever wonder if things would have worked out differently if we talked things through instead of always jumping into bed when one of us was angry?"

"I'm not the one who got angry. And you're the one who left."

"Thanks for the constant reminders."

What else did you expect?

"I'm sorry," Jazz said.

Whoa. Had he heard her right? She had never apologized for anything before. Not to him, not to anyone as far as he knew. For a moment, he wondered if he was hearing things.

"I'm not good at this," she said. "I don't talk about feelings with anyone. When you would get upset, I didn't know how to respond. Not with words anyway. Sex seemed a reasonable solution."

A reasonable solution? She's talking as if you're an equation.

"Is that what this was?" He gestured toward the bed. "A *reasonable solution* for dealing with me when I'm upset?"

"That's not what I meant. I was talking about when we were together before. Not now."

A convenient excuse. She sees you as something to be managed, like she managed you after your shower. She pulled you right back in. She only ever wanted you in bed.

Dammit. Was she really only interested in his body?

"So what about now? What was that after the shower, just a farewell fuck?"

Her mouth dropped open and her eyes filled with tears. Actual tears.

"Go to hell," she snapped. She jumped up and stalked to her boots, then shook them out before pulling them on.

Finn buried his face in his hands. He was prone to losing his temper. He knew that. But he never hurt people. Ever. Not with his body, not with his words. Why was he turning into such an asshole?

It's the effect she has on me.

No. Goddammit, no. He was not putting the blame on her. This was his problem. He needed to sort it out. He had *hurt* her. Hurt Jazz. He had to get her away from this. Away from him. Until he could get himself back under control or at least figured out what was happening to him.

"Are you okay?" she asked.

Why the hell was she asking him that? She shouldn't care anymore. She had tried to talk—finally, really and truly tried. And he had fucked it up so royally, he would probably never get another chance.

Give up.

"Finn?"

He felt her kneel in front of him. She gently touched his arms, her grip feather light. She pulled his hands away from his face and gasped. She grabbed his cheeks, hard.

He was glad. The room was spinning and it helped him feel more connected to his body.

He must have it for her worse than he thought.

"Finn!"

"What?" Nothing felt real. The detachment increased. He felt vaguely nauseated.

"Your eyes are turning blue."

"My eyes have always been blue."

"Not this color."

He closed his eyes tight and shook his head. Not the best move. Her hands shifted to his shoulders as she helped him stay upright.

"Finn? Finn!"

She grabbed his face again and kissed him. Full-on, no build. Her lips were all over his, tongue demanding attention. His body knew her so well, his hands went to the warm skin of her sides like they were magnetized. He pulled her against him, grabbing her legs and pulling them up on either side of him on the bed. He rocked against her, heat building within him.

His jeans chafed his dick as it stiffened. He didn't care —was grateful, even. Because it was grounding him. Her touch, their bodies locked together, it brought him back to himself.

What the fuck is going on?

He was about to start tugging on the strings that held her bikini in place when she pulled back from the kiss—

hands on his cheeks, eyes searching his. She let out a sigh and relaxed in his lap.

"It's okay. They're normal now." She smiled at him.

Then the fireball crashed through the window.

Chapter Seventeen

Heat hit her back as the room exploded into fire behind her. Jazz heard the window shatter. The next thing she knew, Finn had pulled her against his chest and was rolling them across the bed to the floor.

"What the hell?" she yelled.

"Molotov cocktail. We need to go out the back."

The curtains were on fire, flames dropping onto the carpet. Some smoldered out. Others caught.

"Shouldn't we try to stop it?"

As she said the words, another projectile flew into the room, landing on the bed. The sheets caught instantly as the accelerant poured over the mattress.

"Shit!"

Finn leapt forward, blocking her body with his, pushing her toward the bathroom.

"Wait."

Jazz ducked under his arm so she could grab her wallet, phone, and keys from the nightstand. He took her hand and pulled her toward the bathroom, both crouching low to stay beneath the smoke. Finn slammed the door shut as soon as they were in the smaller room, then rolled up a towel and tucked it along the crack at the floor.

There was a small window above the sink. She could fit through easily. She wasn't sure about him.

"Finn…"

"It'll be fine."

He jumped up onto the sink, then opened the window and punched out the screen. He scanned the area outside. "I don't think they're back here. They might have taken off to avoid the cops, but we can't assume anything."

"Is it those guys from the bar?"

"Probably," Finn said. "Come on." He helped her up onto the counter. "Be sure to check the SUV before you get into it."

As if he wouldn't be with her.

"You go first," she said.

"Jazz—"

"I will balk. I swear to fucking God, I will kick and scream and fight you on this. I'm not going through that window until I'm sure you can fit through it. You go first."

He stared at her for a moment.

"We're wasting time," she said.

He sighed, then turned and pulled himself up into the window. Shifting his shoulders, he managed to get himself halfway through. She shoved on his legs, helping him the rest of the way. There was a loud *thump* as he hit the ground on the other side. She hoped it was mostly sand.

There were noises coming from the other room that she

didn't understand. Crackling, popping. Smoke was seeping in around the edges of the door. She turned and practically dove through the window. Finn was on the other side to catch her, which was good, because she was still holding on to her things with one hand. It wasn't like her bikini had pockets. Thank God she had put on her boots.

He grabbed her empty hand and ran with her through the brush that edged up to the back of their room. He pulled her to a stop just before they hit the parking lot.

Jazz didn't see anyone around. Finn waited a few moments longer, then said, "Okay."

They ran across the lot. Jazz hit the button to unlock the doors as they neared the SUV.

"Get in on the passenger's side," he said.

It was the closest. She pulled the door open and jumped up. Finn put his hand on her ass, pushing her across the space. She climbed into the driver's seat as he sat next to her.

Her hands were shaking so hard, she had to use them both to get the key in the ignition and start the SUV. She peeled out of the space Finn had told her to back into. At the time, she wondered why it would matter. Now she understood.

Two loud pops sounded and Finn yelled, "Get down!"

She ducked low. Finn put his arm around her, trying to shield her with his body and yet not interfere with her ability to drive. She floored the accelerator, tearing out of the lot and onto the highway.

Her heart was pounding so hard she thought it might burst. Finn pulled back from her, wrapping his arm around her headrest as he stared out the back window.

He turned to look out the windshield, and said, "Take the next turn. Slow down. You're going to miss it."

"That isn't a road, it's a dirt track."

"I know. They won't think we'll turn here. Trust me."

She turned, praying the SUV wouldn't get bogged down. A few minutes later, he had her turn again. Then again and again, until she wasn't sure she would be able to find her way back to the highway. He seemed to know where he was going, though.

"Pull off here."

Sphagnum moss brushed the roof of the SUV as she took the last turn onto a graveled stretch that was so overgrown she doubted anyone had used it for years. She stopped the car in the shade of a huge gnarled oak tree, knuckles white on the wheel.

Finn reached over and turned the key, killing the engine.

"Where are we?" she asked.

"About a ten-minute walk from Travis's house."

Jazz turned to look at him. "How do you know that?"

He swallowed hard. She saw his throat work at it.

"I don't know."

"What is going on, Finn?" She was scared. So was he.

She could see it in his eyes.

He shook his head and said, "I wish I knew."

She reached across the small space between them and put her arms around his neck, pulling him into an awkward hug. He hugged her back as best he could.

She kissed the side of his head and said, "We're going to figure this out. Okay? I promise you."

He nodded as he pulled back.

Her wallet and phone had fallen to the floor when they jumped into the SUV. She tossed her wallet into the drink tray, but held on to her phone. She handed Finn the keys, then opened her door and slid to the ground.

Her knees felt weak. She left her door open, holding the grab handle and closing her eyes as she regained her equilibrium. She heard Finn's door open and shut and waited for him to walk around the SUV and join her.

She opened her eyes when she heard him stop a few feet away. His face was pale and drawn. He was staring at the bottom of her door.

"What is it?"

She followed his gaze, her stomach clenching with icy dread when she saw what he had noticed. There were two small holes near the bottom of the driver's side door.

That was why Finn wanted them to go in through the passenger's door—the side that was away from the street. He wanted the SUV to provide them with cover from gunfire.

Jazz felt dizzy. She was angry and scared and for once in her life she had no idea what to do. The look on Finn's face made her think he wouldn't be much help. He just kept staring at those holes.

"If they had been a foot higher—"

She didn't let him finish that thought. Either of them could have been hurt. Killed. She wouldn't let him say it—think it. She grabbed his arm and turned him to face her.

"They weren't. Deal—" She cut herself off again. Closing her eyes, she took a deep breath, then let it out slowly. "We're okay."

She opened her eyes to look at him again. He was swaying on his feet. She grabbed his face in her hands and forced him to look at her. "We are okay."

He nodded.

Now that he was reassured, she needed to get a handle on herself. A foot higher and one or both of them would be dead. Fate could have taken him away so easily—but hadn't. Jazz dared to let a little more hope into her heart.

She finally remembered that the shirt she was wearing had a pocket on the chest and dropped her phone in it. The shirt was unbuttoned, so she fixed that immediately. She really wished she had pants. Or bug spray. Wildlife was the least of her worries, though.

The group from the bar had seemed dangerous. She still had trouble believing they were capable of this. Burning down a hotel? Shooting at them? Jazz hoped no one else was hurt.

The hotel was a single-story building laid out like a strip mall, with each room opening out to the parking lot. Finn had mentioned that he had asked for a room away from other guests. Maybe he'd thought something like this might happen.

No. If he had, he would have insisted that they go back to Summer Park immediately. He probably always asked to be secluded. His job made him cautious about everything.

She couldn't believe this was his life. He'd even parked his car strategically. The self-defense lessons he had given her were just the tip of the iceberg. She wanted to learn more, to be able to help him assess situations. She had his back already—when he would let her. She wanted to be sure it counted.

"We can't head back to town," he said.

Her hope picked up. He wasn't trying to bench her, to push her out of his life.

"It's too dangerous. They're probably cruising the highway, and we don't know which direction is safe. They might be using more than one vehicle, based on the attack at the hotel."

Okay. Necessity was keeping her with him. She would take it.

"We should call the police," Jazz said.

"And tell them what? Did you see who threw the

bottles? All we have is conjecture."

"But we could tell them what happened at the bar."

"Which would lead to more questions. Clearview is still the closest town. It's obviously strapped for resources. All the emergency personnel will be tied up with the hotel. Besides, I don't want to answer their questions yet. Not until I've had a look at Travis's house."

"That's too dangerous. You can't keep reading things. It's affecting you—"

"She was my sister, Jazz. Do you have any idea what that's like?"

She bristled, felt the familiar walls come up.

No. Not this time.

She was so keen on him not pushing her away, but he'd been right before. She had kept him at arm's length for their entire relationship. He said he wanted in. She wanted to let him. And if Fate decided to try to take him away because of that, he, she, it—whatever that force was— would have to go through Jazz. She was sick of her curse. Sick of stifling herself and living half a life. It ended now.

"Yeah, I do, actually. I have a younger sister back in Kansas. If anything happened to her…"

Shit. Yeah, if anything happened to her, Jazz would let *nothing* stand in the way of getting justice.

Finn stared at her blankly. She wondered if he was having another episode. At least his eyes were still pale blue.

"What?"

"You have a sister?" he asked.

"Yeah. Her name's Mei."

Jazz forced herself to stand still, even though she wanted to pace—as if putting physical distance between them would make it easier to let him closer emotionally. She couldn't stop herself from crossing her arms tight across her chest. It reassured her. A little.

"That's the first time you've told me anything about your family," he said.

She was aware. She tried to shrug it off, to maybe fool herself into thinking it wasn't as big of a deal as it was.

"What do you want to know?"

His eyes were wide and he smiled. He genuinely smiled. She felt her lips tug up at the corners. She hadn't seen him look so happy in a long time.

"Everything." He shook his head. "I want to know everything."

Her stomach felt like she was on a roller coaster. She hadn't even talked to Elsa about her family. Neither of them discussed their pasts, so they never pushed each other for details or information they'd be uncomfortable sharing. That was one of the reasons they were best friends.

Now that Jazz thought about it, she and Elsa never sharing their histories was also what had made Jazz accidentally give Dante some advice for handling an argument with Elsa that had nearly destroyed their relationship. Maybe she and Elsa needed to start talking more too.

Finn had wanted to share Jazz's life. It was obvious he still did. And she wanted to share it with him.

She took a deep breath. She could do this. She could tell him about her family. Especially if she stuck with the facts and didn't wax poetic about how much she loved them all.

"Her husband's a professional football player. They have three daughters. They live with my mom in a huge house. My brother-in-law dotes on them all. My mom still insists on doing all the cooking, but I think they at least have a maid service."

"I didn't mean right now." Finn laughed. "Although I should probably make the most of it while you're in a talking mood."

"I'm not in a talking mood. I'm *never* in a talking mood." Even without the curse, she just wasn't that kind of person.

"Then why are you telling me this?"

"Because you asked. It's important to you to know."

His mouth was actually hanging open.

"You don't have to look so shocked."

He closed it and laughed again.

This was the Finn she remembered. Always laughing. He had seemed so carefree. It was probably part of what drew her to him. They were opposites in that regard. They both had laser focus when it came to their careers, but he knew how to shut it off. Jazz was always thinking. He knew how to let go and just have fun.

"What about your dad?" he asked.

Shit.

Her insides turned to ice and her mouth went dry. This was one of the reasons she hated talking to people about personal things. It was never enough—always led to more questions, whether she was ready to answer them or not.

She swallowed a few times, then shook her head and murmured, "Not yet. Okay?"

His smile faded, his expression turning gentle. His voice was equally so as he said, "Yeah. Sure."

She tried to shake it off, focusing on the task at hand.

"If we're not going to call the police and we're stuck here for now, should we try to find Travis's house? You said he lives nearby. We could hang out in the bushes and watch for him."

The idea made her skin crawl. There would be bugs and lizards and snakes. Who knew what else this far into the swamp. Alligators, probably.

She pushed down her fear. She would help Finn however he needed it.

"He's probably out checking traps right now. He does it every morning and evening."

"Checking traps?"

"He's a taxidermist."

"Oh." Jazz felt a shiver. She had never understood the allure of stuffing an animal and displaying it. "Family reunions must have been creepy as hell."

Finn laughed again, and shook his head. "I don't doubt it. Look, it's not safe for you to stay with the SUV."

"Not safe for you, anyway." She glared at him. "If you try to leave me here, I will kick your ass."

"I don't doubt it."

"Good. Besides, you can't touch anything. The way your eyes keep changing... It's scaring me. I don't want you to get lost in these memories. You need to stop reading things."

"I'm not sure if I can promise not to. If it means helping Siobhan."

Dammit. She was so keen on helping Finn. She needed to remember that he was just as adamant about helping his sister. She couldn't really blame him for taking the risk. She'd do the same and more to help her loved ones.

He took her hand in his. "I need you with me. Are you up for this?"

She nodded. "Yeah. Let's go."

Chapter Eighteen

Wild fennel brushed against Finn's face and arms as they headed toward Travis's house. Finn didn't know how he was finding the way, but was sure they were going in the right direction. A saw palmetto grazed his jeans, reminding him that Jazz's legs were unprotected. He glanced back to see how she was doing.

Damn, she looked sexy. Okay, the boots were a little silly, but she was pulling it off. He loved seeing her legs stretch out from beneath his shirt. The view of her chest when she bent forward to duck under something was riveting. He felt guilty enjoying the sight of her, knowing that she was assuredly not having a good time herself.

"Eyes on the road." She smirked at him.

He turned back to look where he was going just in time to be smacked in the face by a low-hanging branch. He heard her let out a stifled laugh.

Okay, maybe she was having a little fun.

He was glad there weren't paths cleared to the little stretch of side-road where they were parked. It was a good sign that Travis didn't get out that way and wouldn't discover them. They were lucky to have a base of operations to investigate his house. Still, it would have been nice not to be swimming through foliage to get there.

My kingdom for a machete.

You got that right.

He sighed. Now he was talking to himself. At least it was just in his head. He stopped abruptly. Jazz appeared at his side.

"What is it?" She peered around at the wall of green surrounding them.

"This is it."

He pushed back one of the fennel plants as if it was a curtain. On the other side, the brush had been cleared for a few dozen feet leading up to a run-down house. The paint was light brown and peeling and the roof was covered in moss.

He checked the windows and layout. From what he could tell, it probably had two bedrooms, one bath, a kitchen, and maybe a small family room. All of the rooms had to be tiny. The screen door facing them was barely hanging on its hinges.

Behind the house was swampland. True swamp. A small aluminum fishing boat was tied to a dock that stretched a few feet out over the water. The dock and boat were in much better condition than the house.

Finn remembered what Michael had said about well-fed alligators. He imagined Travis on the dock feeding them... leftovers.

He snorted.

What the fuck?

"Is something funny?"

"No." Nothing about that was funny. Why the hell had he laughed? "Come on."

He started for the yard, but Jazz held him back.

"How do we know he's not home?"

Finn pointed to the gravel drive that led up to the side of the house. "His truck isn't here."

He headed forward again, feeling an almost magnetic pull toward the house. When he reached the front door, he didn't hesitate to open it.

"Finn, let me do that! You shouldn't be touching anything."

"There's a trick to it."

He lifted the door slightly in its frame to keep it from falling off the hinges. Jazz stared at him.

"What?" he asked.

"How did you know to do that?"

How indeed.

"Just...let's go inside."

She kept staring at him as she slipped past into the house. Dim light filtered through the curtains. The inner door was open. Finn shut the screen door behind him and looked around.

It was even more depressing inside than out. Aside from the worn furniture, faded wallpaper, and truly disgusting carpet, there were pelts and stuffed animals everywhere.

"They look so real," Jazz said. She leaned a bit closer to a raccoon, then backed away.

"Travis did develop quite a knack for it over the years."

She turned and stared at him again. "What did you say?"

Finn shrugged. His head was starting to hurt. "They look real. Like you said. He's pretty good at this."

"That's not what you said."

"What does it matter?"

"Finn, you don't sound right."

Troublesome woman.

Finn shook his head. The room shifted as he did. "I'm fine. Let's look around."

"Just don't touch anything."

She's always telling me what to do.

She reached for his hand, but he pulled it away. Why did he do that? He loved it when she touched him. And to have her reaching for him... It was a nice change.

He didn't miss the hurt look that crossed her face.

"I just...need some space."

No he didn't. Why had he said that?

"Are you okay?"

He wasn't sure. He glanced around the room, at the ratty green couch with an old blanket over the back. He was sure Travis was sleeping there at night—on the nights when he slept at all.

Travis had always been plagued by insomnia. His nervous energy was everywhere. Finn could practically see Travis pacing the room. Always pacing. *Taking up too much space.*

A wave of nausea flooded his body. Finn felt dizzy. He had to get out of that room.

"Let's go to the kitchen." He walked past Jazz, being careful not to touch her, and headed to the archway that led to the small tiled room.

Finally, he could breathe again. Travis's energy was much lighter here. He must not spend much time in the kitchen. Finn didn't doubt it, with how emaciated Travis appeared. He walked to the fridge and opened the door.

"Don't touch anything, remember?" Jazz grabbed the door from his hand. They both looked at its contents.

Mustard. A jar of dill pickles. Half a loaf of bread that looked like it was starting to go green. That was it. Aside from being kind of pathetic, it wasn't scary at all. No severed heads or body parts. Finn chuckled.

What. The. Fuck.

"Why do you keep laughing?" she asked. "What's so funny?"

Nothing. If there had been something frightening in Travis's fridge, like trophies from Michael's victims, they might have come from Finn's *sister.*

What the fuck was wrong with him?

"I need... I need to go outside," Finn said.

He staggered to the side door that led to the yard. Jazz was right behind him. This door was closed, but not locked. He jerked it open and practically ran out into the fading sun. He bent over, hands on his knees, and took deep breaths.

Someone put their hands on his back. He yelled and whirled away, swinging his arms to fend them off.

"It's just me," Jazz yelled. She was holding her hands up in the air and had backed away.

Thank God she was so fast. He might have hit her while he was flailing. His heart was pounding and he couldn't seem to catch his breath. He needed to get control of himself again. She took a step toward him and he jerked back.

"Don't touch me!"

Her mouth dropped open. She stared at him for a moment, then shut it.

Where had that come from? He still couldn't breathe. His chest felt tight, like something was crushing him. The light was starting to dim, his vision tunneling. He fell to his hands and knees, retching.

"Finn!"

Jazz wrapped her arms around him. The tightness in his chest vanished.

"Finn, hold on to me. We have to get out of here." She helped him kneel, cradling his face with one hand. "I hear an engine. We have to go. Please, Finn. Come on. Get up."

She was trying to pull him to his feet. She was making better progress than he would have guessed, given how much smaller than him she was. He draped an arm over her shoulders and lurched up. They staggered through the yard together.

"Come on," she said. "Keep moving. You can do this."

They made it through the brush and collapsed, panting. Jazz turned back to the house, crawling on her stomach to get closer so she could see without being seen. Finn flopped forward to join her, dragging himself along. The fennel was thick enough that they should be hidden from the other side.

He won't see.

Finn remembered lying not far from where they were, watching the house, laughing as Travis and Auntie had another of their fights.

Wait, no. That wasn't Finn's memory. Another of Michael's rising to the surface.

He closed his eyes and took a few deep breaths, centering himself, reminding himself that this was *his* body. His mind. He was Finn.

Jazz was right about not touching anything. It was too dangerous. They would have to find another way.

A dark gray truck pulled up to the house. Travis leapt from the driver's seat. He looked shaken. He practically ran to the house's side door. The kitchen door.

The one they had left open.

Shit.

Travis slowed as he approached it. He stopped a few feet from the house and turned, scanning the yard and the brush. Finn felt Jazz stiffen. He put his hand on the small of her back, hoping to comfort her, to silently tell her to stay still.

Normally, Finn would absolutely be able to take Travis down. But not now. Not when Finn could barely stand without Jazz's help.

Travis seemed to stare at them for a moment. He took a step forward. A squirrel ran out from the fennel nearby, charging him. Travis screamed, stumbling backward. The tiny squirrel was terrifying him.

Finn started to laugh. Jazz clamped her hand over his mouth. Lucky for them, poor Travis was still screaming. Because of a squirrel.

Poor Travis. The voice in his head was mocking.

What the fuck was happening to him? How were memories surfacing, causing outbursts, when he wasn't even touching anything? And why *the fuck* was he thinking things—thoughts that obviously weren't his—that weren't even memories?

"We have to go," Jazz whispered. "Now."

Finn nodded. They backed away from the edge of the fennel. She pulled his arm over her shoulders again and helped him to his feet. They had to get away. Away from

Travis and the house where Michael had grown up. Away from his childhood stomping ground.

Even as they ran, Finn felt an oppressive energy, like it was riding on his back, weighing him down. He stumbled more times than he could count, but Jazz was always right there, pulling him up, alternating between whispering encouragement and threats.

Distance wasn't helping. They finally reached the SUV. She popped open the back hatch and helped him sit. When that was too much for him, he lay down on the tarp that covered the big space.

"Finn, what the hell is going on with you?"

"I don't know." He covered his eyes with his hands.

"No you don't," she said. "Cut that out."

He felt her crawl up next to him.

"Let me see your eyes. Finn, come on."

She grabbed his arm and started tugging on it. When she couldn't get enough leverage to budge him, she straddled his stomach, gripping his hands tightly and pulling. He let her win, but kept his eyes closed. He didn't want to know what she'd see. He was too afraid.

"Please Finn. Let me see your eyes." She put her hands on his cheeks, her touch gentle. "Please."

Begging. I like it.

Shut up shut up shut up! Finn's stomach started churning again. The thoughts popping into his head weren't memories. They were new.

A horrifying theory presented itself.

He had been focused on avoiding getting lost in memories while he was reading things. As long as he made it out, he figured he was fine. But what if he was wrong? What if he was picking up Michael's energy with each reading and it was somehow staying? What if Finn couldn't get rid of it?

He felt like Michael's memories had become ingrained in Finn's mind. Worse—like part of Michael's *personality* was stuck in him.

Finn felt a darkness within him laugh. Whatever it was, it wasn't even bothering with trying to hide. Not anymore.

Shiiiit.

"Finn, please. I'm scared. You're scaring me."

He was scared too. He couldn't move. The darkness was creeping along his limbs, paralyzing him. He was trapped in his own body.

"Please, I can't lose you again," she said. "Do you understand? Can you even hear me?"

Jazz's hands were trembling. Her grip tightened. Then she kissed him.

The darkness evaporated. Finn felt it retreat. He wasn't sure what it was or where it had gone, but for the moment, he was just himself again. It was only him and Jazz.

She pulled back from the kiss. He opened his eyes.

She smiled, her gaze searching his face. Then she laughed and lowered her head to his chest.

"Oh thank God."

She slid her arms around his neck and held him, thighs tight against his sides, chest pressed to his. He wrapped his arms around her and held her to him. He didn't ever want to let go. She was his anchor. Somehow, she had pulled him back from that darkness.

At least for now.

Chapter Nineteen

His eyes were normal. Pale blue. Finn's eyes. Jazz had half expected them to be bright blue. The same blue as Michael's.

The things he said back at the house and the way he was acting... It wasn't him. Finn was confident, but not arrogant. And he knew way too much about Travis's home. Finding it was one thing. Being aware of the trick with opening the door? That was another.

He had only mentioned being concerned that he would get lost in a memory while using his powers. Why was he acting weird when he wasn't touching anything? At least when she touched him it seemed to snap him out of it.

She didn't know what was happening. Didn't know how to protect him. She couldn't stand the thought of losing him again. Not to Michael's memories. So she did the only thing she could. She held on.

Finn nuzzled her neck. She shifted so that she could kiss him again.

He brought his hands to her face, brushing her hair out of the way. His tongue slid into her mouth, coaxing her to relax into him. He brought his hands to her hips, holding her tight to his body as he rocked against her. His erection prodded her through his jeans.

They needed this—needed to connect on a deep level. Words had never been their strong suit. Touch was their best form of expression.

She leaned back, slowly unbuttoning her shirt. He massaged her hips as he watched. She left it on, hoping it would add to his pleasure, keeping him focused on what they were doing. The fabric whispered against their skin as she moved.

She lifted his shirt so she could explore the chiseled rows of his abs with her fingertips. There was no padding to soften his muscles. Only lines and curves, dips and valleys defining every inch of him. He was exquisite.

She tugged on his shirt to let him know she wanted it off. He sat up and lifted his arms so she could pull it over his head and cast it aside. Dark hair graced his pecs, fanning over his chest and running down his stomach like a waterfall.

Running her fingertips over the softness of it, she took her time, watching his gaze intensify with each stroke. She pushed him back onto the floor of the SUV, then started to undo his jeans. As she opened his fly, he gripped her hands to stop her.

"Jazz…"

"What's wrong?"

"I don't have any condoms."

Condoms. Right. And they'd used the only one she had. One that had been sitting in her wallet since they dated, now that she thought about it. But why didn't he have any?

"Please tell me you've been practicing safe sex," she said.

He let out a short laugh and sat up next to her. "I haven't been practicing much of anything. Not with a partner, anyway."

She stared at him. They had talked about their histories when they were dating. She had been surprised that his was as brief as her own. When he explained about being able to read people and the logistic issues with not being able to touch someone during sex without reading their mind, it made more sense. Still...

"Finn, it's been years since we were together. Surely you've slept with someone. I mean, everybody has urges."

"I don't need anybody else to deal with my *urges*." He laughed and shook his head. His tone was more serious when he went on. "I haven't been with anyone since we broke up. I tried a date or two, but just...wasn't interested."

"Oh."

She hadn't been interested in even trying to date anyone. She had thrown herself into her work. The only romantic indulgences she allowed herself were her attempted hook-ups for her friends. Knowing that he hadn't been with anyone either, hadn't even really felt like trying… It gave her hope. He still cared. She wasn't the only one who hadn't been able to move on.

"This is the part where you say something," he said.

"Okay."

"Okay…what?"

"Okay, we don't need to use a condom." They never really did, in her mind. "Neither of us engaged in risky behavior before we started dating or since."

He winced, then looked away. "Great. Good to know."

"I didn't mean…" She let out a sigh. "I haven't been with anyone else either. Since you."

"Oh." His face actually lit up.

Apparently he was feeling relieved about their mutual lack of activity too. She had to admit the thought of him with other women was upsetting. She really had wanted to keep him all to herself, not even sharing him with her friends. She would fix that mistake too, if he gave her a chance.

He grinned and said, "I suppose I ruined you for other men."

She laughed. She couldn't say that he had ruined her for other men. There had really only ever been him. No one else had made their way into her heart.

"Don't be so cocky," she said.

He feigned a confused expression. "But I thought we were going to—"

She covered his lips with her fingertips briefly. "How

could I have forgotten what a comedian you are?"

"There are many things I'm eager to remind you of."
He lifted his hands to her back, running them along the
sides of her spine.

"There's something else you should know," she said.

His smile dimmed. She knew she must sound serious.
Then again, she was broaching a serious topic. Possibly a
deal-breaking one.

He leaned back and said, "I'm listening."

Her heart was beating in her throat. She forced herself
to swallow as her moment of truth approached.

"You don't have to worry about me getting pregnant
either," she said.

"Okay."

He was too flippant. He didn't understand, probably
thought she meant she had an IUD or something.

"I can't get pregnant," she said. "Ever."

"Oh."

She waited for him to say something else. Ask
questions. Offer comfort or something. He just stared at
her.

"That's it? *Oh?*"

He shrugged. "Lots of people can't have kids."

"It's not a condition. For me, it was a choice."

His mouth dropped open. Here it came.

*Why would you do that? What if you change your
mind? But you're so young.*

Instead, he laughed.

"What's so funny?"

He kept laughing for a moment, shaking his head. "We could have saved so much money on condoms."

"That's very practical of you." She wasn't sure which was worse, him grilling her about her choice or joking about it.

"We were really going hardcore on birth control."

Yeah, this was worse. She bristled and shifted away from him, but he reached out and picked up her hand.

"Jazz, I'm laughing so hard because I did the same thing. I made the same choice."

"What?"

He shook his head and laughed. "It took me five years to find a doctor who would finally give me a vasectomy. They all kept saying, 'You're too young to make a permanent decision like this. Wait for a while. If you find the right person…' And on and on. Such bullshit. As if I don't know my own mind."

Jazz had heard the same lines. It had taken her *seven* years to get her doctor to perform a tubal ligation.

"But you love kids."

"I do. For about an hour. Then I'm ready to move on." He smiled at her, then brushed a lock of hair from her face and tucked it behind her ear. "Come on. I'm sure you love those adorable nieces of yours. But that doesn't mean you want your own. I get that. I'd sure as hell rather figure it out before having kids than after."

She couldn't argue with that. But this was so unexpected. It felt surreal.

"I thought... I thought you wanted a family."

"What? Why?"

"Your dad named the bar Connelly's. You kept talking about your family up north."

"Because I miss them sometimes. And I was trying to draw you out to talk about yours. My dad named the bar that because he opened it with his brother originally." He grinned at her. "Man, talk about jumping to conclusions. I am never going to let you hear the end of this."

Jazz couldn't believe it. She had built up such a fantasy around Finn—a story of why they couldn't be together. Maybe she had just been trying to feel better about keeping him at a distance.

He shook his head, still laughing. "We *really* should have talked more."

"Do you want to get married?" she asked.

His smile vanished and he paled. "Wow. Okay, that is sudden. Look, we have a lot of things to work out. And marriage..." He shook his head.

"Wait, I'm not asking you to marry me. I'm asking if marriage is something that you're interested in."

"Oh." He visibly relaxed, shoulders lowering as he let out a deep breath. "That's reassuring."

"Well?"

"Damn. I know I wanted us to talk more about meaningful things, but this is venturing into 'be careful what you wish for' territory."

"Finn."

He smiled, but it was subdued, then he shook his head. "No. I'm not interested in marriage. I've seen too many people break vows and ignore the spirit of the arrangement. Paperwork doesn't make a union. Partnership does."

She couldn't speak. How could this be so...perfect? For the first time she could remember, she felt as if Fate was smiling on her.

"Besides, it always struck me as a lot of trouble for what? A tax break on buying a house together? No thanks."

"You like it above the bar. If someone tried to get you to move, they wouldn't be right for you."

He smiled at her. "You never asked me to move."

Jazz smiled back. Her stomach was doing somersaults. She had always felt that she and Finn were a match. She just didn't know how much of one. Talking definitely had its advantages.

Then again, so did other activities.

"I'm going to ask you to move now."

His smile faltered.

She put her hand on his chest and said, "Lay back."

He grinned as he did as she asked, shifting so that he

was in the middle of the empty space. She had never been gladder to have a roomy vehicle. And the padded tarp made it downright comfy.

Kneeling at his side, she picked up where she'd left off. She pulled off his shoes and socks, then unfastened his jeans and slid them down his muscular legs. He was already tenting his boxer-briefs. She gave herself a moment to enjoy him through the thin fabric. She ran her fingers along the length of his shaft.

He closed his eyes and folded his arms behind his head, using them as a pillow. She wanted him relaxed. She also wanted better access. He lifted his hips as she pulled off his boxer-briefs, leaving him naked before her.

Finn naked. She hadn't taken the time to look at him before in the hotel. There had been too much need, too much fear. She had thought if she said or did the wrong thing, he would bolt again.

Things changed. Quickly, sometimes. She smiled as she ran her hand over the strong muscles of his stomach, gently skimming his shaft before tracing her nails along his thighs. His breathing relaxed.

Never in a million years had she thought she would be back in this situation—back with Finn. She wouldn't waste a moment.

She kicked off her boots and slid her shirt from her shoulders, then untied her bikini top. After slipping out of the bottoms, she looked back at Finn. His eyes were open as he watched her, smiling.

"You know you're the most gorgeous woman I've ever seen, right?"

She smirked. "Yeah, I get that a lot."

He laughed, but then a shadow crossed his face. He murmured, "I bet you do."

"I don't think I'll be hearing it nearly as often now, though."

"Why's that?"

"Because you'll be with me."

His expression remained guarded. "I guess I'm pretty good at playing the heavy when we're out in public."

"I was thinking of a different role."

"Which is?"

What word could she use? *Boyfriend* seemed too trite for what she wanted them to be. She was so relieved to know he had no interest in the title of *husband*. *Mate* just made her feel ridiculous. But she wanted him to know she was all-in, just like he'd once told her.

She settled on the phrase that made the most sense to her.

"Partner."

He practically beamed at her. "That sounds good to me."

Chapter Twenty

The day had definitely taken a turn for the better. Finn's life might have been flipped upside-down, but Jazz had tumbled back into it. Naked. Ready to finally talk—to *commit* even. It was a little overwhelming. Still, he said a silent prayer of thanks to any benevolent force that might be listening.

Then he sat up and kissed her. He slid his hand to the back of her neck, tracing her skin with his fingertips. His tongue delved into her mouth. She leaned into him, their chests brushing. She pushed him back, her fingers trailing over his chest as he lay down.

She had let him lead last time, but apparently this time she wanted to take the reins. He was fine with that. More than fine.

Her hair lightly brushed his skin as she moved her kisses along his neck, then further down. Focusing on the feel of her, he was more at ease than he had been in months. It was like her touch was grounding him in his body.

Her hand found his dick first, slender fingers wrapping around him and squeezing. Then her lips pressed against him. His breath hitched as her mouth took him in, waves of pleasure rippling through his body. He ran his fingers through her hair, brushing it away from her face so he could watch her.

Her tongue swirled, her hand kept moving, her lips pulled on his flesh. He was getting too close.

"Jazz…"

She let up at last, shifting to lie next to him. He cupped her cheek, kissing her again and rolling her onto her back. He skimmed his hand over one breast, gently squeezing it, brushing his thumb across her nipple.

Her breath picked up. She arced her back, pressing herself into his touch. He dusted the backs of his fingers against her stomach, not stopping as they trailed through her soft curls. Two fingers slid into her with ease. She groaned against his mouth. He circled her clit with his thumb.

She was so hot and wet. And he was going to be able to feel that, burying himself in her without a condom, with nothing between them. He was sure she was ready. He hoped she was ready. He didn't want to wait anymore.

He moved his hand away so he could grip her thigh and use it to pull her over on top of him as he rolled to his back. He wanted her to enjoy this every bit as much as he did. If being on top helped, he was good with that.

She kissed him deep, rubbing her wet center along his dick. Damn, she felt so good. He thought about sports, traffic, food, anything to try to keep the beautiful contact from sending him over the edge. She lined him up, then slid down over him slowly. He sank into velvet fire.

He felt every pulse of her body as she stretched to fit him. She sat back on his hips and brought her knees to his sides, then rose, bracing herself on his chest. Without asking, he knew what she needed. He brought his hands to hers, interlacing their fingers and supporting her so she had better leverage to move.

She rose up on her knees, leaning against his grip, then sank back along the length of him. Over and over again. He rose up to meet her, hips thrusting against hers. He wanted to go off so bad, but even more he wanted to hold on to the connection they shared. No powers, no walls. Just them.

Her muscles contracted around him, clenching as she upped her pace. He let himself go a bit more, still fighting the ecstasy that beckoned from deep in his gut. She groaned, her eyes shut tight and head tilting back as he felt her pulse around him. Finally, he stopped trying to hold back.

He pumped himself into her, fast and hard. Her grip tightened on his, holding on as she matched his pace. His skin felt like it was lighting up as the pressure built in him, finally exploding through his body. He felt himself fill her, mixing with her heat, her wetness. He landed as deep as he could and held himself there, back arcing off the floor, breath held tight in his chest.

It was a while before he came back down.

Jazz collapsed on his chest, breathing hard. He brought his hands to her back, wrapping his arms around her.

"That was incredible." He panted between each word.

"Yeah."

He didn't want to leave her body, but felt himself softening. There would be time for more later. He just needed to rest a bit.

And this is what it would be like *every time* now. At least, he hoped so.

She nuzzled his neck, then lifted herself from him. He felt a brief surge of panic, wondering if she was pulling away. Instead, she nestled against his body and let out a contented sigh. He kept his arms around her, holding her tight.

It seemed Finn only blinked, but when he opened his eyes again, the sun had already set. He felt better than he had in weeks, even after only a few hours of sleep.

Uninterrupted sleep. No nightmares, no dreams.

Jazz must have the light on the ceiling of the SUV set so that it had to be turned on manually. Either that or the battery had gone dead. It was completely dark. She was fidgeting next to him, then sat up suddenly.

"Shit, we left the back door open," she said.

She lunged for it, but he grabbed her and held her in place. The door was open, she had just woken up, and it was pitch black in the SUV. He didn't want her to fall out.

"Relax."

"You relax. We're going to be eaten alive by mosquitoes—if it hasn't happened already. Bugs and snakes…"

"How exactly would a snake get into the SUV?"

"I don't know. They could crawl up the tires or something. Climb the tree and drop down."

He laughed. He knew Florida had a reputation for bugs and other wildlife, but had never been bothered by them before. Honestly, he didn't know what the fuss was about.

"What about bats? They can fly in. And there are tons of flying insects, even in the city." She shifted closer, leaning against his chest. "And lizards. They can climb."

"Nothing is going to bother us."

She snorted. "Right."

"Has anything bitten you yet?"

After a brief pause she said, "No."

"So don't worry about it. We're more likely to suffocate from the heat if we close the door."

"This is weird. Why hasn't anything bitten us? We're totally naked and without bug spray. I can hear them chattering away right outside."

He shrugged. "Bugs have never bothered me. They steer clear."

She snorted again, but then he felt her lean a bit away. "Wait, seriously? Is it part of your powers?"

"I don't know. Not that Dad ever said."

She pushed him back and straddled him. Waking up for this was fine by him. He could catch up on sleep later. He put his hands on her hips, then slid them back over her ass. He was already getting hard.

"It kind of seems like a big oversight," she said.

He sat up, bringing their chests together, massaging her back as he drew her closer. It wasn't enough to steer her from the current topic.

"Being able to control animals would be awesome," she said.

Control…

"I don't get how it would relate to psychometry, though. Unless you can somehow extend your energy field. Maybe push your energy into others."

He stopped rubbing her back.

"What?" she asked.

"There's one aspect of my powers I never told you about because I never use it. Dad taught me it's like the ultimate taboo."

"I thought the worst thing you could do is read someone's mind with the intent of using what you learn to hurt them."

He wasn't surprised she remembered that. It still made him smile. She had been amazing when he told her about his powers. She'd been studying the whole field of metaphysics—not just psychometry—for years. Finn had never really ventured much outside of his abilities.

She had taught him about metaphysical principles, especially what boiled down to basic karma. *Don't use your abilities to hurt people.* It tied in with what Dad had said about not using his abilities for profit, along with the other warnings he'd been given.

If he was helping people, he was still okay. If he ever gained from using his powers at other people's expense... Finn wasn't sure what would happen, but his dad had implied there would be a swift and terrible reckoning. That was what he meant when he talked about walking the gray line.

Then there was plain stepping over it.

"You know I can read people's thoughts if I touch them long enough with my hands."

"Present company excluded."

"Yeah." He smiled and laughed, then said another little silent prayer of thanks that she, of all the people in the world, was the one person he could touch in peace. "There's something else I can do once that level of connection is achieved."

When he hesitated, she said, "Which is?"

"I can sort of...get them to do what I want. I've never actually tried it out before, because my dad seriously scared the shit out of me when he told me about that. But I can feel it when I'm listening to people's thoughts. One small step and I'd be in their head running the show."

She went completely still. She seemed to be holding her breath even.

"I would never do it. I mean, risks aside, it's just wrong. I'd have to be morally bankrupt to do anything like that."

"What kind of risks did he talk about?"

"Aside from it majorly pissing off the universe and invoking instant karma? You can get lost, I guess. Some of their memories can get embedded in your mind and you can forget which ones are yours."

"Kind of how your powers are acting up now."

He hadn't thought of it before because he never thought about this aspect of his abilities. He had locked it away in a corner of his mind under a glass dome labeled, *Don't.* What he was experiencing did sound like the consequences Dad had laid out.

"Yeah. But I didn't make anybody do anything. I've never used my powers that way. I never would."

There had to be another explanation—a reason his powers were acting up in this particular way. He wasn't controlling anyone. Hell, if anything, he wished he could use those powers to gain better control over himself. That moment when the darkness had spread across his body... He felt more like his powers were being used against him somehow. But that wasn't possible.

Jazz sat back on his thighs, her arms draped over his shoulders. Powers or no powers, he could practically feel her thoughts filling the space as her mind raced trying to put the pieces together.

"Do you think…" She didn't finish her question.

He prompted her to go on. "Do I think what?"

"What if Siobhan has the same powers? Could she be using them to try to push you into getting her justice, and somehow putting Michael's memories in your mind?"

It was a chilling thought.

"Dad said the ability is passed from father to son."

"Even with twins?"

"Honestly, that never came up." When they went back to Summer Park, Finn was going to have a long list of questions for his dad. If he was up for it, anyway.

Even if Siobhan did have the same powers and had retained them on the other side, using the forbidden aspect of those powers wouldn't make Finn take on another person's memories. She would be the one who had to pay the price.

Right?

"I don't think that's it," Finn said. "Michael had a really strong personality. I can feel it in everything I read that was close to him. His energy was dark and twisted, but powerful."

"So it might be enough to leave a kind of retina-burn in your brain."

He laughed again. "That is an excellent way of putting it." He really, *really* hoped she was right. Her other theory, though… It kept running through his mind.

If Siobhan had the same powers and retained some version of them in death… Who knew how that would affect Finn? With his dad, there was always a kind of feedback loop, like static in the channel. Finn hadn't felt anything like that yet. If anything, his powers were stronger, everything he read clearer.

Maybe instead of feedback, she was amplifying him? That would explain the sort of retina-burn Jazz had mentioned. Michael's memories might not be implanting themselves in Finn's mind, but just be strong enough that it was taking him a while to shake them off.

Finn hadn't felt any kind of weird disorientation or disconnection since they had reached the SUV. More accurately, since he and Jazz had started having sex. Being with her chased away all memories and thoughts beyond each moment, each touch.

Yeah, his life had turned into a shitstorm, but Jazz was back with him. And this time, she was all-in. Whatever the universe dished out next, they would face it together.

"I can't see your face at all," she said. "What are you thinking?"

"That I am a lucky bastard. And very glad you're here. No matter how lost I get, when you touch me it pulls me back from the edge. Reminds me that I'm me."

"If that's a line, it's working."

She kissed him, pushing him back to the floor. He gratefully let all thoughts fade away in the presence of her touch.

Chapter Twenty-One

Jazz never dreamed she would think of a restroom at a gas station as a luxury, but after a night in the swamp something as simple as running water made her ridiculously happy. Finn hadn't been keen on the idea of driving to anywhere near civilization so they could freshen up and get food, but had relented when he saw she wasn't going to let it go.

She was not an outdoorsy person. She usually wore leather pants, for crying out loud. She wanted air conditioning, filtered water, and chlorinated pools.

The compromise they had reached was that she would wait for him to get her the key to the bathroom and not go into the store. She was okay with that. Her outfit—or lack thereof—would attract too much attention.

After the run-in with the guys from the bar and what happened at the hotel…she was scared. Dammit, she hated being scared. As soon as they could, she would call the police and tell them everything she knew about the group. She was sure they were behind the fire. The police needed to know how dangerous those guys were.

Finn had assured her that his powers were back on

track, or she would have gone in with him anyway. He said he was feeling better after a night of good sleep. Not that they'd slept through all of it. They were definitely making up for lost time.

Finn had gone back into the gas station to return the key. She chewed on another power bar while she waited for him to come back. He'd been in there for a long time. Too long.

She was starting to open the driver's door when he walked out. He paused, hands in his pockets. He had pushed the door open with his foot, so he was still avoiding touching things. Probably wise. She didn't understand why he wasn't making a beeline for the SUV. In fact, he was kind of meandering around. She started the engine, then drove up next to him, rolling down the passenger's side window.

"Finn?"

He didn't respond. That wasn't good.

"Finn!"

He seemed disoriented when he glanced over at her. Shit, had his powers gone off again? He wasn't touching anything, so how could he be lost in someone's memories?

She hoped she wouldn't have to make out with him in the gas station parking lot. But then he opened the door and climbed in, saving her from bringing unwanted attention to them. It was a start.

"You okay?" she asked.

"Yeah."

"You don't sound too sure about that."

"There were a lot of memories on that key."

Probably some pretty gross ones now that she thought about it.

Do not think about that.

"I thought your powers were behaving."

"They're better. Not perfect."

He sounded tense. After last night, she was kind of surprised. She had felt more relaxed than she had in months when they woke up. As soon as they were alone, she'd try to help him back to that state.

"What do we do now?" she asked.

"Head back to Travis's house. I want another look at it. Maybe this time we won't be interrupted."

"That's not a good idea."

"Why, because you didn't come up with it?"

She was stunned for a moment. She felt her mouth drop open. "Where the hell did that come from?"

He looked confused again, then he shook his head and turned to look out the window. "I don't know. I'm sorry. Could we just get out of here? I need to be away from people."

That part made sense at least. She wondered again if his powers might somehow be working long-distance. They could figure things out once they were back in the wilderness.

She drove onto the highway, heading toward their little grove near Travis's house.

"I don't know if we can do this on our own," she said. "No matter what you said earlier, your powers are still acting up."

"I've got it under control."

She snorted. "That didn't seem the case a minute ago."

"There were too many people back there. Too many memories to sort through."

"And you think it's going to be better at Travis's house? Last time we were there, you looked like you were suffocating."

"I'll be ready this time. Besides, that was before last night."

He put his hand on her leg. Heat immediately flared deep in her belly. He leaned over and kissed the side of her neck, trailing his hand further up her thigh.

"You're trying to distract me."

"Is it working?"

Yes. She wouldn't tell him that, though.

"We should call the police. Someone besides us should know about what we're doing."

He sighed, then sat back in his seat. "I already told Daphne what we've learned. I called while you were in the bathroom."

"Do you think that's a good idea? Tommy shouldn't get too worked up."

"I know. She won't tell him more than he needs to know. Right now, all she's telling him is that we're following some promising leads that took us out of town. I don't want him to worry about us, but they need to know where to look in case…"

She glanced over at him, caught the grim expression on his face, and knew what would come next. He was worrying about her again, wondering if he should be doing this alone.

"Don't even think about it," she said. "I'm not going back to Summer Park."

"I know." His voice was barely over a whisper.

"Seriously? I thought you'd fight me on it."

"We're not just investigating the case anymore. We have some seriously pissed-off locals who are willing to commit major crimes to settle the score. After what they pulled at the hotel, you can bet those thugs are watching the highway. There's a long stretch from here to Summer Park. Before we head back, we need to talk to the police."

Thank God.

"But that will take up time," he said. "Alert more people to our inquiries. Nell and Travis are tight. I think she's a little sweet on him. If she hasn't already told him about us, you can bet it'll happen soon. He'll destroy any evidence that might be left before we can get to him."

Crap. Jazz hadn't thought of that.

"And if he gets really spooked, he can disappear into

the swamp."

Camping anywhere had never appealed to her. She was more of a five-star-lodge vacationer. Not that she actually took vacations. She loved the pools, the sky, the palms, and even the heat of the city—as long as she had air conditioning close by to retreat to.

"Ugh, how can anyone stand that? The swamp must be full of bugs and alligators and all kind of dangerous animals." She shivered.

Finn laughed. "Tasty, you mean."

"What?" She glanced over at him. He was staring out the window.

"Travis loves living off of what he can forage for himself. Squirrels and vermin. He used to disappear for weeks into the swamp when he was in a mood."

"Finn?"

He looked over at her, a blank expression on his face. But his eyes were turning bright blue. He wasn't touching anything, and his eyes were changing.

Jazz gunned the engine. The road that led to their hiding spot came up and she slammed on the brakes, taking the turn faster than was probably safe.

Finn reached for the grab handle above his door. "What are you doing?"

She didn't have time to head back to their safe spot. As soon as they were out of sight of the highway, she hit the brakes and put the SUV in park.

"What are you doing?" He bit out each word.

She ignored him—rather, the memories that were trying to assert themselves again, if that was what this was. Whatever was happening, she needed to stop it. She unfastened her seat belt and crawled into his lap.

He raised his hands and tried to back away, but had nowhere to go. She grabbed his face and kissed him. At first, he was tense, but the more she leaned into him, the more he relaxed. His hands drifted to her waist, then around to cup her ass. His tongue slid between her lips and she let out a sigh.

This was Finn.

The new immediate problem was that she didn't want to stop and they weren't exactly out of the way if someone decided to use that road. Like Travis, maybe. She forced herself to pull back.

Finn smiled at her. "What brought that on?"

She felt half-sick. He wasn't even aware of how he had changed. She kept her hands on his cheeks, then leaned in and touched her forehead to his. She wouldn't let him slip away.

"Jazz?"

"Your eyes changed again." Her voice came out hoarse. Her throat was tight with emotion.

"What? No they didn't."

She sat back on his thighs and glared at him. "They did."

"You were driving. You can't be sure—"

"I can and I am. I know what I saw. What I heard. It wasn't you, Finn. It wasn't you."

Chapter Twenty-Two

Finn's stomach was in knots. He couldn't have been lost in a memory. He wasn't touching anything. And yes, sometimes Michael's memories had seemed to try to resurface in his mind, but he had *felt* them. He had always known when it was happening. Like when that darkness crept along his nerves.

What does she know?

Finn shook off the thought. She knew him. Always had. If she said he was losing it, he was losing it.

Christ, the thought was scary, though.

"Keep your hand on my leg," she said.

"What?"

"I need to get us out of sight. Touching keeps you grounded in your body, so I need you to hold on to me till we get parked. Then we can sort this out."

Could they, though?

The memories he had read so far were powerful— especially the ones back at the gallery. They had manifested physically on multiple occasions. The link was already strong enough that reading Michael's kitchen chair made Finn share in Travis's bloody nose after Michael hit him in the memory.

What if it was permanent?

Finn couldn't believe that Siobhan would do this to him. He knew she was a good person. He could feel it through his dreams. She would be trying to help him, not throw him to the wolves.

Jazz slid back into the driver's seat and put the SUV in gear. He left his hand on her thigh, trying to keep himself from gripping it too tight. For the first time, the softness of her skin, her warmth, wasn't a turn on. It was a lifeline.

"Tell me about ghosts," he said.

She glanced over at him quickly, then back to the bumpy side road. "What do you want to know?"

"Everything. How do they stick around? What can they do?"

She turned down another road as he pointed out the way, nearing their destination. "From what I've learned, it's usually the standard story—they feel like they have unfinished business or suffered some sort of trauma that keeps them from letting go."

"Like Siobhan."

"It's hard to say what made her stay. It could have been how she died. Maybe she wants justice or closure or something."

"How do we find out? Can we talk to them like with a séance or something?"

She let out a scoff. "Those aren't as effective as you

might think."

There was a bitter edge to her voice. He started piecing together what he knew about this other mystery. She had talked to him about her family at last. A mother and sister. Three nieces. But she couldn't talk about her dad. Not wouldn't, *couldn't*. Adding that to her fascination with the paranormal and her comments and knowledge of ghosts...

"I'm sorry," he said. "About your dad."

Her grip on the wheel increased till her knuckles were white. A muscle he wasn't used to seeing stood out along her jaw. Mystery solved.

"Thanks."

She pulled into their spot and killed the engine, but didn't look at him. Instead, she turned her face to the window and quickly ran her arm under her nose.

He didn't know what to say, so he gave her a minute to pull herself together. She had never liked showing emotion. She was crystal clear about that. He wanted to give her privacy, but he couldn't let her go without risking losing himself again.

After a few moments, she said, "Sudden massive coronary. Completely unexpected."

Shit. His own heart started pounding in his chest. He couldn't believe she was sharing this with him. No wonder she had freaked out when Finn told her about Dad. Jazz loved him about as much as Finn did. He couldn't imagine how scared she would be to hear about his dad when her own had been taken from her that way.

"It happened in an airport." Her voice lowered nearly to a whisper. "They were on their way to see me—to celebrate my graduating from college."

"Jazz…"

She went on quickly, like she was afraid her courage would give out. "I was obsessed with finding him after it happened. I just wanted to talk to him one more time." She sniffed again, still staring out the window. "It's good that I was obsessed. The things I learned are helping people now."

As if that made what she had gone through okay. He understood her attachment to Dad that much more.

"There's something else you should know about me. Something I should have told you a long time ago."

"Okay."

His stomach started to twist. They'd covered a lot of ground already, but she seemed so much more serious about whatever she was about to tell him.

"Being close to me is dangerous."

"Dangerous how?"

She paused for a moment, then said, "I'm cursed."

He would have laughed if it weren't for everything they'd been through. His reality had shifted way too far for him to not take this seriously.

"What kind of curse?"

"Whenever I care about people, things happen to

them."

"What kind of things?"

"Bad things. Like what happened to my father. I want to fight it to be with you. But you need to know the risk going in."

Shit. She blamed herself for her dad's death?

"Jazz, you can't take that on."

She shook her head. "You of all people know that there are forces at work that we don't understand. Fate is one of them."

"Yeah, but you don't control people's destinies."

"No. I facilitate them."

"How does that work?"

"I'm a nexus. Supposedly I gather people together at the right time and place. It's one of the reasons I'm so good at running the gallery and finding the next hot thing."

"I can't argue that point, but I don't know about the rest of it."

"I've been to dozens of psychics. They all say the same thing. I'm an instrument of Fate. And for whatever reason, she doesn't want me to be happy."

"No. No way. I'm not buying it."

"Finn—"

"I'm not saying you aren't a nexus or whatever that is. That part actually makes sense. But caring about people can't put them in danger. I mean, what kind of fucked-up universe would it be if that was the case?"

She chuffed out a breath and shook her head again. "The one I live in."

"Not anymore. Bad things happen to people all the time. You can't take responsibility for it. Siobhan was a good person. I can feel it. And she…" His throat tightened up and he had to cough to clear it. "None of us know how much time we have. No one gets to decide that. But we can make choices that make us happy while we're here."

"Being with you makes me happy," she said.

Finn felt like his stomach dropped through the ground.

"And I'm sick of living this way. Always afraid to let myself…" She shook her head, her voice trailing off.

He reached over and picked up her hand, then kissed the back of it. When she looked at him, she was so raw. He could barely stand it.

"Listen to me." He spoke each word crisply, making sure she knew he meant it. "Fate. Isn't. A dick."

Jazz busted out laughing.

"Good things happen," he said, his voice growing softer. "Bad things happen. What we've been through in our lives, and what the people close to us have gone through—it's all brought us here. This is where we're meant to be. Everything happens for a reason. I honestly believe that. And I don't believe that Fate is an asshole."

Her eyes filled with tears. She looked away quickly. It would probably be a while till she was comfortable really letting all her walls down with him. That was okay. He could wait. At least he was starting to feel that there was hope for them on the other side.

"Rachel would be a better source of information," Jazz said. "About ghosts."

He could sense that she needed to move on from the topic. She had just faced down one of her demons. He could play along.

"Your assistant?"

"Yeah. She's clairsentient—she can communicate with them."

"You're kidding. She always sounded so normal when you guys talked about her."

Jazz shrugged. "You seem pretty normal too."

She pulled the key from the ignition and tossed it in the drink tray, then opened her door to let in some air. He did the same to give them a cross-breeze.

Finally, she turned toward him. Her cheeks were dry, but her eyes were red around the edges. Seeing it felt like being punched in the gut. Jazz looked away quickly. She pulled her phone from the pocket of her shirt and stared at it for a moment.

"No signal." She put her phone in the drink holder with her key. "We should try to call her as soon as we can and tell her what's going on. Ask her advice. When we head back to Summer Park, we should head straight to Garrett's house."

"She's staying with Garrett?"

"It's a good thing," Jazz said. "She needed to get out of her mom's house. That woman is evil."

Finn snorted, playing along with the conversation. Jazz wanted to gloss over what she'd shared. He could help do that for her.

"But how do you really feel about her?" he asked.

Jazz smiled and shook her head. "Maybe this time, they won't be idiots and will finally hook up."

He laughed outright. "Wait, she's into him too?"

"Big time. She tries to play it down for some reason, but it's obvious how they feel about each other."

"Well shit. He's been pining for her for years. Why didn't they just…"

"Talk about it?" She arched an eyebrow.

Finn shook his head. "At least you had a really good reason."

"I thought I did. Maybe they do too."

"Okay, I guess I shouldn't be pointing fingers."

"I think I'm going to call those years we didn't talk, *the lapse*."

"The lapse?"

"Yeah. As in, *lapse in judgment*." She became more serious as she said, "I should have fought for you harder."

"I should have insisted we talk things through."

She smiled again. "While I'm willing to work things through verbally when we need to, I really am not used to all this talking about feelings. Now that we've settled all that, can we please crawl into the back and have sex again?"

"Absolutely."

He unfastened his seat belt so he could lean closer, pulling her in for a kiss. He heard the click as she undid her seat belt, and then she was in his lap again, pushing him back into his seat. Her tongue slid along his lips, her fingers burrowed through his hair.

He knew what it was like to seek solace in her touch, could feel that was what she wanted—needed—from him. She was still raw from what she had shared. He grabbed the lever to push the chair back, giving them more room to work.

She didn't waste any time. She reached between them and undid his jeans. With her attentive hands, his dick became rock hard in about six seconds. He was still amazed at how her touch could relax him so deeply while working him up at the same time.

The intrusive thoughts and disconnection that had been plaguing him also vanished. Maybe Siobhan *was* to blame, and seeing her brother go at it made her run away. He'd be the same way.

Not the time to be thinking about ghosts, man.

Jazz moved her kisses along his jaw and down his neck and he stopped thinking period. She grazed his skin with her teeth and nipped at him. Damn, she remembered just what he liked. She pumped her hand up and down, increasing the pressure. He leaned back and closed his eyes letting himself relax into the chair.

She slid down between his legs, pushing his shirt up so she could kiss his stomach and trace the lines of his abs with her lips and tongue. That was something she had always liked—playing with the lines of his muscles.

She never had trouble talking about how much she loved his body. It didn't bother him anymore now that she had given him hope that there might be more to it. She wasn't just in it for the physical part of their relationship. Knowing that let him sink into the sensations, to enjoy them on a level he'd never reached before.

The wind had picked up a bit. It drifted through the open space, lifting her hair across his stomach. She kissed him lower on his abdomen, on the sensitive skin below his navel. She held his dick so she could draw her cheek along the length of it, then wrapped her lips around his crown.

So damn good.

She took him in deeper, swirling her tongue, running her fingertips lightly over the base of his shaft. He trailed his fingers through her hair, resting his palm on the back of her head to feel more of her movements. Up and down, a steady rhythm rippling through his body, reminding him that he was Finn and he was hers. He always had been.

She picked up on the pulsing beat starting to build at the base of his shaft and eased him from her mouth. She kept herself pressed against his side, kissing his stomach as she reached down and slid her bikini bottoms down her legs. Then she crawled back up to straddle him in his chair.

Bracing her arms against his shoulders, she lined herself up. He rested his hands on her hips as she inched down over him, her body stretching to hold him tight.

"We need to keep doing this forever," he said.

She smiled, then leaned forward and kissed him, tongue plunging deep, hips rocking on his body. He thrust himself up into her, meeting every movement. The pull of her flesh against his was bringing him too close. He wanted to be sure she was right with him.

He pulled away from the kiss and said, "Sit back."

She kept her hands on his shoulders as she leaned back, using the leverage to steady herself as she slid up and down along his length. Damn, she felt too good. He was going to go off any moment.

He put one hand between them to find her clit, circling it as she moved. Her breath hitched and her eyes rolled shut. He used his free hand to push her bikini top up over her breasts, then drew one into his mouth as he cupped the other, lightly tracing his thumb over her nipple till it was a tight bud.

"Finn…"

His name came out as a moan. God, he loved it when she said his name like that.

His dick was pulsing, pressure building deep. The pull

of her skin against his, wet and hot, the softness of her breasts—it was too much. He let go of her breasts but kept the hand at her clit, circling, flicking, feeling the pre-quake tremors start echoing out through his body.

He pressed his back against the seat, his feet against the floorboards, and started thrusting up into her harder, faster. She flung back her head, eyes clenched tight, fingertips digging into his shoulders as she moaned his name again.

At last he let himself go, ramming up into her as he held on to her hips. Her body tightened around him, drawing out his orgasm as he spilled himself inside of her. He buried himself as deep as he could and held himself there, holding tight, pinning her against him, feeling the pulsing in their bodies answering each other.

She fell forward against his chest, breathing heavily. He felt her heart pounding against his.

When they were together like this, it was like they created their own tiny world. It was just the two of them. He wrapped his arms around her, enjoying the moment of peace while it lasted.

Chapter Twenty-Three

After the truly glorious session in the passenger's seat, they had moved to the back for round two. Jazz had been only too happy to fill their time in each other's arms as they waited for the best moment to go back to Travis's house.

Finn said Travis checked his traps out in the swamp in the mornings. She didn't want to think about how he knew so much from so few readings. There was still something going on they hadn't figured out, and it was scaring her. But they needed to focus on what they were doing. They would sort everything out in time. She had faith in them.

He held her hand tightly as they made their way through the brush surrounding the house. Jazz pulled him back before he could step out into the yard.

"His truck is still here."

Finn pointed to the small dock behind Travis's house. "Yeah, but his boat's gone."

Her heart was beating fast. She didn't like the idea of going into the house for many reasons. At the top of the list was her fear that Finn would get drawn into a memory again. After the incident in the SUV, where he seemed to be falling into Michael's memories without touching anything, she was even more afraid of that happening.

What if the next time she couldn't pull him back?

"We won't be able to hear him," she said. "The boat doesn't make noise like the truck."

"You can stay outside as a lookout."

"Like hell I will. Where you go, I go."

"Then you're going into the house. I have to get some answers, Jazz. I need to know what his role in all of this is. It's the only way to make this stop—to help my sister. I'm sure of it."

She didn't like it. Her instincts were screaming for her to run. "We can try to call Rachel again."

"You just did. No signal, remember?"

He cupped her cheek and kissed her—a gentle kiss, not building to anything. Just a reassurance. It didn't do much for her nerves.

He pulled back and said, "You don't have to go with me."

"I do and I will. I'm all-in, remember?" She let out a deep breath that did nothing to ease her nerves. "Let's just get this over with."

She stepped into Travis's yard, pulling Finn after her. This time, she insisted on opening the front door. She didn't want him to touch anything. She managed to not knock the door off its hinges.

Inside, things had changed. The animals, the pelts, they

were all gone.

"Someone's been redecorating," Finn said.

Jazz felt a chill. She stepped closer to Finn.

"How is it that it's somehow even creepier now?" she asked.

"Travis's talent lies in being creepy."

She looked over at Finn. That didn't sound like him. He was looking around the living room, a strange smile on his face.

"Finn?"

"Yes?"

The lighting was dim. She couldn't see his eyes clearly enough to note their color.

"Let's go to the kitchen."

"Okay."

Two steps forward, and he stumbled into her side. She grabbed his chest to try to hold him up.

"Finn!"

"Whoa. Whee…" He laughed.

"This isn't funny."

She draped his arm over her shoulders. Damn, he was heavy. They staggered a few feet closer to the kitchen before he fell to his knees.

"Dammit, Finn, get up! I am not making out with you in this shithole!"

He laughed again. "Honestly, is that all you ever think about?"

He listed to the side. She grabbed his face in her hands and tried to see his eyes. They were closed.

"Show me your eyes. Finn, dammit, show me your eyes!"

The grin on his face was unnerving. It was worse when he finally opened his eyes.

They were glowing. *Glowing* blue. She could see the color creeping over his irises, making his own color look gray in comparison—blotting it out.

"Shit. Finn..."

She kissed him. She hoped—prayed—it was enough.

He shoved her away. She scrambled after him as he bolted for a door that led from the room. He ran into the small bathroom, retching into a sink. Dim light filtered in from the living room. The window in the bathroom had been painted over and an acrid scent of chemicals overpowered her sense of smell.

She didn't care. She brought all her attention to Finn. She wrapped her arms around him, holding him tight. When he was done, he managed to stand up again. He tilted his head back and let out a huge sigh. He didn't push her away.

"Finn?"

"Yeah. It's me. Shit, at least I think so."

Thank God. She buried her face in his chest, gave herself a moment—just a moment—to feel him, to regroup, to try to figure out what to do next.

"This doesn't make sense," she said. "If your sister wants you to help her—sees that you're trying to—why is she making your powers go crazy? She has to know that messing with you is making Michael's memories have a stronger effect."

"I don't know what's going on. I wish I understood." He held her tighter. "I'm scared, Jazz. I feel like I'm losing myself. Like he's taking me over."

"That sounds like possession."

"How can he possess me if he's gone? You said he can't be haunting me."

"Rachel said he was cremated. Without physical remains, he should have been forced to cross over." Jazz had learned that in her own studies, even before Rachel had told her. "I'm calling Rachel. Something's not right."

She pulled her phone from her pocket. The signal strength was weak, but there. She hoped it would be enough. Finn rested his head on her shoulder as she dialed the number.

Rachel answered after only a few rings.

"Hello?"

Jazz barely gave herself time to register relief that she had reached Rachel. It was too early to be reassured anyway. Who knew how long their signal would hold?

"Are you absolutely sure that Michael is gone?" Jazz asked. A sharp bite of static hit her ear.

Through the noise, Jazz could hear the hesitance in

Rachel's voice. "He was cremated."

"I know, but if he found a strong connection, could he possibly possess someone?"

If Finn's twin had the same power, maybe Michael's personality had implanted itself in her. Jazz had seen documentaries about twins and their psychic links. Or even worse, maybe Michael had latched on to Siobhan's psychic energy and was using it to stick around. Michael could be using their connection to get to Finn, to try to influence the corporeal world.

Finn reached behind Jazz and flipped on a light switch. The room went from dark and creepy to bright and...gross. Jazz turned away from the sink. String crossed the room just above her head, filled with photographs hanging from clothespins. Was this a dark room?

She forced herself to finish her thought as she glanced at the pictures. "Maybe someone with psychic abilities?"

"Possession?" Rachel's voice rose to a squeak.

Jazz looked more closely at the pictures. Her heart pounded, her breath catching in her chest as full-on panic set in. The pictures hanging on the string were of Elsa and Rachel. Rachel through the windows of her mom's tea room, taken with a telescopic lens. Elsa standing at the window of her loft, arms around Dante's waist. He had bandages on his face.

These were recent.

"Oh God—"

In a huge burst of static, the call went dead.

"Jazz…" Finn was looking at the pictures, his eyes wide.

"Yeah. I see them."

He reached up and plucked one of the pictures from the line.

"Finn, don't!"

Her warning was too late. She waited for the change, for him to stiffen and pull away, to look at her with that condescending smile. His hand was shaking.

Her chest was so tight, Jazz felt like she was going to pass out. She pulled herself together. Finn needed her, dammit. From the look of things, all of her friends did.

Travis was stalking Elsa and Rachel. Maybe that was the real reason that Siobhan was messing with Finn. She wasn't trying to get help for herself—she was trying to save Elsa and Rachel.

"This… It's her. I know it." Finn's eyes were perfectly, pristinely gray-blue. And full of tears.

"Who?"

"Siobhan. This is my sister."

Jazz looked at the photo. "That's Rachel."

"No. No, this is Siobhan. I'm sure of it."

"It can't be. Finn, that is Rachel."

"This doesn't make any sense."

"Okay, we need to figure this out—back at the SUV. We need to call the police."

He nodded. Jazz let out a tiny breath. There was so much more at stake than she had imagined.

"Put the picture back. We don't want to tip off Travis that we were here."

She kept one arm around Finn's waist as she twisted around to turn on the water in the sink and rinse it clean. She hoped it would dry before Travis came home. Finn kept staring at the picture in his hand.

"Finn, put it back."

Slowly, he lifted his arms and placed it back on the line. He kept staring at the other photos.

She had to get him out of there.

"We're going to figure this out," she said. "If Travis has these, he probably has other trophies around. We let the police know, they search the place with a warrant, and they stop him before…"

She couldn't finish that thought. She had no idea what Travis had planned for Elsa and Rachel. Jazz couldn't convince herself it was nothing. She turned off the water in the sink and flipped the light switch, then pulled Finn back into the living room.

A quick survey of the room showed her they hadn't disturbed anything else. She pulled the door to the bathroom shut, then headed for the front door. She kept her arm tight around Finn's waist. He didn't seem to want to leave.

The sooner they were out of this house the better. They

stumbled out the door and through the yard. Fennel brushed against them as they made their way back to the SUV. A lingering scent like licorice floated around them, cleansing her nose from the stifling bathroom.

She opened the back door of the SUV and helped him sit down. He looked like he was in shock.

"How can Rachel be my sister?" he asked.

"She can't. I've met both her parents. Your powers must be acting up again."

"No. Not this time. I'm sure of it." He shook his head. "Is she adopted, maybe?"

"Not that she's ever told me. Then again, her mother is a lying, manipulative—"

Wait… Her mother *was* a liar and a master manipulator.

Jazz remembered what Tommy had said about Finn's mom. The picture he painted was not rosy. It did, however, remind her of Lillian Montgomery.

"What?"

"Your dad said your mom left for a lawyer."

"Yeah."

"Rachel's dad is a lawyer. Tommy said your mom warned him not to try to find them. What if they moved and changed her name?"

"How could we all wind up in Summer Park?"

"Summer Park is a magnet for psychics. I'm friends with the owner of the local metaphysical bookstore. There's a huge population of them here."

"It still seems like too much of a coincidence."

"Maybe it isn't a coincidence. Maybe it's Fate."

She was starting to wonder.

"I don't know. If Rachel is Siobhan, that means my powers aren't off the rails because of being haunted. I'm back to square one solving that problem."

"I don't think so. When exactly did your powers go out of control?"

"It was the day Michael died. No, the day before."

"The day Rachel was abducted. You started dreaming about what Rachel experienced that night—as it was happening. Twins often have a psychic link. With both of your heightened powers, maybe the trauma of it activated a connection and it sort of went haywire."

"That's a hell of a lot better than being haunted or possessed." Finn shook his head. "Do you really think it could be her?"

Jazz looked at his pale blue eyes, remembering again how similar they were to Rachel's. But it was more than that. They were both tall and had similar athletic builds, like Tommy. Straight noses, strong features... How could she have not seen it before?

She laughed. She couldn't help it. She was so relieved, almost giddy. Finn's sister wasn't dead after all. And she was *Rachel*.

"Yeah," Jazz said. "I think so."

"Damn," he said. Then he laughed too. "I have to tell

Dad. I mean, I'll check with him on the details first, but he has to know about this."

He jumped up and pulled his phone from his pocket. He looked at the screen, then he started walking around waving it in the air.

"There has to be a signal around here somewhere."

Jazz couldn't stop smiling. This was the best news she'd heard in a long time. Tommy would be so happy. Even Rachel would be glad to know that she actually had a decent family. It was perfect.

Except something wasn't right. Rachel's trauma might have Finn's powers out of whack, but that didn't explain how Michael's memories were strong enough to take him over. From what Finn said, Michael's memories were potent, but they shouldn't be enough to change his appearance...

Could they?

"Let's drive somewhere that has a signal," he said. "We need to call Dad and let the cops know to—"

He gave a sharp cry. Jazz heard creaking and a loud crack from the other side of the SUV. She bolted around to see Finn hanging upside down, his body slowly rotating in the air.

"Finn!"

She ran to him, grabbing his sides to stop his movement. A rope was caught around his ankle. He had stepped in some kind of snare. It looked like it had been set up to pull him against the tree. He must have hit it hard to make such a loud noise. He was out cold.

"Shit! Finn…"

His chest was still moving. He was breathing. She had to get him down. Maybe there was something in the SUV that could help. She turned back to it, vaguely registering Travis standing right behind her, his arm seeming to fly toward her face. She felt a brief moment of pain. Her vision filled with blinding lights and then went dark.

Chapter Twenty-Four

Wake up. Wake. Up.

Finn's head was pounding. He blinked his eyes and looked around, trying to figure out where the voice was coming from. His shoulders ached. He couldn't move his arms. Pain lanced through his wrists as rough rope bit into his skin. He was tied to a chair.

A moment of panic shot through him. He had dreamt something too close to this over and over again. He had to calm himself down. Assess his situation, his surroundings. Directly across from him, Jazz was tied to a chair too. Her head was bowed forward, her dark hair obscuring her face.

More panic, but longer than a moment. She wasn't moving.

"Jazz!"

Finn tugged against the ropes, tried to hop his chair closer. The floor of the place was sand. He couldn't get enough purchase to move.

"You pathetic fool."

He jerked his head to the side, trying to find the voice. The world spun around him and he felt nauseated. He closed his eyes till the feeling passed.

"I can't believe you let him catch you. I only left you alone for a few minutes."

Finn looked around more slowly. They were in some kind of shed, the dark wood pitted from time and exposure to the elements. The door was open, giving Finn a view of the swamp outside. And it was actual swamp.

The water line was only a few dozen feet from where they sat. If a gator decided it wanted a snack, it could walk right in.

He looked around the room some more. Gators became the least of his worries.

Tables lined the walls of the shed. They were covered in a mix of pelts, hunks of wood in vaguely animal-like shapes, and tools. Sharp, jagged tools. Some of them he recognized as being for woodworking. The rest he could only imagine were for carving…other things. It looked like they were in a torture chamber.

He pulled against the ropes again.

"You disappoint me."

Where the hell was that coming from? The guy's voice sounded like it was right in Finn's ear. Even closer.

He looked around the place again. It must be Travis's taxidermy studio. He and Jazz were the only ones there. Finn craned his neck around to try to look over his shoulder.

Two forms lurked in the shadows.

Shit.

They were small, but in his current state, there was nothing he could do to protect himself or Jazz. If only he was free. He could take them—

"What kind of private investigator were you?" The voice was thick with mockery.

Finn's neck hurt, but he kept looking. The figures didn't move. They were holding too still. Mannequins. They were female mannequins. More specifically, they looked like the frames sitting on the tables. The ones Travis must use for...

Oh shit!

He turned back to Jazz, his breath coming so fast he was almost hyperventilating.

"Yes," the voice practically purred. *"Frames for my little mad elf's workshop. I see you can imagine what he plans to do with them."*

"Who are you?"

"Tsk. It's just the two of us in here. I'd rather keep our conversation private. Besides, you don't want Travis to hear, do you? Once he knows you're awake, he'll come back inside."

Finn looked at the open doorway. Yeah, he didn't want Travis coming back. Not until Finn had figured a way out of this and could kick the sick bastard's ass.

"So violent. You need to learn control. There's so much that you're capable of. You didn't even scratch the surface of your powers."

Finn closed his eyes and took a few deep breaths.

"Who are you?" he thought.

"Better. Much better. But too little, too late."

The light dimmed as Travis stepped into the shed. He was wearing a faded gray and white checkered shirt, jeans, and heavy boots. He glanced at Finn and did a double-take.

"He thought you'd still be sleeping. He didn't know I'd be here to prod you awake."

Finn ignored the voice. "Travis. It's Travis, right?"

Travis's mouth tightened into a line, his lips disappearing almost completely. The guy was a rail. His cheekbones stuck out on his face, his thin arms were corded with muscle and sinew—no fat to soften him anywhere.

He walked behind Jazz and checked her ropes. She stirred. Finn's heart was pounding. He had to get her out of there. Travis headed toward him, stepping behind Finn's chair.

If Finn could reach him—touch his skin—he would push him to let them go. He didn't give a shit about the consequences. He just wanted Jazz safe.

"Do you think it's that simple? That you can turn on that power like a switch, without studying it, practicing it?"

Travis checked the ropes, pulling on them tight enough to make Finn wince. He reached for Travis—tried to anyway. His hands didn't respond.

"That is how it's done. Finesse. Slip in between the cracks so they don't even know you're the one in control. Learn how they think so they can't tell which voice in their mind is their own."

Shit! Travis walked to one of the tables. Finn had to think of another way to reach him.

"What is it that you want?" Finn asked.

"He wants to be like me," the voice whispered.

"Shut up!"

Finn's stomach seemed to drop through his body, carried away with a feeling of déjà vu. This conversation wasn't new. It had been going on since yesterday at least. Intrusive thoughts that Finn believed were his own, even though they weren't like him at all.

He'd thought Michael's memories were affecting him —getting under his skin—until Jazz shared her theory in the darkroom that Michael was the one haunting him. That somehow his spirit was still hanging around. Hanging around *Finn*.

Maybe he had used Finn's bond with Rachel or used the connection Finn made when he read objects. Either way, Michael was back. And he was in Finn's head. Under his skin.

The voice in his head laughed. *"'Under your skin' is going to have a very literal meaning for you soon."*

Travis turned from the table, a long thin blade in his

hand. A skinning knife.

Shit!

Finn drew out the word in his mind. He couldn't help it. That panic from earlier was back in full force.

"Come on, man," he said. "You don't have to do this."

"He wants to do it. Don't you see? He's trying to live up to the standard I set—to prove he's as good as me. It's pathetic, really."

"Travis, please. This isn't you. I saw the kid you were before Michael started messing with your head. Don't let him turn you into this."

"Oh, please. I've been sculpting his mind for decades. Do you think you can undo my work with platitudes? When I came to live here, he was a plump little thing just approaching manhood. Disillusioned with the world, but still open-minded enough for me to squeeze in. I would pick at him till he attacked me, then set his mother against him as well. They were excellent practice for learning to control others. You, though. You have so much raw power. Power you never bothered to use."

Dammit. Finn almost felt bad for Travis. The guy's hand was shaking. He really didn't want to do this. Michael had fucked with his head so bad.

"I can help you," Finn said.

"No you can't," the voice said. *"You can't help anyone. Not yourself. Not Ms. Zhou."*

Finn was trying to figure a way out of this, but coming

up empty. The sand kept him from getting enough purchase to shift his chair. Travis was right there with them, armed and absolutely dangerous. Jazz was unconscious, at his mercy.

"Please," Finn said. "I'm begging you. Let her go."

Travis was staring at the knife in his hands. He was working up his nerve. Finn had to reach him quickly.

"As if he would ever let either of you go. You both know about what he's done. He's too much of a coward to go to prison. He'd rather kill you."

"Of everybody in this room, I think you're *the one he'd most like to kill."*

Wait… That just might work.

"Travis, I know Michael hurt you. Made your life hell. I know you hate him and you want to prove that you're better than him."

Travis finally spoke, his voice rusty as if he seldom used it. "You don't know a damned thing."

"I do. I know because he's here. Michael is here."

Travis finally looked at Finn. His eyes were wide and his mouth dropped open. He glanced around the small space, shifting the knife in his hand so he wielded it like a weapon.

"You've felt him too, haven't you? You know he's still around."

"My traps…" Travis murmured. "They were all set off last night."

How could Michael have managed that? Finn wished that he and Jazz had talked more about what ghosts could do instead of focusing on Finn's problematic powers. In the movies, sometimes ghosts could move things. Setting off a bunch of traps seemed a bit much.

The voice in his head laughed. Mocking him again. *"You really are clueless."*

Finn was missing something. Michael had already taunted Finn about not knowing what he could do with his powers. And Michael had said he was practicing using them. Finn looked at Travis again, the way his eyes glazed over, the terrified look on his face.

"They weren't empty, were they?"

Travis's gaze flicked to Finn's again and he snapped his mouth shut. Finn went over everything he knew about Michael, remembered the dream about Travis.

Traps.

What if Jazz was right and Finn did have the ability to control animals? What if Michael had been practicing on them while working his way up to controlling Finn's own body with his powers, overriding his mental commands?

"It was squirrels," Finn said. "They had run into the traps and set them off."

Travis's eyes nearly bugged out of their sockets. He flashed the knife toward Finn. "How do you know that?"

"Because Michael is in my head. You want your revenge? Take it. He's right here for you. But let Jazz go."

"Pathetic. As if ending your life would end me."

Travis turned back to the table and set down the knife. He kept scanning his tools, shifting them, lining them up in perfect rows.

"He'll never let her go. You only have one chance at making it out of this alive."

Finn knew the devil was about to offer him a deal. He could feel it. And he didn't have any options to counter whatever Michael was about to say.

"Which is?"

"Let me talk to him."

It couldn't be that easy.

"Step aside and let me take over."

"As if."

"I'll convince him to let us out of the chair and remind him of his place."

There was no way Finn was letting this sick bastard take his body for a spin. The things he might do... No. No way.

"Then die here. Both of you."

Shit.

"You know he's going to kill you. You're helpless to stop him. If I can talk to him directly, I can convince him to let you go. After that, all you have to deal with is me."

That last part caught Finn's attention. Michael noticed.

"This is your body. Do you really have so little faith in yourself that you don't think you can reassert control after

you're free?"

Finn wasn't sure. It was too risky. He had to think of another way. Fast.

"There is only one way out—if he lets *you go. He will never cut you free. But he will free me. It's been fun to mess with you, but if he kills you, I can always find someone else to possess. Either way, the choice is yours."*

Chapter Twenty-Five

Holding still while Finn talked to Travis was taking all of Jazz's willpower. She kept her head dangling loose on her neck, letting her hair shield her eyes as she surveyed the small space where they were held captive.

She could see tables out of the corners of her eyes. Their phones were sitting on one of them, along with carving tools, blanks waiting to be used, and some that had already been shaped into frames for more of Travis's work —including two life-sized female forms just behind Finn.

The hair on her arms lifted as she thought about the implications of those two mannequins. They were the same size as Elsa and Rachel.

Her stomach knotted. There was an acrid scent permeating the air as well. Something had been burned nearby recently. The wind carried the smell just inside the shed occasionally as it shifted. Char and chemicals. Lighter fluid.

There was sand beneath her feet. Her legs were tied to her chair at the ankles—around her boots. If they could get Travis to leave, she would be able to get her feet out of her boots. She could walk to the table and get a tool to cut herself and Finn free.

It was a big if.

Finn was trying to convince Travis to free Jazz. He had been, anyway, before he lapsed into an unexpected silence. Travis was standing at his tables, sorting through his tools. She risked a glance at Finn. His head was bowed against his chest. Had he given up?

No, he was a fighter, like her. What was he doing then? All of his focus seemed to be directed internally. Maybe he was trying to sort through Michael's memories to figure out a way to help them.

That didn't seem safe. The more he delved into them, the more of a foothold Michael seemed to get. And in this dark place... They were in his home territory. She could feel it.

She had listened to their conversation. Finn hadn't been able to reach Travis. Maybe she could. She lifted her head cautiously and kept her voice low and neutral.

"Travis."

He stiffened, but didn't look at her.

"Hi. I'm Jazz."

He kept picking up one tool after another and setting it back in place.

"You haven't done anything wrong yet." It wasn't exactly true, but she needed to win him over. "You can still let us go. Put a stop to this. You have the power to do that —to make that choice."

He said something, but his voice was too low for her to hear.

"What?"

"Be quiet."

"Travis, please. You need to listen to me."

"Shut up." He was still picking things up and putting them down. Over and over.

"It isn't too late."

"Shut up. Shut up. Shut up!"

He turned to her, eyes wild, then he leapt at her. He grabbed her by the throat with both hands, squeezing till she couldn't breathe.

"You are *materials*! Materials don't talk!"

The sound of blood rushing through her ears was distorting what she heard. It had to be. Because Finn was laughing.

"Pig!" Finn shouted. "Pig, pig, piggy!"

Travis's grip went lax. Jazz sucked in air, the room spinning around her.

Travis turned around, his voice eerily quiet. "What did you say?"

Finn laughed again, then made a horrible squealing sound. His eyes were closed, and his head listed to the side. A bizarre smile stretched across his face.

"Finn…" Her throat was sore. She couldn't manage more than his name.

"I said shut up!" Travis backhanded her.

Pain blurred her vision and blood started to pool in her mouth. She blinked away the tears so she could see Finn more clearly. His head had rolled forward, his chin resting against his chest.

"Travis, how many times do I have to tell you?" Finn lifted his head, his smile spreading to show all of his teeth. He paused after each word when he spoke. "Don't damage the canvas."

He looked up at her. His eyes were bright, bright blue.

"No…" Jazz whispered.

Travis pulled back his fist, aiming for her face. He froze when Finn yelled, "Pig!" again.

"You will listen to me, you filthy little pig."

Travis took a menacing step toward Finn. "Stop calling me that."

"But it's what you are. My piggy bank." Finn laughed again.

Travis's face went pale. He lifted a hand to touch his chest just above his heart, his breath coming fast. If they were lucky, maybe he would pass out and Jazz could try to figure out a way to fix this, to bring Finn back to himself.

Travis stumbled toward Finn. So much for luck.

"You… You can't say that. You can't say these things. You can't know these things."

"I know everything about you. All your dirty little secrets."

"No. You can't be him. She killed you. That Rachel, she

killed you."

Finn grimaced. "She was *paint*. Do you really think she could end me? Do you think *anyone* can end me?"

Travis shook his head. His hands were twitching, forming fists that Jazz doubted he was even aware of.

"This is a trick," Travis said.

"You know it isn't. Otherwise you wouldn't look like you're about to wet yourself."

"Shut up."

"That's it. Hide in the mud, piggy. Hide from the truth, the truths I know. Like that you're a gutless coward." Finn cocked his head to the side and pursed his lips. "Is that why you like to play with dead things? Hollow them out so they're like you? Is that why you stole everything Auntie cooked for *me*. Trying to fill yourself up?"

"Stop it." The calm of Travis's voice worried Jazz more than his shouting. Shit, Michael had done a number on this guy. She couldn't imagine living with a psychopath.

"You never even had the courage to kill any of your playthings without your pathetic little traps. I had to do it for you. You'd have nothing without me. You *are* nothing without me!"

"Stop!" Travis punched Finn in the jaw viciously.

Jazz gasped. Maybe the pain would snap him out of it, let him escape from Michael's memories. Finn spat out a mouthful of blood and smiled again.

"I'm sorry," Travis stuttered. He dropped to his knees

next to Finn. "I'm sorry, I just get so mad. You know how I get mad."

"It's all right, Travis." Finn's voice was smooth and cool, like a snake's skin. "I forgive you. I understand. That's always been your problem. Your violence is always a reaction. Never a *decision*. Never a choice. My violence always has purpose."

Travis was nodding, his gaze on the floor and his hands clasped in front of him like some sort of sick disciple. "I know, Mikey. I know."

"Let me show you," Finn said. "Let me give you purpose."

"What do you mean?"

"You have a grand goal. I applaud you on that. But you need to practice. Beyond your little pets."

Finn looked at Jazz for the first time. Hope swelled in her heart, then burst when she saw the coldness of his eyes. Finn wasn't there.

No. Dammit, no. She could still save him. Help him save himself. She wouldn't give up on them again.

"If you let yourself become angry, you'll bruise the skin and ruin the piece," he said.

"You're right. You always think of these things." Travis looked at Jazz too, an assessing gaze, one that didn't see her as a person. She was just materials to him, to them both. Maybe she could use that to her advantage.

"These ropes on my wrists sure as hell are chafing.

Might want to do something about that if you're trying to keep my skin all pretty."

Travis took a menacing step forward, but Finn... No, *Michael*, stopped him.

"Ah-ah, Travis."

"She keeps talking to me." Travis bit the words out, his jaw so tense, muscles were twitching on both sides of his face.

"Then stop her. But do it better."

"How?"

Michael-in-Finn's-body leveled a malicious stare at her, grin wide, head lowered like a predator. "Cover her mouth with your hand and pinch her nose shut."

"Oh, that's perfect."

"Wait..." Jazz said, but Travis was already on her, covering her mouth and nose. She tried to bite him, but he was too strong. When she flailed her head, he grabbed her hair with his other hand and kept her still. Her lungs started to burn, her eyes watering.

"Not too much," Michael said. "We're not done with her yet."

Travis let go, and Jazz gulped down air again.

She was getting a good idea of how this would end. The worst of it wasn't even that she was going to die. Finn was going to keep on moving, trapped in his body while he was being controlled by Michael.

She had to do something. Any time she opened her

mouth, it set Travis off. But words were her only weapon.

The first thing she needed to do was get Finn free—his body, anyway. If she could reach him, it would only help if they weren't both tied to chairs.

"You think you're in charge, but you're tied up just like me." Jazz swallowed hard, then leaned back. "*Mikey*."

Something dark crossed his features. Jazz really hoped she could reach Finn quickly. She was sure Michael would come up with some creative ways to punish her for pointing that out.

"Let me up." Michael somehow made each clipped word a threat.

Travis was thinking about what Jazz said, but she doubted he would be able to go against Michael's wishes.

"You're going to be mad because I hit you," Travis said.

"Not as mad as I'll be if you don't get these fucking ropes off of me right now!"

Jazz had never known Michael to swear. The fact that he did so now terrified her. He even dropped the condescending way he normally spoke. She might have gone a bit too far.

Travis could sense the change too—the danger. He started working on the ropes on Finn's feet. When they were loose, he moved behind the chair to free Finn's hands.

"I didn't know you were in there. I wouldn't have tied

you up if I'd known, Mikey."

"Stop calling me that."

As soon as Michael was free, some of the menace seemed to drain from him. He rubbed his wrists and shook his shoulders. After a deep breath, he smiled at Jazz again, a look she'd seen dozens of times at the gallery.

"Where is it?" Michael asked.

"I kept it safe for you, Mi—"

Travis stopped himself, which was probably a good thing given the menacing look Michael cast at him. Travis reached into his shirt and pulled out a leather pouch on a loop of dark cord. He took it off and handed it to Michael.

Whatever was in there, Michael was delighted to have it back. He cupped the pouch in his hands, closing his eyes and taking a few deep breaths as he smiled. Then he draped it around his neck, pressing it against his chest above his heart—above *Finn's* heart.

Michael opened his eyes and smiled at her. "Now then. Let's get started."

Travis was staring at Jazz too. He was shifting his weight from side to side. "What's first? Should I get my knives?"

"The skin, Travis. You have to think of the skin." Michael started moving around the room, picking over Travis's tools.

"Right."

Travis joined him in the search for something to use to

kill her. He paused and stared at her. Jazz's heart was pounding in her chest.

"Oh, I know!" Travis said. "We can drown her in the swamp."

"That is a wonderful idea."

Michael turned around, holding a large blank for carving a frame for one of Travis's creepy companions. Never slowing his momentum, he smashed the block of wood into the side of Travis's head.

Travis crumpled to the ground. Jazz wasn't sure if he was alive after that vicious blow.

Michael tossed the blank aside, then dusted his hands together. "Well, my dear. Now that we're alone…"

Shit.

But they weren't alone. Finn was still in there, somewhere. She had to believe it. She had to reach him. And if he wasn't…

Her vision blurred. She closed her eyes, feeling tears roll down her cheeks.

"Finn, I'm so sorry," she said. "I never thought it would end this way. I didn't think it was going to end at all. I thought Fate had given us a second chance."

She opened her eyes to look at him. Michael was glaring at her, but there was confusion and uncertainty on his face. He grabbed a knife from the table and stalked toward her. She smiled.

"I'm glad we had a chance to work things out. I wish

we had more time for me to make things up to you."

"Stop talking to me like I'm him. Finn is gone. Permanently. You know who I am now."

She nodded. "If that's true—if Michael is all that's left —then I'm ready to go. I don't want to be in a world without Finn."

He let out a snort. "You and he are a pair. Both disappointing. Everyone is always so impressed with you. You're supposed to be a fighter. You're supposed to be strong. How can you give up so easily just because one man is gone?"

Jazz shook her head and smiled.

"I love him."

Michael's mouth dropped open.

"I hope you're in there, Finn. I truly do, if nothing else so that you can hear me say this. God, I hope you can hear me. I love you, Finn. I'm sorry it took me so long to tell you."

He clamped his mouth shut, his eyebrows pinched together above his nose. He was breathing hard, she could hear it, see his chest heave. He walked around behind her, put his hand on her forehead and pulled her head back. He put the knife against her throat.

She looked into his eyes, praying that somewhere in there, Finn was still fighting. She was fighting too, in her own way.

His gaze was so intent on her, he didn't seem to notice

that the hand holding the knife trembled.

Then he dropped to his knees and cut her free.

Chapter Twenty-Six

Finn's hands were shaking. He could feel Michael's will flowing along his nerves, moving him around like a marionette. Before, Michael had been the one fighting to control Finn's body. Now, Finn was the interloper.

"Thank God," Jazz said. "Finn…"

He threw the knife away. He had to help her, to give her the best possible chance of surviving this. And the best chance she had was to run.

Finn glanced at her and saw the terrified look on her face. He could guess what she saw. His eyes were still wrong. She grabbed his face and leaned in to kiss him. Finn couldn't even feel her. But he could feel Michael.

He started to laugh.

Jazz pulled back, eyes wide, mouth open. It only made Michael laugh harder.

"Surprise," he said.

She punched him in the throat. Michael's hands went to his neck and he fell to the side, coughing and sputtering.

Finn let out a whoop inside Michael's head. He had never been more grateful she let him teach her basics of self-defense. Sure, that was going to hurt like hell later, if he ever fully made it back to his body, but he didn't care. It seemed like she had pulled her punch at the last second. Finn's body would heal.

She scrambled to her feet, grabbed her phone from the table, and ran.

"Yes! Run, Jazz. Run!"

"We're on an island, you idiot." Michael's voice was cold inside his head. *"There's nowhere for her to go."*

Michael pushed himself onto his knees, using the chair Jazz had been tied to for leverage. He hung there, breath rasping. Maybe she had hit him harder than Finn thought. Good.

"Veronica. Veronica!" Michael's voice was hoarse. Finn hoped it hurt him to talk.

Who the hell was Veronica?

Michael had his eyes closed, so Finn couldn't see anything. He couldn't *do* anything. He was trapped in his body, watching as Michael drove it around.

"Tend me."

Michael opened his eyes.

"What the fuck?"

The clearing outside the shed was filled with people. Women, more precisely. They milled about, clustered in groups, stared at Michael with terrified eyes. They looked almost solid, but Finn could see the faint outline of trees and brush behind them—through them. Sometimes they would sort of shiver and wink out, only to reappear somewhere else.

Michael laughed. *"Meet my life's work. It turned out even better than I imagined. I'm glad I had a chance to see them like this."*

One of the ghosts—and Finn was certain that's what he was seeing—approached and knelt in front of Michael. She had blonde hair and blue eyes. Finn looked around through the windows of his body's eyes. All the women had blonde hair. They were too far away to make out their eye color, but they had similar builds.

"I see you have a type."

Michael laughed in Finn's head. *"I get nostalgic. I had a sister too. If I had known about ghosts and earthly remains, I might not have burned our house to the ground with her and mother inside. Then they could have joined us as well."*

"You sick—"

"It was better than they deserved," Michael snapped.

Shit.

"Killing Rachel will be so much more gratifying when I use your body—your powers—to do it. Only she won't get to cross over."

Aloud, he said, "Rachel will be joining us. Right, ladies?"

The ghosts inched closer to the swamp, turning their faces away. All but the one right in front of them. Maybe this was Veronica?

Michael lashed out and grabbed her throat. He moved so quickly, Finn barely registered the strike. Michael stared at the ghost he was throttling.

"I want you to see." Michael thought the words. It must be a special message just for Finn.

The ghost was whimpering, then she started making choking sounds. How could Michael choke a ghost? Where his hand touched her neck, the translucence of her skin became more opaque. There had been a shining quality to it, but it dulled and turned gray. Dark cracks appeared, centered on his hand.

"Stop it! You're killing her."

Michael laughed. *"Idiot. She's already dead."*

Dead or not, she was in pain. Finn tried to pull his hand away, to make Michael stop. He didn't budge. After a few more moments of Finn screaming in his head, Michael let her go. She collapsed on the ground, flickering in and out of sight.

"That is so much better." Michael moved his head from side to side, testing out his neck. His voice sounded fine.

"What did you do?"

"Used your powers."

"I've never done anything like that." Finn actually wasn't certain what Michael had done, aside from hurt that poor ghost.

"Because you're a coward who lacks imagination."

Michael stood up and glanced around. Had he healed

himself? What the hell…

"You have no idea what this body is capable of. You don't deserve it."

He took a deep breath, then let it out and said, "Let's see if we can't track down Ms. Zhou. I'd love to catch up."

He walked into the sun, glancing around. A few yards from the shed, the remains of a huge bonfire smoldered. Finn could see a few shapes in the pile of charred wood at the center of the scorched earth. Animals.

Pops and crackles were still sounding from deep in the mass and cans of lighter fluid were piled nearby. Michael wrinkled his nose as the scent of chemicals drifted toward them. He shook his head and stepped away from it.

"Travis is so sensitive. Running the squirrels into his traps was genius on my part. You should have seen the terrified look on his face. And when he came home, I shifted his pieces around at just the right moments to have him out of his mind with fear. He gathered everything up— all his precious friends—and burned them."

Michael sounded gleeful. Finn felt sick.

Michael walked to the edge of the water and looked out. *"I have my own friends."*

Half a dozen alligators floated nearby. Their eyes were glowing blue.

"Shit! Shit fuck fuck!"

Michael laughed again. *"Such language. Do you kiss your mother with that mouth? Oh wait, you haven't met her yet. She's an amazing woman, actually. I think after I'm done with Rachel, I'll stop by for a little reunion."*

"Leave her alone."

Finn didn't care about the things Jazz or even his dad had said. The woman was his mother. Finn would do his best to protect her.

"You misunderstand me. I think Lillian and I will get along very well, once I can get her attention. She could actually be quite helpful." He turned and walked inland. *"There are things going on in this town. I can feel it. I intend to be a player rather than a pawn. And you'll have a front-row seat."*

A ghost flickered into view before them. Most seemed to be staying out of sight.

"Nicole."

Michael reached up and ran his finger along her chin. She shimmered. When she spoke, her voice rippled and echoed, an audio accompaniment to the visuals that seriously creeped Finn out.

"She's this way."

"Fuck! No no no. Please, don't lead him to Jazz."

"She can't hear you. And even if she could, she does as I say. Nicole doesn't even fight me anymore. She's learned her place. You will too, given time."

"Thank you, my dear." Michael gestured before them. "After you."

Chapter Twenty-Seven

Bugs were crawling over her legs. Lots of them. Jazz didn't care. She had run like hell from the shed and found a hiding spot, trying to figure out what to do next. So far, she had come up with exactly nothing.

Touching Finn wasn't working. From what she could tell, it was as if Michael had completely taken over Finn's body. She had no idea how to bring Finn back—if he was even in there anymore.

No. He was. He had to be. Dammit, Fate wasn't an asshole. After her talk with Finn, she refused to believe that anymore. It wouldn't bring them back together, really together, in a way they'd never been before, then take him away. Not like this.

She had to reach him. She needed help.

Checking her phone, Jazz choked back a sob of relief. There was finally a signal.

She dialed Rachel's number, praying with each ring. *Please be there. Please be okay.*

"Hello?" Garrett answered. Not Rachel.

Jazz started to panic. "Garrett? Where's Rachel? Is she okay?"

"I'm here. I'm fine." Rachel was safe. Not only that, she sounded strong, focused.

Jazz let out a huge breath. "Thank God."

At the same time, they both said, "Listen to me."

Jazz cut in. "Me first. He'll find me any second."

"Who will?" Rachel asked.

"Finn. I mean Michael. I don't even know anymore! I'm losing him. He's losing himself. Michael is possessing him."

Jazz wiped her nose with the back of her hand. Her vision blurred with tears. Dammit, she didn't have time to break down. She had to warn her friends of the danger they were all in.

"He's coming for you and Elsa. You have to warn her. He's going to kill you and..." She thought back to the female forms in the workshop. "You don't want to know what he has planned then. If I can't save Finn—"

Rachel interrupted her. "Stop. We're saving everybody. And we're taking Michael out in the process. Permanently. Where are you?"

Rachel had never sounded so strong. It bolstered Jazz, reminded her to hold tight to her hope. They were going to get out of this. All of them. They just needed to work together.

"I don't know exactly," Jazz said. "I was knocked out. But I'm in a swamp. Probably somewhere near Clearview."

"Why Clearview?" Rachel asked.

"Finn and I were trying to find out more about Michael's other victims. It's Michael's home town. We found the house where he grew up."

"Listen to me carefully," Rachel said. "I am certain that Michael's body was cremated but there must be something of him left behind. Something acting as an anchor in the physical realm. With how powerful he is, it can't just be a lock of hair. It has to be something with more substance."

Knowing Michael, he would want to keep it close. He'd only recently re-obtained a body—and the first thing he'd done was take that pouch from Travis and hang it around Finn's neck.

"I think I know where it is. What do I do with it?"

"Burn it," Rachel said. "Can you do that?"

There was a bonfire right next to the shed. It looked like it had nearly burned itself out, but Jazz remembered smelling lighter fluid. If she could find some, she could get it going again fast. All she had to do was get the pouch from Michael and make it back.

Yeah, just that.

She would do it. No matter what it took, she would do it to save her friends. And Finn... How could she help him? Was he really beyond Jazz's reach?

Rachel was the expert. Jazz almost didn't want to ask, but she had to know if Finn was still in there. If there was still hope.

"Yes. But what about Finn?"

"Once you destroy the anchor, I'll be able to take care of Michael and Finn will be free. We'll be working from here to try to weaken Michael, but we need you to help Finn keep fighting."

She could do that. She *would* do that. Finn was a fighter. Jazz had given up on him once before, she wouldn't make that mistake again.

Garrett came on the line, his voice raw. They were best friends, he and Finn. Like brothers.

"Jazz, you have to reach him. Any way you can. He won't be able to live with himself if he hurts anybody."

"I know," she said.

"Watch out for wildlife too," Garrett said. "Michael can control snakes and gators and the swamp's full of them."

She remembered Finn talking to Travis about squirrels. Before Michael had taken over.

"It's good if he's spreading himself thin," Rachel said. "The more fronts we can hit him from, the better. Work on your connection to Finn. Try to reach him and help him to hold on."

Jazz heard a twig snap nearby. She lowered her voice as much as she could while still being heard.

"Hurry."

She ended the call.

Holding her breath, she scanned the area in front of her. She was lying under a saw palmetto, flat against the sand.

Its sharp leaves poked her legs. They were easier to ignore than the bugs. She was never leaving the city again after this.

Something particularly big crawled onto her thigh and she jerked reflexively, swatting it away.

Shit…

She looked back out at the clear space in front of her. Nothing.

Suddenly, the leaves above her bent away, leaving her exposed. She looked up to see Finn standing over her. His face seemed to blur as he grabbed her and lifted her from the ground.

"Hello, darling."

She kicked at his knees, punched, clawed, even tried to bite him. He was too strong, too big. He held her at arm's length while she flailed, exhausting herself.

"Are you done?"

"Let me go."

He laughed. "Why on earth would I want to do that? Travis is an amateur, but he did hit on an interesting concept. It would be a shame to waste those forms, don't you think?"

He tucked her against his chest, pinning her arms at her sides and keeping her facing away from him. She tried to head-butt him with the back of her head, but he swerved out of the way.

"Ah-ah-ah. None of that."

He headed toward the shed. That was a good thing. The fire was there. She held still, building her energy, coiling it within her so that she could lash out when they were close. If she could grab the pouch as he dropped her...

Who was she kidding? Finn had always been strong and fast. Michael was somehow even faster, stronger. Inhumanly so.

She needed Finn's help. She needed to reach him, to help him fight, like Rachel and Garrett had told her to.

"I would think that you of all people would be happy to sacrifice yourself for art," Michael said. "Then again, I suppose you've always been more of a merchant than anything else. I do appreciate your believing in me, though. For that, I'll make sure you're unconscious before I drown you."

"Thanks."

"Of course."

"I'd rather have a moment with Finn, though."

He laughed. "I don't think so."

"You don't have to give him control. I just want to talk to him—for him to hear me. There's something I didn't get a chance to explain."

They were back at the shed. Jazz could see Travis lying on the floor inside. She hoped he was still alive. At this point, she counted him among Michael's victims. The guy needed help. And Garrett was right—Finn wouldn't be able to live with himself if his body had been used to kill someone. Even if he wasn't in control when it happened.

Michael walked with her to the water's edge. As if the thought of drowning wasn't terrifying enough, six huge alligators were floating nearby. Their eyes were glowing blue.

What the hell...

She looked away. If she thought about the water, she was going to panic. Panic wouldn't help anyone.

"You were one of the most talented painters I've ever met." It was a revolting truth, but one that might help her. He had twisted his talent so horribly.

"Thank you. But I already knew that."

"Branching into a new medium can be difficult."

He laughed. "It won't be new to me. Who do you think introduced Travis to his little hobby?"

She was grasping, trying to find any way to keep him talking, to give her a chance to reach Finn. If Michael killed her quickly, Finn would lose his hold on himself. She was sure of it. Physical touch couldn't help him anymore, but emotionally she still had a chance to reach him.

"I don't get why you're so scared of me, though."

He stiffened. "What makes you think I'm afraid of you?"

"You won't even let me talk to you—to Finn. You're so afraid of what I'll say that you want to just knock me out and drown me."

"I am a little busy right now. I regret to tell you that you don't hold my undivided attention."

"Of course. I don't need it. This is a done deal. We both know it. Can you blame me for wanting a little more time?"

He set her down on her feet. She craned her neck so she could look at him. His eyes were glowing, just like the alligators'.

Shit.

She pushed down her fear.

"I suppose not." He smiled at her and it actually looked semi-genuine. "You know, I always liked you, Jazz. You're remarkably calm. Even in the face of this, it's just another business transaction. That's probably why it didn't work with you and Finn. He's so emotional."

That was it. She'd found her in.

"I am a businessperson first and foremost. So you can understand why I'd rather not go out with a debt that I can resolve."

"What do you mean?"

"I owe Finn information."

He frowned. She pushed forward.

"All I'm asking is for you to stand there and listen to me for two minutes. I gave you a chance at the gallery. Can't you give me one now?"

"I know you're trying to manipulate me."

"Do you think I actually stand a chance of doing so?

Come on. I'm good, but not that good."

He grinned. "All right. This should be entertaining at the least. He's practically having conniptions in here at the moment."

Jazz could only imagine. But that was good. Finn was in there. Michael had just admitted it. And Finn was already worked up, already fighting. He just needed more ammo, a line to grab on to. She had a feeling she knew just the one to cast.

Chapter Twenty-Eight

Something was happening to Finn. Something he didn't understand and didn't like at all. If he could still feel his body, it would probably resemble a panic attack. With only a sense of his energy, he felt like he was made up entirely of fireworks that were starting to burn out, one after another.

The ghosts sometimes shimmered and flickered, winking in and out of sight. Finn felt the same, except if he blinked out even for a second, he wasn't sure if he would come back.

Michael was winning. He was pushing Finn out of his body. Finn could sense it. The more he fought, the more disconnected he became. He was getting to the point where all he could do was hold on. He wasn't able to help anyone, not even himself.

He was going to have to watch Michael kill Jazz.

No. *Goddammit, no!* That wasn't happening.

"Finn," she said.

Michael had granted them this audience. As if he was some fucking benevolent being. He was a monster. Finn felt the darkness in Michael growing, a sense of sharing his body with something that wasn't human anymore. Michael had moved beyond being a serial killer. His soul was twisting into something even worse.

"Shut up and listen. This is all you're going to get."

Every time he spoke, Michael's voice was stronger in Finn's mind. Every time, Finn felt smaller, more distant.

"We covered a lot of ground," Jazz said. "I'm glad we had a chance to fix things between us."

Finn was too. That was the only comfort he had to hold on to. Dammit, there had to be a way... He felt a pressure on what used to be his heart, a weight dragging him down that had nothing to do with the physical.

Jazz stepped closer. She put her hands on his chest. Did she know that Finn couldn't feel her? He only knew what she was doing because Michael was watching her every move.

"We didn't get a chance to cover everything, though. I want you to know, I never had a problem being seen with you. I wasn't embarrassed that we were together. That isn't why I never told anyone about us and asked you to keep us a secret."

"This should be good," Michael thought. *"Of course she was embarrassed to be seen with you. She's above you."*

"Shut up."

Jazz slid her hands up to Michael's neck. Finn sensed Michael's amusement.

"Do you think she knows who she's touching? Do you think it's on purpose?"

Michael was mocking him now, baiting him. Finn kept his attention on Jazz. She was up to something, he could tell. He just didn't know what or how he could help her.

"I felt like I was being punished when my father died. Every time I was really happy about someone in my life, every time I talked about it, they were taken from me."

"Oh look," Michael thought. *"It's about to happen again."*

"If I could find your face, I would punch it."

Michael chuckled.

"That's why I never talk about people I care about. Why I was so desperate for no one to know how much I loved you. I knew if people saw us together, I couldn't hide it. I thought if Fate found out, you'd be taken from me. I talked up my father to all my friends at college, and he died right before I had planned to show him off. That wasn't the first time something like that happened. And with you... I was so afraid, I didn't even want anyone to know we were dating."

"Interesting. My gallery exhibit was set to open just before I died."

"Shut up, you sick fuck. This isn't about you."

Michael laughed in his mind.

Finn wanted to hear more of what she had to say. Having these answers, *finally*... It lifted a weight from him, made him stronger. He felt as if he was drifting toward her, like he could almost reach out and touch her.

"The bar felt safe," she said. "Like it was an oasis. Our little corner of the world where we could be together. I thought as long as we kept our relationship there, everything would be okay. It was the only place I believed I could let myself love you."

She ran her thumb over Michael's lips, then back down to either side of his neck. She kept brushing her thumbs along his jaw. Finn's spirit might not be in control, but his body sure as hell remembered her touch. He focused on what Michael must be feeling, willed himself to connect with the sensations.

Finn could feel Michael suppressing a shudder, vague ripples of nausea flowing through him. He dropped his hands from her arms, as if he couldn't stand to touch her. For whatever reason, Michael didn't *want* to feel this.

Finn was granted a little more space in his body. He prayed that Michael was distracted enough that he wouldn't sense Finn slipping back in.

"What does she think she's doing?" Michael thought.

Finn wasn't sure. But he made himself ready.

"I was afraid if I showed you off, I would lose you. But I hid you and lost you anyway. I understand now that I should have fought for you. I should have let everyone know, stood by your side proudly. I should have fought for you."

Finn needed to fight. That was what she needed, what she was warning him about. She was about to do something, and he needed to be ready to help her.

"I'm so glad for everything we've shared through this, Finn. We have a second chance. To do things right. But we have to fight for it."

She grabbed the cord hanging around Michael's neck with both hands and pulled. It snapped free. She dropped under his arms and leapt past him, running toward the shed.

Michael was still reeling from Finn's body reacting to Jazz's touch. Finn felt himself connecting, fighting for control as he pushed his awareness along his body's nerve-endings. It was enough to slow Michael down.

"What are you doing?" Michael asked. "There's nowhere for you to run. Nowhere to hide that I can't find you."

Jazz was standing near the bonfire of Travis's work. She bent down and picked up a can of lighter fluid, then shook it. She smiled as she stood.

"I don't plan to run."

"Foolish—"

Michael's thought cut off as Jazz lifted the pouch she had taken from him. His hand went to his chest. He felt around frantically, as if he couldn't believe what he was seeing, that she had taken it—had gotten the better of him.

"Give that back!" he roared.

She chucked it on the fire as he ran toward her. Tried to run, anyway. Finn managed to trip him.

He felt Michael's surprise, a wave of rage pummeling him, searing him. Finn screamed. He couldn't stop himself. The pain was beyond anything he had ever experienced.

But Michael's attention was on him. It gave Jazz enough time to spray down the pouch with lighter fluid, soaking it. Flames crept up around it and the leather started to burn.

"No!"

Michael scrambled to his feet, heading for the fire. Jazz ran past him, not toward land but toward the water. Toward...

Fuck. There were six full-grown alligators out there.

Finn grabbed at his arms with his awareness, clawing at them, making the muscles of his physical body cramp. Michael curled into a ball, clutching them.

"You have a choice, Finn." Jazz was standing at the water's edge. "Save the pouch, or save me."

Then she turned and walked into the water.

"No way. No fucking way!"

"The pouch!"

Michael turned to the fire, fighting against Finn. More fireworks erupted in his body as they clashed. Finn visualized himself tackling Michael, taking him to the ground. He pushed all of his energy into that thought.

They fell.

"Yes!"

Michael started to crawl. His hands dug into the sand, pulling them closer to the fire.

"Dammit!"

Finn could feel Michael's spirit crowded against his own—his body overfull from both of their presences. And if he could feel Michael, he could touch him. Finn dug his elbow into Michael's back. Michael screamed.

Darkness suddenly engulfed Finn as his external senses cut out. He was standing in a pitch void, staring at a vaguely person-shaped form made of glowing blue energy. He lifted his hands and saw that he was the same—only his energy was gold.

He didn't have time to notice more. Michael flew at him. Literally flew. He hit Finn in the middle, knocking him to the ground. Finn managed to grab Michael's wrists and hold them, keeping him at a distance. Michael writhed and snapped at Finn, trying to bite him. The energy he was putting off became more frantic, more violent.

Less human.

It was also fading.

Michael threw his head back and let out an inhuman screech, then vanished. Finn's regular senses turned back on as if someone had flipped a switch. He felt himself sort of flood back into his body.

He looked up and saw the pouch fully engulfed in

flames. The fire started to die down, all the fuel consumed. Whatever had been in the pouch was destroyed.

He lay on the ground for a moment, trying to get his bearings, to remember how his arms and legs worked. Then he heard Jazz scream.

He jumped to his feet and bolted for the shoreline, leaping from the ground, body forming a perfect line as he dove into the water.

Please, please...

He couldn't be too late.

Chapter Twenty-Nine

Jazz hoped Finn was winning against Michael. She really, really hoped so.

Her boots were full of water. At least they kept her from feeling the greenish stuff that she was walking through. Her skin was crawling. The water closed around her thighs, cooler than she expected.

Any time, Finn.

It was a gamble. A huge gamble. Being knocked out and drowned seemed a lot better than having half a dozen alligators rip her to shreds...while she drowned. The water was up to her waist. She didn't hear Finn behind her.

He would fight Michael off. She knew he would. But he had to feel that the danger was real.

Shit, the danger is *real.*

When the water had reached her ribs, she paused and looked around. She didn't see any alligators on the surface. That didn't seem like a good thing.

Her heart was pounding and her breath coming fast. Passing out would also not be good. She tried to get herself to calm down, to keep herself from hyperventilating.

Something brushed her leg.

She screamed. The shrill sound echoed around her. She leapt back, water slowing her progress. She couldn't run to shore. If Finn thought she was safe, he wouldn't have as much incentive to fight Michael, to save her.

Too much time had passed. What if Michael had won? What if he had already pulled the pouch—with whatever piece of him was inside of it—from the fire? They might have already lost.

Something clamped around her chest.

Shit! She was about to be eaten by alligators.

What was she supposed to do? Go for the eyes. They would try to roll with her, to take her underwater and drown her. Except she was still upright. Upright and screaming at the top of her lungs.

Her voice trailed off as she realized she didn't feel any pain. She looked up over her shoulder. Finn was standing behind her, face scrunched up as he winced at her.

"That was really loud," he said.

She spun herself around and grabbed his face, pulling his eyelids open. His irises were blue—pale blue, not bright. And they weren't glowing.

"Finn!"

She wrapped her arms around his neck and kissed him. He only half-heartedly kissed her back. That wasn't normal. She pulled back and looked at him warily.

"That is you, right?"

"Yeah. But could we maybe get on shore before making out?"

She nodded vigorously.

He smiled as he turned and started toward dry land, pulling her along with him.

"I fucking hate the outdoors," she said.

He laughed.

As soon as they were on land, he wrapped his arms around her and held her against his chest. He buried his face in the nape of her neck.

Smoothing down his hair, she held him too. She never wanted to let go. But they needed to.

"Finn, we need to check on Travis."

She felt him suck in a breath, his body going stiff. Her stomach knotted with worry.

Please let him be alive.

Finn slowly released her, then nodded. He held her hand as they walked into the shed.

Travis was lying right where he had fallen. A small puddle of blood surrounded his head. Finn knelt down, his hand shaking as he pressed his fingers against Travis's neck. After a few seconds, Finn let out a huge breath.

"He has a pulse. It's thready, but there. I don't think we should move him. We should try to get a signal and call the EMTs and police."

Finn stood and grabbed his phone from the table. He put his hand on her waist and pulled her against him as they walked outside.

Her mind was whirling. Their part of it was done. But what about Rachel? Was she okay? And Elsa? Jazz hadn't spoken to her best friend since...she couldn't remember.

She pulled her phone from her pocket. The water hadn't reached quite that high on her body. Finn was busy messing with his own phone.

"I have a signal," he said.

Jazz looked at her phone and saw one as well. She dialed Rachel's number frantically, pressing the speaker button. The moment the call picked up, she half yelled, "Are you guys okay?"

Rachel's voice came over the line. "We're fine. What about you two?"

"We're okay." Jazz stifled a laugh. She was so relieved.

Garrett's voice was rough and actually cracked over the words as he spoke. "Finn, you SOB. What the hell did you get my friend Jazz mixed up in?"

She felt Finn's grip on her side tighten and nestled against him.

"Are you crying?" Finn teased.

"Shut up."

"Oh, I am never going to shut up about this."

Finn kissed the top of Jazz's head. She rolled her eyes.

"Ugh, bromance."

"I think it's adorable." Rachel laughed.

Finn's grip on Jazz tightened again. She looked over at

him and saw his eyes glistening with tears. He was talking to his sister for the first time. Of course he was overwhelmed with emotion.

"Finn, you okay?" Garrett asked.

"Yeah, man. Yeah." Finn's voice was rough.

"Wait a minute. Now are you crying?" Garrett said.

Finn smiled at Jazz. "You'll never prove anything."

Jazz laughed. "Don't worry, Garrett. I'll get some pictures."

That would have to wait. Finn had other immediate plans. He shoved his phone in his pocket and tilted Jazz's face to his, claiming her lips for a deep kiss. The warmth of his mouth, the softness of his skin against hers...she let herself get lost in the feel of him for a moment. But only for a moment.

She kept one arm around his neck when she pulled back, and left their foreheads pressed together.

"Look, we've got a mess to clean up here," Jazz said.

Garrett laughed. "Funny, I was about to say the same thing."

"Ours is going to take a while. We need to call the Clearview police—"

"Already texted them," Finn said. "They're on the way."

Jazz leaned back, one eyebrow arched and a scowl on her face. How the hell had he managed that? She knew she was off her game, but to not even notice...

"When did you text them?" Her voice had more bite than she intended, which riled him up, of course.

"As soon as you called Rachel! I didn't want them to check our phone records and see that we called our friends before them when—"

"Enough!"

Jazz shook her head. They had to work on their dynamic. It would take time. Time that they now had.

"We can explain all that later," she said. "Bottom line is, you two need to call Elsa and Dante and give them the all-clear. We are all clear, right?"

"Yes," Rachel said. "Michael is gone—for good this time."

Jazz felt Finn relax a bit. She was relieved to hear it as well. Jazz would be sure to ask Rachel exactly how she had managed that.

"Thank you," Finn said.

"We couldn't have done it without you," Rachel said. "We make a good team."

Jazz covered her mouth to stop a choking sob from coming out. Finn fairly crushed her against his chest. She couldn't wait to tell Rachel about her new family.

They had to tell Tommy first. He would be so happy. They'd have to break it to him easily, ask questions to be certain. But Jazz was already sure. Psychic powers or no, she could feel it.

Rachel just went on, oblivious to Jazz and Finn's

reactions. They must have been doing a good job hiding them.

A dull whirring noise was approaching. Jazz looked out at the swamp. It was coming from the water.

"I'll text you after I call Elsa to let you know they're okay," Rachel said. "But I'm sure they are. We let them know what they needed to do to protect themselves and it sounds like we were all keeping Michael pretty busy."

The whirring increased. It was an airboat. Jazz relaxed another iota as she saw the reassuring symbol for the police on the boat's side.

"Okay," she said. "The cops are pulling up."

"Is that an airboat?" Garrett asked.

"Yeah," Jazz said. "We better go. But we're headed your way as soon as we're done. And I'm bringing guests, so clean up."

"Guests?"

Rachel didn't seem all that keen on company, but she would handle it. Especially the company Jazz was bringing.

"Deal with—"

Shit. No. Jazz was done dismissing people's emotions —including her own. She took a deep breath and said, "I know you can handle it." Then she ended the call.

"What are we going to tell them?" Finn nodded toward the airboat.

"The truth. At least, as much of it as they can believe.

We were investigating Michael Angelo's case, trying to ID his other victims. We came across a possible accomplice, found evidence that he was considering a crime, but were abducted before we could tell anybody."

Finn laughed. "Damn, you're good at thinking on your feet."

She shrugged. "We all have our talents. We need to tell them about the thugs at the bar too. In case they were involved at the hotel."

"We're going to be here for a while."

"Fine by me. As long as we're together." She rested her head against his chest.

"I love you," he said.

She smiled. "I love you too."

Chapter Thirty

Finn stretched out in his bed. After one of Daphne's amazing meals, then a hot shower with Jazz and…follow-up activities, he felt like a new man. No, not new. He felt like himself. For the first time in months.

Jazz was curled up against his side. They might have fallen asleep a little, which meant they were running behind for meeting up with Garrett and Rachel for a late dinner at Elsa's house. Garrett had called and asked for the switch in location. Apparently his house had been damaged while dealing with Michael.

Jazz had suggested they reschedule for the next day so that Dad could rest, but once it had been established beyond any doubt that Rachel was Siobhan, there was no stopping him. Finn didn't blame his dad for wanting to make up for lost time. It wasn't like he could sleep knowing his daughter was alive and well and thirty minutes away.

The door to Finn's bedroom opened and Dad practically ran in. He clapped his hands together a couple of times.

"Come on, let's go!"

"Dad! Give us a break, man."

Finn covered his eyes with his elbow. He was excited to meet Rachel too, but also exhausted. It had been a hell of a day.

Jazz pushed herself up on her elbows, staring blearily at Dad. She rolled over and pulled the sheets up higher, then laughed.

"This is where I came in," she said.

Right. The first time she and Dad met, he had barged into the room, thinking Finn was alone. Instead, Jazz had been by herself in Finn's bed.

Having a history with someone filled his chest with warmth. Especially since it had led them to this moment— this family.

"I'll be waiting for you downstairs in the bar. Five minutes," Dad said. He pulled the door shut, then yelled, "Five minutes, or I go without you!"

"Come on!" Finn let out an exasperated breath.

Jazz laughed and leaned against his chest. "We better get ready."

They jumped out of bed and dressed. Daphne had loaned Jazz a set of clothes that fit reasonably well. In four and a half minutes, they were all standing in the bar, ready to go.

Well, he and Jazz were standing. Dad was sitting down, one arm resting on the table next to his hat.

"Dad? You okay?"

Daphne was the first to realize something was wrong.

She ran over to Dad and knelt at his side, pressing her fingertips to his neck. Finn and Jazz joined her in seconds.

"Dad!" Finn's heart was pounding.

Please, God, don't let Dad's heart give out. Not now.

It was too cruel. To be so close to reconnecting with his daughter and never get a chance to meet her.

Jazz's hands were shaking violently as she pulled out her phone. "I'll call an ambulance."

Finn took in the look on Daphne's face, the blue tinge to his dad's lips, and knew there wasn't time. Dad's eyes were clenched shut and his breathing was labored. He was fighting. If only Finn could do something to help him.

Something Michael had said popped into Finn's mind. Of all the people to be thinking about right then…

"You didn't even scratch the surface of your powers."

He remembered how Michael had siphoned off that poor ghost's energy and used it to heal himself—heal Finn's body. Finn knew his powers went both ways. He could read people, and he could control them. If he could heal himself, maybe he could heal other people as well. He was too desperate not to try.

Finn rested his left hand on Dad's chest, just above his heart, and willed some of his energy into him. Healing energy. He remembered how it had felt fighting Michael in the swamp—their energies clashing as they tried to end each other. This time, he visualized his energy entering Dad's body and wrapping around his heart, strengthening it.

The damned feedback started up, just like every time Finn and his dad's powers interacted. Finn tried to focus through the static. He could feel the jerky movements of each beat of his dad's heart, the muscle's struggle to get blood to flow. Finn saw the veins opening up, the blood pushing through, getting to where it needed to be.

His breath rushed out of him as he felt the connection synch up. His entire existence became that one organ—Dad's heart. He heard each beat clearly in his ears, the sounds of the room muting around him.

Golden light flowed from his hand into his dad, illuminating his heart, clearing it out. The beats became stronger, the light-imbued blood traveling throughout Dad's body, healing him not just there, but everywhere.

Finn felt his dad's joints become less creaky, his bones more firm, his muscle tissue becoming more elastic. Finn wanted to laugh. It was such a rush, like he was a conduit between Dad and...something else. Something so much bigger than anything Finn had ever connected to before.

He felt someone grip his wrist, pulling his hand away and breaking the connection. It was Dad. His grip was so strong, Finn could hardly believe it.

"Enough, son. Enough."

Jazz was the first to recover. "What the hell was that?"

Finn laughed. He knew his dad was going to be fine. Better than fine. Better than he'd been in years.

No imagination, my ass.

Finn could heal people. He could heal everyone he loved.

As soon as he had enough energy to stand up. That was going to be a minute.

Dad, Daphne, and Jazz helped Finn into a chair. They all stood around, staring at him with wide eyes. Finn felt a laugh bubble up in him. He couldn't stop it.

"Finn," Jazz said. "What *the hell* was that?"

"A taste of Heaven." He grabbed Dad's hand and squeezed it. "How are you feeling, Dad?"

"I think you know," Dad said. "I saw everything through our connection. Everything you did."

"We saw something too," Daphne said.

Both men looked at her. That was a surprise.

"Your hands glowed," Jazz said. "While you healed him. That is what you were doing, right?"

Jazz was scowling at him. How could she be mad? She loved Dad as much as Finn did.

"What?" he said.

"There's always a price, Finn. Scales that need to be balanced."

"Fine," he said. "I'll deal—"

Her glare increased. He stopped himself from using her old catchphrase.

"She's right," Dad said. "You can't take a risk like that again. Not until we understand this new aspect of your power better."

"I'm not going to go running around healing papercuts and headaches," Finn said. "But if someone I love is at death's door, you can bet your ass I'm going to make that bastard step off."

Finn's fatigue was already lessening. He didn't feel that bad. A dull ache lurked between his eyes, and his hands were still tingling. He was more bothered by the stares of everyone around him.

"I keep telling you, I refuse to think that Fate is some neurotic asshole fixated on *balanced scales* and making people miserable. Maybe Fate is looking out for us, and the only reason we went through all that shit was for us to be right here, right now—the best versions of ourselves to handle choices like the one I just made."

Jazz was staring at him. Dad and Daphne just smiled.

"If we hadn't been through all this, I wouldn't have known how to save Dad just now. You and I wouldn't be together. Hell, neither would Garrett and Rachel. And we wouldn't know about her and she'd be stuck with her shitty-assed family." He shook his head. "What happened sucked. Royally. But I can't say I'd change a damned thing."

He pushed himself to his feet, glad when his legs felt strong beneath him. "Speaking of which, I have a twin sister to meet. You guys coming along or what?"

Dad and Daphne exchanged a glance. She nodded

slightly, then wrapped her arms around his neck. She hugged them both all the time, but not like this. Dad buried his face in her neck. That was new too. And about freaking time.

Jazz found Finn's hand and interlaced their fingers. He looked down at her to find her beaming. Finn was even gladder he'd been able to save his dad. There was too much the lucky guy had to live for.

Another laugh escaped Finn. "Should we leave you kids alone?"

Dad turned to him. "Shut up."

Jazz laughed. Daphne gave him a shy smile.

Dad ran the back of his fingers along Daphne's cheek, then said, "You sure you can handle the bar on your own?"

"Of course. But are you sure you're all right?"

Dad smiled. "Never better."

Then he kissed her.

Finn felt his eyebrows shoot up his forehead. Jazz leaned into him, her grip on his hand tightening. The kiss went on for longer than Finn expected. He glanced down at Jazz again, and she elbowed him in the ribs.

When they broke off the kiss, Daphne said, "Go and spend some time with your daughter."

She hugged his dad again, then came over and hugged Finn as well. "Take good care of him, okay?"

"Always," Finn said.

Daphne surprised him by hugging Jazz too. Which

wasn't half as surprising as Jazz hugging her back. A real, full-on hug—not a polite pat on the back.

It was like they were a family again. An even bigger one, now that Daphne and Dad were together. And it was going to keep growing as soon as they figured out how to tell Rachel the truth.

"See you all soon," Daphne said.

"Yeah." Jazz cleared her throat and glanced at Finn. She scowled at him when he grinned. She was just as moved by the whole thing as he was.

When they were on the sidewalk, Finn said, "So, you and Daphne, huh?"

"Yeah, me and Daphne." Dad glared at him.

Jazz laughed and they both turned to her. She shook her head.

"Sorry. Just, when I met Daphne, I was afraid she and Finn were… Never mind."

Dad snorted. "Like he stood a chance next to me."

Finn led them to his sleek black muscle car. The darkened windows made it perfect for surveillance. The lack of rust spots helped quite a bit as well, given the neighborhoods he often parked in.

"Wow," Jazz said. "Maybe I won't miss the old car as much as I thought."

Finn grinned at her, opening the passenger's door and pushing the seat forward so she could climb in the back.

"Are you sure you're up for driving?"

"Yeah. I feel fine. Great, even."

She gave him a skeptical look. "Prove it."

"How? You want me to do some pushups or something?"

"Kiss me."

He heard Dad chuckle. Finn looked around the street. It wasn't too busy, but there were a few people walking around. And it was broad daylight.

"Now? Here?"

"Yeah. Unless you're not up for it."

"But there are people around."

Things had changed between them, but she'd drilled this into him so much he hesitated. No public displays of affection. Ever.

She stepped up to him and wrapped her arms around his neck. "Kiss me and I'll be able to tell if you're okay."

He'd have to stop smiling first. He wasn't sure he'd be able to.

She pulled him closer, helping him along.

He brushed her lips softly at first, then deepened the kiss. He put his hands on the small of her back, pressing their bodies together. His tongue delved into her mouth, his lips caressing hers. She melted against him.

After a while—Finn wasn't sure how long—Dad cleared his throat. Reluctantly, Finn pulled away.

Jazz's eyes smoldered. Her lips pulled into a grin.

"Yeah. You're fine."

"Sheesh." Dad was holding the door. He gestured impatiently for her to get in. "If you guys are done showing off, let's go."

Chapter Thirty-One

Elsa lived about thirty minutes outside the city. Finn made it in twenty.

Jazz was grateful for the time to collect herself after the scare with Tommy. Being in the back gave her some privacy to deal with it.

Scare wasn't really a strong enough word. *Terror* was better.

Michael had almost taken away everyone she loved. If Fate had taken away Tommy after she'd just reconnected with him... Jazz wasn't sure what she would have done. Not returned to her belief in her curse, though. She was done with that. Especially after Finn's speech earlier.

Finn had explained about Michael using Finn's powers to heal himself. If they hadn't been through their ordeal, Finn wouldn't have learned about his new power. He wouldn't have been able to save Tommy.

"Everything happens for a reason," Finn had said.

And *"Fate isn't a dick."*

Jazz let out a slow breath and smiled.

Finn's hands had glowed with a beautiful golden light. She'd watched it flow into Tommy's body. The color had returned to Tommy's face, his lips had turned pink again, and his breathing eased. He even sat up straighter.

She was a little worried about Finn, but he'd given her yet another amazing gift—hope. Hope that the universe wasn't out to get her. Hope that maybe it wanted her to be happy.

She knew she would experience sadness and hardships in the future, but didn't think she would take it personally anymore. She was still going to call Chloe as soon as possible to get her take on it all. In the meantime, Jazz enjoyed the silence.

Tommy and Finn seemed content to drive without conversation. It was a nice change from answering questions and filling Tommy and Daphne in on everything that had happened. Well, almost everything. They left out some of the scarier details for Tommy's sake. Thank God, after what had happened at the bar.

Jazz wondered how Tommy would hold up to meeting Rachel. His daughter was a handful, even as an adult. Now that Jazz thought about it, Rachel was a lot like Tommy. They both had outgoing, friendly natures.

Jazz had never met someone as energetic, outgoing, and cheerful as Rachel. She was the antithesis of Jazz's best friend, Elsa, who was reserved, shy, and…well, a huge control freak. But Jazz would never say that out loud.

The two women balanced Jazz's life. Now she had Finn and Tommy back—plus Daphne. And Garrett and Rachel were finally together. Jazz's heart felt over-full. She saw Elsa's drive appear and pulled herself together.

Nobody said anything until they were standing at the front door of Elsa's mansion. Tommy turned to them and said, "How do I look?"

He looked pale. Frightened. Excited. A little overwhelmed. He was holding his fedora so tight the brim was bending.

Finn gripped Tommy's shoulder and gave it a squeeze. "You look great, Dad."

The door opened. Elsa stood there, smiling broadly. Jazz had never seen Elsa smile like that.

Emotions Jazz wasn't ready to deal with started rushing to the surface. She stepped forward and grabbed Elsa, pulling her into a crushing hug.

"Dad, this is Elsa Sinclair," Finn said.

"I know."

Tommy sounded a little irritated. He probably thought Finn was afraid Tommy would think Elsa was Rachel or something. Jazz felt Tommy step closer.

"I've read all your books," Tommy said. "It's nice to meet you."

Elsa laughed, wrapping one arm around Jazz and shaking Tommy's hand with the other. "And you."

Jazz finally let go. She sniffed and wiped at her eyes, then murmured, "I'm glad you're okay."

Elsa bit her lower lip for a moment, obviously fighting

back tears of her own. Then she said, "I'm glad you are too."

And that was it. End of moment. Jazz was sure they'd be having more in-depth conversations about…a lot of things. Their relationship would change, but she was sure it would be stronger for it. And so would they.

"Please come in." Elsa shifted to the side so they could all enter the foyer. She closed the door and locked it when they were all inside. It would probably be a while before any of them really felt safe.

Jazz took a deep breath. She hadn't realized the big step she was about to take. Introducing Finn to her friends—as her life partner.

"This is Finn," Jazz said.

Elsa smiled at Finn and shook his hand too. "It's nice to meet you."

Finn was beaming. "You too." Under his breath, he added, "You have no idea."

Jazz scowled at him. Then she wrapped her arm around his waist and rested her other hand on his stomach.

Elsa's eyes about popped out of her head. Her jaw dropped and she stammered a few strange sounds. Then an even bigger grin spread over her face. Her brown eyes shimmered as if she was about to cry.

Jazz sighed. "Keep it together, Elsa."

"I'm a romance novelist," Elsa said. "You can't expect me to not have a reaction when my best friend introduces me to her boyfriend for the first time after all our years together."

"Finn's more than a boyfriend," Jazz said.

Elsa actually made a choking sound. Jazz rolled her eyes.

"Oh, come on!"

"It's okay," Elsa said. "I'm okay."

It was definitely time to change the topic. "Where is everybody?"

"On the patio," Elsa said. "Can you show them the way? I'm helping Winston in the kitchen."

Jazz's stomach sank. "He's not letting you cook, is he?"

After the bombshell Jazz had dropped—introducing Elsa to Finn—Elsa was certain to be even more distracted than usual. She had tried to make food for them both a couple of times when they were roommates in college. The results were revolting.

Elsa had a tendency to grab the wrong item, like putting cayenne pepper in oatmeal instead of cinnamon. The worst was when she thought she was using honey but had grabbed amber-colored dish soap instead. Jazz shuddered at the memory.

"I'm just bringing him what he needs and carrying things." Elsa glared at her.

"Yes, but you didn't give him any of the ingredients, did you?"

Elsa let out a little huff of breath. "It's just

sandwiches."

"I've had your *sandwiches.*" Jazz made sarcastic air quotes.

"He smelled everything to make sure it was right. Now *if you'll excuse me.*"

Jazz and Elsa had been friends for so long, they had their own secret language hidden in regular conversation. Elsa had effectively told Jazz to eff-off. It was an added treat that Jazz was the only one Elsa was comfortable enough to let loose with that way.

Jazz grinned. "Sure."

Elsa stalked away.

"What was that all about?" Tommy said.

"I'll explain later. Come on."

Jazz led them to the patio through the solarium that Elsa had converted into her art studio. The windows that made up the walls and ceiling had steamed up, but still let the last of the evening's sunlight into the room. More filtered in from the double doors that opened onto the stone tile sun and walkways surrounded by plants that hugged Elsa's house. Laughter and conversation floated toward them.

Garrett was sitting in a chair next to the patio table, with its big umbrella coming out of the middle. Dante was lying on the sun lounger. Half of his face was covered in bandages and he was wearing pajamas. He started to sit forward when they walked outside, but Garrett put a hand on Dante's chest to keep him in his chair.

"You know the deal," Garrett said. "You can rest in the sun lounger or go back to your room."

Dante sighed, then leaned back. "I suppose I can forgo formalities for once."

"And no alliteration." Garrett looked at Jazz and her group. "Dante's been driving us nuts with it. It's only funny for the first five minutes."

"I do believe it comes round again." Dante grinned.

Garrett laughed.

"Wow," Tommy said. "You're Dante Lucerne?"

"I am. Have we met?"

"No, I just…" Tommy glanced at Finn. "I've heard a lot about you."

Finn stepped forward and offered his hand. It must be such a relief for him to not be afraid to touch people anymore. He grasped Dante's hand and shook it gently.

"Finn Connelly. This is my dad, Thomas."

Tommy stepped forward and shook Dante's hand as well. "Call me Tommy."

"I am very pleased to meet you," Dante said.

Tommy was beaming. No wonder. He loved reading historical fiction of any kind. Meeting someone who had actually lived in a different era must have him over the moon.

"If you guys can keep an eye on Dante here," Garrett said, "I'm going to go check on my other patient."

"Other patient?" Tommy asked.

Jazz's stomach clenched. She thought everybody was okay. Winston must be fine if he was working in the kitchen. They had seen everyone except Rachel.

"Is Rachel all right?" Jazz said. "She sounded fine when we talked to you guys on the phone."

"She got cut up pretty bad, but she's going to be okay."

Jazz let out a breath. Garrett passed close to them as he walked toward the house. He put his hand on Finn's shoulder.

"Are you kidding me, man?" Finn shook his head. "After everything we just went through?"

Finn grabbed Garrett and pulled him into a hug, clapping his back and then just holding on.

"Garrett, check out my makeshift wheelchair." Rachel's bright voice rang out behind them. "Elsa said I can use this old broom as a paddle."

Finn stepped away from Garrett, turning to face Rachel who was...pushing herself onto the patio using a broom, just like she'd said. She was sitting in a wheeled office chair, holding her feet off the ground. Jazz would have laughed at the spectacle if Rachel's feet weren't wrapped in bandages. There were more on her arms.

Garrett headed over to Rachel and put his hands on the back of her chair. "That's a pretty slick system, but on this rough stone, I think I'll feel better pushing you."

"I didn't mean to interrupt your bromantic moment,"

she said.

Tommy let out a laugh. Finn was just staring. Jazz realized she was as well. She couldn't help it, seeing the two together for the first time.

They had the same hair, eyes, and smile. Even their builds were similar—both tall and athletic. Well, when Rachel was standing, anyway.

Garrett wheeled Rachel closer. She patted his hand when they paused in front of Finn.

"You must be Finn," she said.

"Uh…yeah."

Rachel reached for his hand and he let her take it. Jazz stepped forward a moment too late.

"I'm so happy to…meet…" She broke off, eyebrows furrowing. "Wait. I know you. You've been looking for me. I felt you trying to reach me."

Shit. Jazz should have kept them from touching. Who knew how their powers would interact?

She and Finn and Tommy had already decided not to tell Rachel about their relationship until things had settled down. They didn't want to give Rachel any more to deal with than she already had.

So much for that idea.

Rachel's eyes widened and her mouth dropped open for a moment. She snapped it shut and shook her head.

"I've been dreaming about you for months. I don't understand."

"I can explain," Finn said. He tried to pull his hand away, but she wouldn't let him.

"You all have been through a lot today." Tommy stepped forward. "Maybe we should have waited till tomorrow."

"To tell me that Finn is my brother?" Rachel said.

Garrett laughed. "Have you been dipping into Dante's pain meds?"

"I'm serious." She grabbed Garrett's hand as well, keeping her hold on Finn's.

Garrett's brow furrowed as his gaze became unfocused, then his face relaxed and a huge smile spread across it. "Well, I'll be."

"What the hell was that?" Finn said.

"Empathic bond," Garrett said. "It lets me feel whatever she's feeling, including the connection between you two."

Damn, that would be useful. Jazz sort of wished she and Finn had something like that going on. It would certainly cut back on their miscommunications.

Then again, that level of intimacy was not something she was comfortable with. She was pretty sure he'd feel the same. They'd have to muddle through their relationship the old-fashioned way, and just start talking more.

"Well, I can feel enough of what you guys have going on to really want my hand back," Finn said. "Dude, she's my sister."

"And that makes you my brother." Garrett grabbed Finn in a huge hug, pinning his arms to his sides and lifting him off the ground. He laughed the whole time.

Finn let out an exasperated grunt. "God, this is embarrassing. Put me down."

Garrett did, but then ruffled Finn's hair.

"Stop it." Finn ran his fingers through his hair and looked over at Jazz.

She just smiled. "I've got nothing for you. I think this whole thing is disgustingly adorable."

Tommy spoke up in a gentle voice. "Are you two married then?"

"No, sir." Garrett returned to Rachel's side, resting his hand on her shoulder. "But at this point, the wedding feels like a formality."

"A really *big* formality," Rachel said. "With a huge venue, and a jazz band, and... Wait a minute, we're getting off track."

Jazz laughed as Elsa and Winston walked out onto the patio carrying trays loaded with food, paper cups, and pitchers of iced tea and lemonade. She didn't want to leave Tommy's side, and was grateful when Finn stepped forward to help carry everything to the table.

"It isn't fancy," Elsa said, "but since I was helping out, we figured we should keep it simple." She pulled up a chair next to Dante and held his hand. "What did I miss?"

"I do not know where to begin," Dante said.

Winston let out a *hmph*. He angled his head toward the others as he sat in a chair close by.

"Let me help you out there." In his thick cockney accent, he said, "Rachel and Garrett are finally engaged and she wants a big wedding. She and the muscled one who likes to strut are siblings somehow, and their psychic mumbo-jumbo makes them able to read each others' minds or something."

Winston leaned back with a sigh. The silence stretched on for a moment, then he added, "Oh, and Garrett and Rachel have an empathic bond. I miss anything?"

"I don't strut," Finn said.

"You totally strut," Jazz said. "But how did you know all that, Winston?"

"I keep telling you all, I've got ears like a bat." Winston pointed over his shoulder. "That's the kitchen window and the one just past is my bedroom. You people think you're being all sneaky and whatnot, but it's really just a pain in the arse keeping all these secrets."

Jazz had heard that being blind could increase other senses—including hearing. This was outright amazing, though.

Elsa and Dante exchanged looks.

"Do you know about us too?" Elsa said.

Winston laughed. "Oh, my love. I know more about you pair than I ever wanted to." He put on a mock shiver, then smiled at them.

Elsa turned scarlet.

"Great," Jazz said, trying to keep Rachel away from her line of inquiry. "Now everyone knows everything about everybody."

It didn't work.

"Not even close," Rachel said. "I still need to know how Finn is my brother."

"I have to admit, I'm curious about that myself," Garrett said. "You never mentioned anything about that before."

"I didn't know before," Finn said. "We discovered it while investigating the case."

"I don't understand," Rachel said. "Did my dad have an affair or something?"

"No." Finn let out a sigh. "It's complicated."

Her eyes snapped to Tommy. "Why did my question upset you?"

"Uh…" he stammered.

"Enough with the empathic readings already," Jazz said. "Rachel, you know how your mom's an evil, lying, manipulative—"

Three voices of protest cut her off. Jazz was surprised that the Connellys jumped to Mrs. Montgomery's defense. She suppressed a smile thinking of them as a family unit already. Damn, they were good people.

"Am I wrong?" Jazz said. When no one argued the

point, she went on. "Did you ever notice that you look nothing like Edward Montgomery?"

"Well, yes," Rachel said. "But not all children favor both parents."

Jazz pointed at Tommy. "Have you not noticed yet that you look *just* like Tommy and honestly more like Finn than I'm comfortable thinking about?"

Rachel stared at Tommy and Finn for a moment, her eyes growing wide. "Oh my God. *You're* my father?"

Tommy looked over to Jazz, and she nodded encouragement. He stepped forward, crushing his hat in his hands.

"Well, yeah," he said. "I know this must be a shock for you. I don't expect you to—"

She launched herself out of her chair and hugged him. Tommy wrapped his arms around her and held her above the ground as best he could. She was almost as tall as he was.

"Sweetie, you need to stay off those feet," he said.

Rachel let out a sob, her eyes clenching shut and tears rolling down her cheeks. Jazz didn't need empathy to guess what Rachel was feeling. Her parents had treated her terribly. It was probably the first time a parent had shown her true concern.

Tommy rubbed her back. "It's okay," he said. "It's all going to be okay."

Garrett approached and put his hand on the pair's

shoulders. They helped Rachel back into her seat.

"You're so tall." Tommy face was filled with pride as he smiled at her. "You grew up so beautiful."

Rachel held on to his hand, staring into his eyes. Finn picked up a chair and brought it over so Tommy could sit right next to her, then he knelt at their side himself.

"Finn, don't you dare heal her wounds," Jazz said. "We still don't know how doing that affects you."

Garrett's interest perked up. "Heal her?"

Jazz shrugged. "Yeah, it's something new he can do. Turns out, Finn's the most psychic of them all." She looked over at Elsa and Dante. "Well, except maybe for Elsa."

Dante beamed at Elsa. "As someone saved by her psychic sagacity, I certainly—"

"Dante," Elsa said.

His smile became a bit more subdued.

Garrett shook his head. "Yeah, well wait till you hear about how Rachel got the better of Michael."

"I'd be really interested to hear about that, myself," Tommy said.

"Well, first I shot him seven times."

Tommy let out a half-strangled laugh. He cleared his throat, and said, "Only seven?"

"I ran out of bullets."

Tommy pressed a gentle kiss on the back of her hand, then set it in her lap, but held on. "That's my girl."

"This is a lot," she said.

Jazz picked up a chair and brought it closer for Finn to use. "There's one more thing. Finn's not just your brother —he's your twin."

Rachel smiled up at Finn and squeaked, "Twin? Really?"

"Yeah," Finn said. "We were split up in the divorce right after we were born."

More tears flowed down Rachel's face. She shook her head, and said, "God, our mom *sucks*."

Jazz let out a big laugh. She pulled Finn up from where he was kneeling so he could sit in his chair, then sat in his lap. He wrapped one arm around her waist and let the other rest on her thighs. It felt like the most natural thing in the world. Nobody said a word about the display of affection.

Buoyed by that, Jazz said, "I've already warned Finn about your mom. Just in case he gets curious or nostalgic and wants to meet her someday."

"Good." Rachel turned to Finn and said, "Whatever Jazz told you, it's all true—and worse."

"Believe that," Garrett said.

He was scowling more deeply than Jazz had ever seen. Whatever Mrs. Montgomery had done to get on his bad side, she'd better watch out for him. Jazz somehow doubted Mrs. Montgomery's dreams of her husband launching his political career in Summer Park would come true without the Wolfstroms' endorsement. From the look on Garrett's face, she sure as hell wasn't going to get it.

"Well, I'm curious right now," Rachel said. "I want to know everything."

Jazz broke in. "We have time to catch up later. Let's just...be together. Okay?"

Rachel hesitated for a moment, but then nodded. "Sure."

Elsa and Garrett started handing everyone paper plates loaded with chips and sandwiches. Jazz couldn't believe a day that had started out filled with chaos and death could end so...peacefully. Her stomach started to churn as the familiar fear eked in. She felt at any moment the other shoe was going to drop.

Rachel glanced over from her conversation with Tommy.

"Don't," she said. "Don't let fear in. This is the moment we have. Hold on to it."

Everyone was silent for a moment.

"Well said." Tommy raised his cup toward her. "And if I might propose a toast... To family. And a brighter future."

"Here here."

"To family."

They lifted their glasses one by one, then took a sip.

Jazz wrapped her arms around Finn's neck and smiled down at him. This was the moment they had. She was going to hold on to it for all she was worth.

—

Thank you so much for reading *The Summer Park Psychics* series! These characters have always felt so real to me, as if I'm slipping into an alternate universe when writing them. The friends are all together, but I have a feeling their stories are far from over. Wait till you see what happens with their kids.

In the meantime, there's some bold paranormal romance waiting for you in the *Forbidden Knights* series. Or if you'd like to try some Science Fiction - Horror Romance (set on familiar Earth), check out the *Blades of Janus*. If you'd like shorter Science Fiction Romance that's more light-hearted, you can try *The Department of Homeworld Security*. There's also the action-packed Science Fiction Romance of the *Cygnian 7!*

It's been a grand adventure. Thank you for joining my friends and I in Summer Park! But don't leave Cassland yet! There are so many more adventures waiting for you. Check out this excerpt from the first book in the *Forbidden Knights* series, *Forbidden Instinct!*

—

Forbidden Instinct

Forbidden Knights
Book One

Gasoline was spreading onto the street...

June 15 — 2:44 PM

In five minutes, Miranda's car would be a crumpled wreck. She checked her seatbelt with a shaking hand—again—to make sure it was fastened tight, then gripped the wheel hard enough to make her knuckles turn white.

A familiar silver minivan came into view ahead. She hadn't met the driver, but recognized the soccer-mom's short bobbed haircut. Miranda would never forget the woman's face—or the faces of the three children inside. Two of them were on the passenger's side. One of those was an infant.

The SUV is going to hit them from that side.

Her vision had been absolutely certain on that point. She glanced at the clock, then stepped on the gas.

2:46 PM. She had three minutes to get in front of them and slow them down. Three minutes to beat them to the intersection and be the one in front of the SUV that was about to speed through a red light. If she did everything right, the accident would only take out her car.

Her heart pounded in her throat, making it hard to swallow. She couldn't let herself panic. She knew she would make it through this. She'd *seen* it.

How did mom do this, knowing she wouldn't *make it out?*

Miranda couldn't think about the past. If she started to cry, it would blur her vision, dull her reflexes, and facilitate a family reunion she wasn't ready for. The present—and the specific future she was trying to create—needed her full attention.

Her ancient car struggled to catch up as the minivan accelerated. She managed to get behind it, then swerved into the left lane, crossing the double lines. She jerked the wheel back to the right just in time to avoid a head-on collision with a blue pick-up truck.

"Beeeep! Beep-beep!" She sang along with the pick-up's horn, knowing precisely how it would sound. Other cars joined the chorus.

"Everybody's a critic," she muttered under her breath. "I'm trying to save lives here."

She slowed, herding the soccer-mom behind her. The minivan's horn persisted.

"Yes, I know. I'm being an ass." She glanced into her rear-view mirror, taking in the angry expression of the woman behind her. "But I'm also saving yours."

Almost time...

She knew she had to steer away from the SUV right before it crashed into her. Maybe that act was going to offset the force of its impact or something. If she didn't time it right...

She *would* time it right.

A dark shape loomed in her peripheral vision and she jerked the wheel hard to the left. The first crash of metal hit her ears as she was hit. The second followed a split-second later—the minivan plowing into the back end of the SUV that had struck Miranda's car.

The world was set to tumble-dry as the street rolled around and around through the front windshield. Her car balanced on two tires for a last moment of teetering suspense before finishing its final roll and falling to the ground, upside-down. The roof crunched ominously, several inches closer to her head than it used to be—or maybe it was that she was hanging from the driver's seat, her seatbelt the only thing that kept her in place.

Probably both.

Tires screeched. People screamed. Horns kept blaring.

She laughed. It sounded hysterical, even to her. Tears ran over her temples and into her hair. Her eyes burned. She wanted to unbuckle her seatbelt, but couldn't will herself to let go of the steering wheel. She felt oddly disconnected from her body.

Is this what shock feels like?

It didn't matter that she'd known she would walk away from the accident. She'd dreamt this version of the future over and over before waking. But the primal part of her brain had basically seen her chewed up and spit out by a saber-toothed tiger. It was still processing the events.

She hadn't bothered to count all the iterations of what could be. In the end, there was only one possibility that didn't end in death. Miranda had to be in that intersection at the exact moment of the accident. It had to be *her*.

Mom would be so proud...

Her tears came harder.

Why couldn't people believe? Miranda wished she could tell people about her visions and let them make their own decisions. She should be able to walk away. Maybe actually have a life of her own, find someone who could understand and support her.

Darren's face popped into her mind's eye.

If only...

Sweet, smart, gorgeous Darren—with his jet black hair and steel gray eyes—who laughed at her jokes, even if he didn't make many of his own.

Getting to know him had made her happy, which was terrifying. She never knew when her visions would call for a sacrifice, and he somehow seemed the type who would throw himself on a grenade for others. She didn't think she was strong enough to endure another vision that sent someone she cared about to their death.

She shouldn't let him get too close. But she couldn't stay away.

No one at the accident scene was having trouble staying away from her car. They probably thought she was dead, and no one wanted to be the one to find her gruesome remains. If she hadn't known to turn her wheel just before the moment of impact, they would have been right.

The surreal cast to her perception started to fade. Her skin tingled and her heart kept pounding in her throat. Each beat sent a spike of pain through her head. She needed to get out of her car.

All she could see through the cracked glass of the front windshield were people's feet as they hurried around the intersection. She noticed a pair heading straight toward her. Black dress shoes polished to a high sheen and nice slacks.

The man stopped just outside her door, probably bracing himself for the worst. She considered making a funny face to lighten the mood, and let out another semi-hysterical sounding laugh. She cut it short as he knelt next to her open window.

Oh, wow...

Steel gray eyes bored through her, surrounded by thick dark lashes. The man's hair was raven-black, skin tanned to a deep bronze, jaw strong, features flawless. She had memorized his face weeks ago.

His eyes widened as he recognized her, too.

"Miranda?" he said.

"Hi, Darren. I'd offer to take your order, but I'm a little hung up right now."

She laughed, but her eyes had filled with tears again. He didn't laugh at her joke this time. She wished he would at least smile. Seeing his dimples always made her feel better. She wanted—needed—something that at least gave her the illusion of normalcy.

"You're going to be okay," he said.

She already knew that. Still, his seriousness brought home what she had risked. It made everything feel more real. She'd liked it better when her perception had that lingering sense of dreaming.

"Can you assess yourself?" he asked. "Do you know if you hit your head?"

"I didn't. I mean, my head hurts, but I think it's from the adrenaline."

He didn't look at all relieved. His eyes flicked to the ground, then back to hers.

"I need you to listen to me very carefully," he said. "We can't wait for the EMTs to arrive to check you out. We need to get you out of the car. Now."

Her visions tended to jump around, leaving large swaths of time unseen. The universe didn't seem to want to spoil all of her surprises. Miranda took in the grim expression on Darren's face and figured this wasn't a good one. She took a deep breath to calm her nerves and finally registered what was making him look so worried.

Gasoline was spreading onto the street from underneath the roof of the car. Her heart started to pound again.

She had seen herself on the other side of this. Walking stiffly among the tables and booths at the diner, holding a carafe of coffee. She was *not* going to burn to death.

Please, don't let me burn to death...

"Stay calm," he said. "I'm right here with you. I won't leave."

She closed her eyes and took a shaky breath, then let it out. She believed him. It made her less afraid, but also brought home the sharp sting of her loneliness. She was usually better at keeping it at bay. It had been a long time since someone had helped her through the aftermath of a vision. A long time since she hadn't felt completely alone.

She opened her eyes as he stood. He tried the door handle a few times, but the metal frame was mangled. The world seemed to spin as fumes burned her lungs.

She wondered briefly why Darren didn't just rip the door off her car, then remembered he couldn't do that yet. No, that was wrong—people couldn't do things like that at all. Reality was warping—memory, dream, and vision bleeding together.

She heard fabric rustling, then Darren squatted next to her again. He'd taken off his jacket and wadded it into a ball that he placed under her head. Brown leather straps hugged his broad shoulders—and held a handgun in a holster. He'd never mentioned being a cop. All she knew about his job was that he kept late hours.

He squeezed as much of himself into the car as he could fit. He was kneeling in gasoline. "Let go of the steering wheel and put your hands on the roof of the car."

She *knew* that she would be okay and was still panicking. He had no assurances of safety and was trying to help her anyway. He was risking himself for her. Her eyes filled with tears again.

"It's okay." He placed his hand on hers. "I won't let anything happen to you."

She let him gently peel her fingers off of the wheel, grateful that the adrenaline flooding her system seemed to be blocking her ability to read futures through touch. His hands were warm, his skin smooth. He pressed her hands firmly on the roof of the car, then reached into his pocket and pulled out a knife.

"I can't reach the seatbelt release, so I'm going to cut it," he said. "When I do, you'll fall." He put one arm across her chest. "I'll slow your descent as best I can, but will need your help to make sure you don't get hurt, okay?"

She nodded, bracing herself. His knife cut the seatbelt easily and gravity took over. She'd barely touched the floor before he was pulling her into his arms. She grabbed his jacket as she passed by, clinging to it. Darren tucked her against his chest and started running away from the car.

"There's gas over here," he shouted. "Everyone needs to stay clear."

A few bystanders glanced over, their jaws dropping open. The soccer-mom was among them, holding her baby while her other kids clung to her legs. Her gaze met Miranda's briefly, and the mix of horror and gratitude etched into her eyes was one Miranda didn't think she'd ever forget. Whatever happened next—whatever Miranda had to deal with after this—it had been worth it.

She turned into Darren's chest, letting it block out the rest of the world for a moment. Either the fumes, his proximity, or the adrenaline firing through her system was messing with her sense of reality again. Nestling in his arms, she felt like she was remembering something that hadn't happened yet.

A normal person could write it off as déjà vu. For her, it held more significance and a hope she shouldn't let herself feel.

He was going to hold her in his arms again.

—

Darren and Miranda have a rocky path ahead of them, winding past a host of supernatural beings and taking them to places they never dreamed could be real. Read more of their story to find if their love is strong enough to help them survive!

You can get *Forbidden Instinct* now! I'd love to keep in touch. Join my newsletter to get sneak peeks and behind-the-scenes insight into my many worlds, and check out other ways to join my community on my website at cassandra-chandler.com/community. I really want to know what *you* think. If you enjoyed this book, please consider leaving a review at your favorite book review site. I'd really appreciate it—reviews help readers and authors alike!

Thank you for reading *Lingering Touch!*

Cassandra Chandler

About the Author

USA Today Bestselling author Cassandra Chandler uses her vivid imagination to make the world more interesting, spawning the ideas she turns into her captivating Science Fiction Romances and enthralling Paranormal and Urban Fantasy Romances. Fast-paced and funny, lighthearted or filled with suspense, her stories will introduce you to characters you'll fall in love with and worlds you long to explore.